S0-AVS-701
ALAMEDA
FREE
LIBRARY
THIS BOOK
IS A GIFT FROM
SUSAN & MIKE SILVERSTEIN

I've travelled the world twice over,
Met the famous: saints and sinners,
Poets and artists, kings and queens,
Old stars and hopeful beginners,
I've been where no-one's been before,
Learned secrets from writers and cooks
All with one library ticket
To the wonderful world of books.

THE MINERVA STONE

When Sarah marries television star Niall Rhodes she has no reason to believe that the rich full life she had led in her family's home at Guinever, a lovely old castle on the English coast, will not continue. But almost from the start, she and her family, including her wild, crippled half-sister, Dido, her domineering father, Kester, and her beautiful folk-singing sister, Nina, become involved in the ominous secrets behind Niall's public image, an image to which he seems intent on sacrificing everything—including Sarah.

Books by Anne Maybury in the Ulverscroft Large Print Series:

THE JEWELLED DAUGHTER
RADIANCE
JESSAMY COURT
I AM GABRIELLA!
WALK IN THE PARADISE GARDEN
RIDE A WHITE DOLPHIN
THE MINERVA STONE

ANNE MAYBURY

THE MINERVA STONE

Complete and Unabridged

ULVERSCROFT
Leicester

First published December 1968

First Large Print Edition
published February 1984

British Library CIP Data

Maybury, Anne
The Minerva stone—Large print ed.
(Ulverscroft large print series:
Romantic suspense)
Rn: Anne Buxton I. Title
823′.914[F] PR6063.A885

ISBN 0-7089-1090-4

Published by
F. A. Thorpe (Publishing) Ltd.
Anstey, Leicestershire

Printed and Bound in Great Britain by
T. J. Press (Padstow) Ltd., Padstow, Cornwall

1

IN the livid afternoon, three things happened at once. The first clap of thunder broke the insufferable stillness, the telephone rang and a boy on a bicycle came weaving and whistling up the avenue under the pale green lime trees.

From the huge basket chair with its shell-shaped back, my father scowled at the boy. "That young fool is going headfirst over the handlebars."

Indolent as cats, my sister, Nina, and I lifted sundrenched eyelids and watched the boy disappear round the side of the house. Then Nina rolled over and laid her cheek against the grass. I threw a fallen peony head at her, but she didn't stir. She lay with her calm, delicate face hidden from me, her black hair fanning over the grass. "My changeling daughter" Father called her, for she was so dark. The rest of us—Penn and Theo and I—were fair, although none of us had Father's wild, sovereign gold hair or his dark blue eyes. Penn once said that as a child, Father's hawklike nose must have saved him from being a "pretty boy."

I turned over and looked at him. Elbow on his knees, chin on fist, he sat like Rodin's "Thinker." Startling daubs of vermilion paint spattered his shirt like blood.

The telephone stopped ringing. I pulled at a blade of grass and the sun struck my wedding ring in a point of blazing light. Instantly I pushed my hand out of sight. The ring belonged to Sarah Rhodes, wife of Niall Rhodes, former schoolmaster and television personality. It was alien to me—the Sarah who lay on the warm grass at her father's house, waiting for the storm.

In July, the southeast winds, blowing from the sea, carried the scent of lime flowers from the long avenue of Guinever Court into the windows, permeating the rooms like incense.

When the four of us were very young, we had listened to Grandfather and Father arguing as to who had discovered our house.

"Damn it, I did," my grandfather shouted through whirls of pipe smoke. "It was a winter afternoon and cold enough to freeze the noses off us. The house agent had just taken us to look over some Victorian horror they called 'a desirable residence,' when—"

"When," my father would shout, "*I* saw the tower through the bare trees and *I* asked the agent what the place was. He said that before Cromwell had flung his cannonballs at it, it had been a thirteenth-century castle. Now, all that was left was a bit of the keep and the great hall. He said the owner was a very old lady who lived in Launford and would have liked to sell the place only no one in their right senses would buy it. And I said, 'Are you in your right senses, Dad?' It was only then that you told the agent to turn back, so it was *I*—"

We would listen, giggling, and we made up a rhyme about it:

Aye. Aye. Aye.
I found the castle,
I saw it rise . . .

And there we stuck until Theo finished triumphantly:

Turreted and towered
Into the blooming skies.

"Blooming," he explained seriously, not in

the slangy sense of the word, but poetically, because in summer the skies above Guinever seemed more blue than anywhere else.

Father was eight when they came to live at the castle. He told us that he had counted a hundred bats flying out when the builders moved in. Grandfather had renamed the place—to our regret, for as children we would have enjoyed telling people that we lived in a castle. It was now Guinever Court.

The hall that was our living room was the only part of the original building that could be made habitable. It was not particularly lofty, but it had graceful vaulting and fine stone pillars, where, as children, we had tried to carve our names, much to Father's fury when he caught us. At the far end, there was still the dais, where the table of the lord would have been set at right angles to the body of the hall. A dark stone passage, dank with age, led from our living room to two small rooms in the tower. They had walls eleven feet thick, narrow window openings and archers' slits. Just outside these rooms, a flight of spiral steps led from the passage up to the battlemented lookout. Perched on the high cliff overlooking the sea, the tower was a landmark as far as the horizon. My grandfather built the main rooms on to it. The exterior of the house merged with the keep's façade, gray stone to gray stone, and did not offend.

We could never swim in what we called "our sea." The currents that swirled round the points that guarded the cove immediately below were too treacherous. All we could ever do was wait for the tide to ebb and then snatch an hour's paddling over the rocks looking for starfish in the salty pools.

During our lovely, uninhibited years, Father made his name as an artist. We would read in the newspapers and the weeklies that "Kester Palfrey's exhibition at the Chantry Galleries in London is drawing great crowds" or that he was being paid a record fee for painting a celebrity's portrait.

Every art gallery of importance possessed at least one Kester Palfrey. Then, at the height of his fame, Father switched to a different form of art. He returned to the medieval fashion for painted ceilings, and although he was certainly no Michelangelo, he revived classical painting on the grand scale. He brought to his work a superb craftsmanship and a sense of great depth so that the scenes and figures he dreamed up seemed to move and breathe.

The acres of land that had once belonged to Guinever were now farmed by Penn, my elder brother. From a farmhouse across the ravine, his fields stretched inland as far as the village of Azurstone. Only the lawns and the great mound where the oaks stood belonged to us now. But somewhere under the grass and the flowerbeds was all that remained of medieval Guinever—chapel and bailey, gate-houses and barbican—whose lord had been Roger de Vaumaris.

Our garden was laid out with grass and flowering shrubs, charming enough, but certainly Guinever was no show place. None of us had time to be imaginative over garden landscapes, and only one corner was really beautiful in a strange and exotic way: my brother Theo's lily garden.

Enclosed in a hornbeam hedge, it was entirely given over to the growing of lilies of every kind. In the round pond were Theo's beloved nymphaeas, gold and crimson and white, embedded deeply in the dark green water. It was in this garden that, as children, we discovered the Minerva stone. Covered with weeds and trailing ivy, it was just a square of stone set deep and flat into the earth. Intrigued, we had torn away the ivy, sending ants and beetles scurrying, and had found two words carved on the stone: "SEMPER. MINERVA."

Nobody knew its origin. Father said it must be the grave of a beloved cat or dog. Penn had said, "Let's dig it out and see." But the idea of finding an animal skeleton did not appeal to the family, so it remained untouched, and its timeworn lettering, "SEMPER. MINERVA."—"Forever Minerva"—eventually ceased to intrigue us.

A voice broke the silence, calling from the house. "Sarah. Sa-ra-ah . . ."

Father shouted across at me. "For God's sake answer her before she shatters my eardrums."

Freda, my stepmother, had been an opera singer before Father married her. Whenever she called us, she used every ounce of her power. She explained that she was "stretching her voice," although Father demanded, "What the devil for? She has finished with opera."

Nina lifted her head from the grass.

"Perhaps Niall has arrived and we didn't hear him."

I got up slowly and brushed an ant from my arm. I slid my bare feet into sandals, dawdling, delaying the moment. There had been no sound of a car up the drive, but Niall could have approached the house from the far side.

Freda stood in the terrace doorway. Behind her, in the living room, was my husband waiting?

Over the single year of my marriage I had moved quickly from the unguarded joy with which I would rush to meet him, through caution and uncertainty, watching for disapproval of what I said or did or wore, to the final mechanics of a greeting without feeling.

Nobody could have warned me. Niall had no friends close enough to him who might have unconsciously given me an insight into his character, nor had I met any of his small family of Scottish uncles and aunts. Whenever I asked him about them, he shrugged the questions off. "We no longer have anything in common." He spoke so finally that I did not tell him that because they were his relatives I would like to meet them.

So far as my family was concerned, I knew

their opinion of me. "You can't tell Sarah anything. She has to learn from her own experience." . . . "Sarah can't grow up quietly. She storms life."

They were right. I had tried to put a check on myself, but temperament is like a leopard's spots—there is nothing to be done about it. I plunged into things, acting first and thinking later. But in the case of Niall, it was he who stormed my emotions.

Long before I knew him I had been a compulsive viewer of his television programs, intrigued by his intelligence, his impatience with stupidity, his ruthless honesty. When I met him, the fascination remained.

All my life I had lived among artists. My father's friends came to Guinever and sat arguing and laughing, making reputations and breaking them, drinking brandy into the early hours of the morning. Before my marriage, I had worked at the Launford Art Gallery so that there, too, my life had been among artists and art lovers.

Niall came from a different world—one more recently created—with an impact on a vastly greater public, vital, high-pressured. I could no more have resisted him than sea resists the magnetism of the moon. Heady infatuation, a sense of excitement that Niall had chosen me over all the other women who must have wanted him and his own character, with its mixture of charm and aloofness, led me to become Mrs. Niall Rhodes.

As I scuffed through the grass, I knew I would go to him as he expected me to and lift my face. I could almost feel his lips, dry and taut, against my cheek.

I had drawn near enough to the terrace to see that my stepmother was holding a cablegram.

Freda was a large woman with hair color-rinsed to a dark red. She was warm and tolerant and she gave to us, another woman's four children, so much love that it shook me when I first realized her dislike of Niall. Not that she was openly aggressive, but though she was always polite to him, her face would grow pink when she looked at him. Father said that Freda showed her feelings in glorious Technicolor.

"A cable—for you." She held it out. "I'd have brought it sooner, but I was talking to Penn on the telephone and that little devil of a mail boy just threw it inside the door and made off."

I opened it and read: "DELAYED A WEEK STOP WAIT AT GUINEVER STOP NIALL."

Relief was like a cool wave washing over me. "It's from Niall," I said. "He's been held up in New York for another week."

Her face lit up. "Then you won't go back to London yet, will you?"

"No."

The only things about Freda that were small were her teeth. They gleamed now as she gave me her wide smile. "It's how I always like it. All of us at Guinever together."

All of us, except Niall.

With the cable crumpled in my hand I went down the terrace steps and across the lawn to the edge of the brick wall that guarded us from the sheer drop of the cliffs. Below the livid, creeping cloud, the sea lay sullen. I leaned my arms on the wall and looked down at the rocks where the sulphur-colored light reflected in the pools and the wet brown seaweed.

Father had had three wives. First, Polly, whom he had married when they were both students at the Slade School of Art. He liked his women to be pretty and well rounded. Polly was both. She was also as quick to fear as a rabbit. Two years after their marriage, during one of Father's outbursts of temperament, Polly had run away, met up with an ugly, golden-tongued, footloose Irishman and, after Father gave her a divorce, married him. Her life with Tom Singleton had been far more unhappy than her brief marriage to Father, which was, according to him, "my moment of idiocy." My own mother was his second wife. They had four children and were completely happy together. My mother died, tragically and ironically, of a prick from a rose thorn.

Eighteen months later, unable to live without a woman, Father married Freda. His first wife, Polly, was forgotten, until a letter only a year later and bearing a Kenya stamp brought her back into his life. Father never kept anything to himself. Like the great extrovert he was, he told us Polly's story as she had written it to him in her scrawling, twenty-page letter.

When she married Tom Singleton he took her first to Peru, where he had some wild idea of mining. But the project, which had existed almost entirely in Tom's mind, failed, and the small family went to Kenya, where they eked out some kind of existence on a miserable little strip of farmland. It was here that Dido was born.

Then Tom, whose sense of responsibility was always tenuous, disappeared. He went without the excuse of a quarrel, without any previous warning, taking with him the pittance they had in the bank—which was owed to creditors—and the jewelry Polly had inherited from her mother.

Terrified and defenseless, she became the housekeeper of a widower who farmed nearby. It was at Ngorokong when she was ten years old that Dido had her accident. The child had been found one afternoon lying injured by a stone wall that was part of a ruined fort so old that its name was lost in history.

When she regained consciousness Dido said that just before she had been struck, she had heard horses' hoofs. A horseman had jumped the wall and knocked her down. The authorities examining the place where the accident happened found that the wall had been freshly damaged. Their verdict was that a stone must have struck her. Dido protested that it was a hoof, that she had a moment's glimpse of horse and rider above her. Had she, then, recognized him? . . . Someone she knew? No, she only saw the back of the man and a chestnut's flying hoofs. The man, she said, hadn't looked round—or perhaps he had when he was well away, but by then she was unconscious. To calm Polly, who was frantic, the authorities had made inquiries in Nairobi. No one, it seemed, had been riding by the old fort that afternoon.

Polly, distracted and stupefied, tied to her employer, who had recently had a heart attack, did not do the obvious thing. Instead of having Dido taken to the hospital in Nairobi, she had her sent to the primitive, makeshift place at Ngorokong, where she could be with her as much as possible. A native doctor operated and saved Dido's life, but part of her spine was damaged and she suffered paralysis of her lower limbs. Dido could not walk.

When the farmer for whom she worked died, Polly, alone with her crippled child in a hut near a grove of thick, squat mango trees, sent a terrified letter to Father.

He showed it to Freda who said at once, "You must go out and bring her here. There's plenty of room for both of them."

"For just a few weeks," Father said. "Until

I can make arrangements for her to live in Launford, where I can keep an eye on her."

So Polly came, bringing Dido. And stayed. No one minded. In her gratitude, she was so anxious to please that she would have willingly become our slave if Freda had let her. Tom Singleton had killed all Polly's romantic dreams. All she wanted was security and a quiet life. The security she certainly got, but the quiet life was doubtful, for Father alternated between beneficence and volcanic eruption. Polly had once more to take his moods. But this time she had our example to help her, and when Father ranted we laughed and applauded him.

A flash of lightning made me see stars. Blinking, I left the wall and went back to the house. Freda was collecting some books from the wrought-iron table on the terrace.

I asked, "Where's Polly?"

"With thunder around, you should be able to guess. Hiding under the stairs." Freda lifted her head, listening to a clock chiming. "Dido's treatment at the hospital is in half an hour. I'd better go and look for her."

I said, "I'll take her into Launford."

Before she came to us, Polly's driving

experience had been on the lonely African roads. The Launford streets, crowded in summer with tourists coming to see the abbey and the quiet, swan-haunted precincts, terrified her.

Freda said, "Thank you. But, you know, it's a long wait at the hospital."

"Oh, I'll have tea somewhere," I said and went to find Dido.

The living room, with its high vaulted ceiling, was huge, and even our large furniture was lost in it. Ruby brocade and sky-blue velvet glowed; there was a litter of papers and books and phonograph records. On an old carved Italian cassone in the hall was flung a green cloak, richly embroidered at the neck. It had lain there carelessly since Nina had flung it down late the night before. I wondered where she had been and who had taken her. Nina told us little about the men she went out with because they made too small an impact upon her life. Her real love was her work, although even in that she was more gifted than hard working.

She sang folk songs to a guitar. The young man who wrote many of her songs adored her—Pascalle, her manager, would have left his wife any day for her. Nina drifted in her own lovely way, always good-tempered, gay, beautiful yet as elusive as a panther in the jungle.

When the intimate review *Methuselah and All* had ended its long run, Nina, who had had rave notices, came to Guinever "to lie in the sun," she had said, "and think of nothing." That was a month ago. Since then her agent had telephoned, written and at last come to Guinever himself to beg her to accept some of the offers that came pouring in. She kissed him on both dark jowls.

"This is one of the loveliest summers we have ever had and I'm going to make the most of it," she said, "so just don't bother me," and sent him back to London.

Father once observed, "Nina has a love affair with idleness." It was the only poetic phrase I had ever heard him use.

I found Polly crouched under the stairs by the side of Dido's wheelchair. Their faces turned, pale in the shadows, as I approached.

I laid my hand on Dido's chair. "I'm taking you into Launford for your treatment."

Polly's left cheek was puffed out with one of the treacle toffees she was always eating. "But shouldn't you be waiting for Niall?"

Again I had to explain that he was delayed.

Dido opened her white handbag, took out a mirror and looked at herself. With light fingers she began to fluff out her hair so that her head was like a mass of pale chrysanthemum petals curling inward. She said petulantly, "Can't I be left alone? I'm bored with Matthews. Day after day in that beastly hospital."

"It's better than being an inpatient, which is what they wanted. Father thought you'd be happier here with us than in a hospital ward. But of course, if you prefer to live at Matthews during your treatment . . ."

"Here, or there. It's just the same. They're experimenting with me." She put the mirror back into her bag and swung her chair violently round, unbalancing her mother, who had been clinging to the arm. "I'm not going."

"Oh, yes, you are." Gentleness never worked with Dido. "Or don't you want to walk again? If you do, you'd better do your share toward the effort. The doctors can't walk for you."

Polly swallowed a lump of toffee and pleaded, "Darling, you must try to understand that after all these years of being . . .

like you are, you can't expect the cure to be sudden."

"And whose fault is it I wasn't cured six years ago when it all happened?"

"Oh, darling, I did my best . . ."

Dido's pretty, bitter face lifted to me, her lips mocked. "Did you hear that? My mother did her best."

I said dryly, "And no one can do more. Now, let's go."

Dido's hands were stiff on the arms of her chair; her eyes looked through me like those of a dreamer. "I hope he's dead. I hope he died a horrible death."

I said, "He? Who?"

"Or she. Whoever did this to me. Whoever jumped the horse that hit me." The chair moved forward at a racing pace, gliding over the parquet floor of the hall.

Polly's voice wailed at her daughter. "Never, *never* wish evil to anyone. Wrong thoughts come home to roost."

"Let them come," said Dido, and the door of her ground-floor room slammed behind her.

The rain had begun pelting the windows. I threw a mackintosh round me and then went to get the station wagon Father had bought so that we could take Dido with us when we went out.

2

DIDO'S mood stayed with her as we drove into Launford through the streets, past the abbey and the gray gabled houses leaning against one another, too old to stand upright. Beyond the green lawns I could see the archways and the wrought-iron gate of the bishop's palace through a silver mist of rain. Launford, a paradox of a city, with its modern center of supermarkets and its cluster of lovely medievalism . . .

At first I tried to talk to Dido, and then I gave up and left her to sit sullenly in the back while I coped with lashing hail and sluggish windshield wipers.

At the main crossroads, when the traffic lights changed to red, I leaned back, my hands resting on the wheel, and looked at the long white line of Matthews Hospital. The storm cloud had almost surrendered to the sun, and light gleamed on the wide windows of the wards, the great research wing, the intensive-care unit, where patients lay watched over by closed-circuit television.

Like London, Launford had its street of doctors and this was it. On the doors of most of the lovely Regency houses of Gordon Terrace were brightly polished brass plates.

"Look. Sarah—look . . ."

Dido's voice, after her long silence, startled me. "At what?"

"That car parked outside the house with the window boxes."

I looked at the car without interest. It was long-nosed, expensive and bright red.

Dido said, "I saw that car the other day when I came shopping with Freda. A man was driving it and Nina sat next to him."

"Oh, Nina's men are legion."

"You can see this terrace from the treatment room they usually put me in at Matthews. Nurse Amelie, the gossipy one, looked out of the window the other day and said, 'There's that man's car.' She said he was a kind of osteopath, but not an orthodox one. He has developed his own method of treatment and he's doing marvelous work. He has only been here a short time but people are flocking to him."

"He has chosen an odd place to practice," I said, "right opposite the hospital."

"He has done that on purpose. Nurse Amelie says *he* says he wants to put a notice on his gate: 'Don't despair when doctors fail. Cross the road and ring my bell.' "

"Well, good luck to him," I said.

"There he is."

A slim, not very tall man came out of the house and got into the car. He sat frowning at the lights, tapping his fingers impatiently on the wheel. Then, like someone sensing he was being watched, he turned his head and looked back at Dido and me. For an instant his eyes, deep-set and startlingly bright, held mine in what seemed to be amused recognition. I said under my breath, "You've made a mistake, pal. I've never seen you before." Then the light changed and I swung right and drove through the hospital gates.

I sped past the beds of vivid pink geraniums up to the big glass door. The porter helped me with Dido's chair, and I left her with a nurse. I had about three-quarters of an hour to wait; I could have tea or I could do some shopping. I did neither. The storm was over and the sun danced on wet leaves. Little curls of steam rose from the drying pavements. I parked the car in the hospital drive and walked out. But I didn't make for the tea shop. I turned into the open gates of Gull's Folly.

They dotted England, these monstrous eighteenth-century nightmares built by men with lots of money and muddled faith, trying to catch the divine eye.

The town's folly stood at the end of the drive: four triangles, each one a room with a ceiling that rose up like a narrow pyramid, capped with a weather-beaten saint. Matthew, Mark, Luke and John sat on their compass points so that whichever way God looked, he would be reminded of Peregrine Gull, who had built the place to his own plan.

Now it was just a gimmicky house where visitors to Launford stopped, paid their shilling, looked around and went off, grinning. I got my ticket from the automatic machine by the door and went inside. The place was almost deserted. A middle-aged couple were just ahead of me, but I could see no one else.

The folly had a whispering gallery. Nobody knew whether it was by accident or design that words, spoken softly, echoed eerily round the ludicrous pyramids. Most children of Launford had, at some time or another, played the whispering game there, trying to scare one another.

I climbed the staircase leading to the gallery and stepped to the balustrade, leaning over to look down at the pieces of heavy Victorian furniture in the room below.

"Mrs. Rhodes. Mrs. Rh-od-es . . ." The sibilant whisper echoed round me, the cadences lifting and falling as they hit the walls.

"Mrs. Rho-o-h-des."

"Who is that?" I could see only the elderly couple tip-toeing, as if they were in a church, round the angle and out of sight.

"Sh-h . . . Sh-h . . ."

A child who knew me, the son or daughter of a friend, keeping up the old tradition, playing the traditional game with me? I laughed, and when the echo had died away, I said, "Who are you? I can't guess."

"Do you believe in ghosts?"

Again I waited until the echo had died down, then I called back, tempering my voice to clarify my own echo, "If you appear in a white sheet and clanking chains I promise to believe in you."

No one giggled. A whispered voice is impersonal. I peered into the dimness of the opposite gallery and could see no one. "Come on," I called. "Let's see you and find out how you can scare me."

"I don't want to-o-o."

"Then why are you doing it?"

"She told me to. She . . ." The word lifted and sank, bouncing from the walls.

"Who is 'she'?"

"She said . . . 'Just ask Mrs. Rhodes if she believes in ghosts and tell her she's going to and she's going to be scared out of her wits.' "

"Now look—"

There was a scuffle of feet. The sound came from the other side of the angle. I sprang away from the balustrade and took the corner in a kind of dive.

A boy of about eight with ginger hair was clattering down the stairs.

"Hey!" I cried out to him. "You were playing the whispering game with me, weren't you? I don't think I know you, but you seem to know me so—" I was wasting my breath. Two skinny legs took the stairs like an acrobat. I tore after him. All I wanted to know, so I told myself, was how he knew my name. The staircase curved. I swung round the bend, missed my footing and crashed into someone coming up. For a moment I rocked giddily. Two hands came out to steady me.

"You always were impetuous," said a laughing voice I knew well, too well . . .

Memories hurtled up from the past and hit me. Luke Ashton's voice . . . Luke's face . . . I'd have remembered them both after a million years.

"For heaven's sake—*you!*" I pulled away from him, startled and out of breath.

Three years had dimmed the hurt and the anger. But nobody had warned me of the impact of the laughter I thought I would never hear again. Luke's laughter always reached his eyes, making me think of light dancing on gray water. He asked, "What was the hurry?"

"That boy who passed you . . . I've got to catch him."

"Then come on." He dragged me after him down the remaining stairs.

I tried to pull back. "It doesn't matter. It's not important."

I could have been talking to an empty desert for all the good it did.

The same Luke Ashton, I thought, never listening to protests, going his way, heedless and headstrong. Admittedly, in this case it was on my account, but it was to such unimportant purpose. I no longer cared that the skinny little redhead knew my name and warned me that I was going to be afraid. In the dazzling daylight as I stormed through the open doorway, the silly threats had no more importance than the dust particles dancing on the sunbeams.

I caught up with Luke just outside the door.

"I've lost him. Now where the devil did he go?"

I leaned against the wall. "I told you it didn't matter."

"There he is."

The boy darted from behind a tree. Luke leaped on him, caught him by the shoulder and turned him round to face me. I went reluctantly toward them and, standing in front of the boy, looked down into the broad, freckled face. "I don't know *you*. How do you know my name?"

He tried to hunch his shoulders out of Luke's grasp.

I said, impatiently, "Well, *have* we met somewhere?"

"No." He had large brown eyes.

"Then come on, how did you know my name?"

"The lady told me."

"What lady?"

"The one that gave me half a crown to say what I did. I said it was silly and you'd laugh, but she said the things about ghosts and getting scared 'ud all come true."

I took a deep breath to give myself patience. "Let's get this straight. Someone gave you money to play the whispering game with me. Right?"

He nodded.

I laughed. "Oh no. It's too idiotic. Let him go, Luke. He's making it up."

"I'm not. It's true. The lady did say what I told you she said."

"Then you can tell me who she is so that I can ask her why."

His eyes were as puzzled as mine. It had been a game to him with half-a-crown prize for playing it. This cross-examination was the forfeit for being caught that he hadn't expected. "I've never seen her before. She stopped me just as you went into that place."

"So that you could tell me I was going to be frightened? You'll have to do better than that if want to be believed."

Luke said quietly, "I believe him, Sarah. He has honest eyes."

The boy said, "I didn't really want to scare you, Mrs. Rhodes."

"You didn't. But I'm interested to know why an adult should pay you to play some silly game. What was she like?"

"Oh." He considered the point. "Grown up."

"That much I guessed."

"Well, she had sort of brown hair and, oh, I dunno . . ." Then he brightened. "She wore long green gloves right up to . . . there." He thumped his right elbow.

I began to laugh. It wasn't important. Grown-ups who played silly tricks had a name. Morons. So there was a moronic woman who knew me and wore long green gloves. "Let him go," I said to Luke.

The boy ran off. He looked double-jointed in his legs.

Luke said, "You've got some peculiar friends."

"Ghost friends, it seems," I said lightly. "Perhaps a headless woman was going to appear on the stairs, only you spoiled it all by being there."

Luke didn't laugh.

Raindrops dripped from the trees on to my neck. I turned away. "And now that the silly business is over, let's sit and talk." I walked to a low wall which the sun had dried and sat down. Between the cracks in the stones, the moss was soft and still damp.

Luke hadn't changed, except that the lines between his eyes and from nose to mouth had deepened. His hair was still light brown and crisp, his nose very straight with nostrils flaring slightly, his mouth long. He sat by my side, graceful and full of self-confidence as if it hadn't been in the least a shock to see me.

"I don't believe in coincidences," I said.

"Nor do I. I didn't just happen to be here. I saw you park your car in the hospital grounds. I saw Dido. I've already heard about her case. And when you wandered off, I followed you."

"What are you doing at Matthews Hospital?"

"Working. Researching in tropical diseases."

"I thought you were dedicated to India. That's what you said before you—" I wanted to say, "Before you walked out on me," but that sounded possessive, which was the last thing I wanted to be remembered for.

Luke didn't press me to finish. He said, "My job in India was done so I came home."

"And now I suppose you are all set for London?"

"No. Even London can't produce anything better than Matthews."

I said, "I'm married."

"I know. To Niall Rhodes, the television man."

The conversation sagged. From a rosemary bush nearby, the rain and the sun had released a nostalgic scent. I realized what people meant when they used the cliché about "the air being pregnant with unasked questions." There were too many between us and neither of us wanted to begin. I said, "They tell us at the hospital that, given time, Dido will be able to walk."

He answered, "They hope so. It could be only a partial cure. But at least she'll be mobile and able to throw her chair away."

"It's terribly slow. She gets disheartened."

"Of course she does. But what do you expect after years of neglect? The hospital doesn't train magicians."

The sunlight on the trees, the familiar paths down which we had once walked together, the white gleam of the hospital between the trees, evoked memories that made me tremble inside. How detached he was. And then I saw myself, sitting on the wall with the sun on my face, quiet, not fidgeting, outwardly as detached as he. We were modern, we were sophisticated. We didn't wave old pains like banners for everyone to see, nor twist our emotions with old quarrels . . .

"How long have you been home?"

"Two months."

"And you didn't come to see us."

He let the reproof lie. Or perhaps it didn't sound like one, just an observation.

It was so quiet I could hear my heart beating. I said softly, "If you've still got our quarrels on your mind and that's why you've stayed away, it's old history, Luke."

He laughed. "*You're* not harboring grievances, are you, Sarah? So if you think *I* am, then you put me to shame."

"I don't. Of course I don't."

He said quietly, "That's all right, because I'm not either."

I wanted to turn my head and have a good look at him, but a certain shyness stopped me. Stupid to be so superficially embarrassed by a man who was once a lover. We had shared such intimacies and Luke had been so gentle with me, teaching me the considerations, the mutualism of the art of making love. In those days, we had dreamed of being together always. Now we sat like polite acquaintances, tapping our heels lightly against the old stone wall, our faces turned to the radiant after-storm light, finding conversation difficult.

I waited for him to say something more personal, to close the emotional gap of those three years. But then, how could he, and what was the matter with me that I expected him to? I said brightly, "Tell me about India."

He gave a long, low whistle. "Tell you about a different world in the five minutes I have free?"

"It was a silly question. But you can tell me in bits at a time over a long period."

He said gravely, "It can't be told that way either. Perhaps in a book—but I'm not the one to write it."

I felt suddenly small and insular and superficial and I knew it was not really Luke's fault. It was the enormity of what he had seen and done and felt. Only three years separated us from our last meeting, and yet in experience he was a long way from me. At the moment, however, I was more concerned with Luke than with his achievements. I wanted him back in our lives.

"When are you coming to Guinever?"

His hesitation was fractional. "May I?"

"Since when did you ever wait for an invitation?" I even laughed. "Once they know you're back, they'll be hurt if you don't come."

Luke said, "I hear that Nina is appearing in some charity concert at Cypress Mount on Thursday. I'll try to get a ticket and see you there."

"Don't. Father has bought a block of them. There's one to spare, which Niall would have had. But he's in New York. That's why I'm here—the weather is too lovely to stay in London." I turned to him. "Come with us to the concert, Luke. After the show, Freda and Father are having a supper party at Guinever."

He said, "Thank you, I'd like to come." He was so calm that it might have been his double who had been my lover. He looked at his watch. "There's a limit to the amount of time I can steal. I must go back." He turned and gave me a long look. In my memory I hadn't exaggerated the clear gray of his eyes. He smiled. "Do I leave you here?"

"No. I don't like this place. Perhaps it's only fun when you're a child."

We walked together between the lines of chestnut trees, turned left and went through the hospital gates. My car was parked halfway up the drive. I stopped beside it.

"Six o'clock on Thursday, for a drink and a snack with us before the concert."

I got into the car and tilted the rear mirror so that I could watch him walk away from me. I suddenly thought, "It could be Niall . . . the smooth brown hair, the throw of the shoulders, the swift, purposeful walk." Like Niall, too, he had a quick mind, impatience with stupidity, ambition. Luke and Niall, men out of the same mold. My type of man. That is what attracts: a type—something created in imagination and recognized in life. Yet had I been in my right senses I would have walked straight past both of them with my fingers crossed.

Luke had been registrar at Matthews when I first met him. Our love affair had been brief, stormy and beautiful. Our passion was real; our quarrels, bitter. We were both sensitive, recalcitrant. If Luke understood me a little, I understood (but could not accept) what he was, what he always would be. I was possessive. To me at that time, love was a complete surrender, an emotional and physical submerging of myself, a strong and unqualified abandonment. I expected the same in return. But Luke had ambition, and the more I showed I wanted him totally, the more he withdrew himself into work. By being possessive I had encroached on the thing he prized most: his freedom. Our last quarrel took place when he told me that he was leaving for India within a week to start a research unit in Bihar. I saw the plan as an escape from me. I did not understand that his going away was a necessity to his temperament. Only too late did I realize that by letting him go willingly, I could have held him. Instead, I took it personally, angrily, accusingly. And so I killed everything.

Nurse Amelie's voice startled me.

"Well, here we are." She had pushed Dido's chair up to the car. "It wasn't too bad, was it, dear?"

"It was a bore," said Dido.

Nurse Amelie raised her eyebrows at me, and I guessed that Dido had been as difficult and uncooperative as she dared—not that, I thought with satisfaction, Nurse Amelie would stand much nonsense from her. We exchanged a few remarks about the weather as we settled Dido in the back of the car. Then Nurse Amelie said cheerfully, "See you tomorrow, dear," and walked briskly back to her next patient.

I got in behind the wheel and said, "Would you like a run into the country?"

"I want to go home."

"That's fine. So do I."

As we drove out through the gates, Dido said, "Luke Ashton is back. He came to see me while I was on that beastly treatment table."

"I've seen him too."

"Why didn't he stay away? *Why?*"

Her ferocity shook me. My foot jerked off the accelerator. "What makes you say that?"

Her voice filled the car with bitter clarity. "You have everything, haven't you? Money, health, a rich husband—and now Luke. They say people are born under certain stars—lucky or unlucky."

"If you were an astrologer," I said dryly, "you'd know that Luke is no longer, and never will be again, in my stars."

3

I HAD a restless night, dreaming and waking between strips of nightmare in which my friends were my enemies. Ludicrously, I even dreamed of Nina in long green gloves.

When morning came I dressed, feeling restless and tense. I needed action. I would go to London. I made the unnecessary excuse that if I were to remain here, I needed a few more clothes and, anyway, I should stop by the apartment to see if there was anything urgent in the mail.

There was a nearly unchanging pattern about breakfast at Guinever. Food was kept ready on a hot plate, and we came straggling in. Freda and Polly would be first in the dining room; then Father, demanding a kind of Henry VIII breakfast; then Theo and I.

Whenever she could, Nina would shut up her Knightsbridge apartment and come to Guinever, but she brought with her one London habit. She seldom had breakfast with us. She would come down, collect coffee and toast and disappear into her room until late in the morning.

Theo and I often met on the stairs. This morning I was first. When he appeared I said, "Am I early or are you late?"

Dido answered for him, her laughter sharp and a little cruel. "Oh, he's been putting umbrellas over his precious lilies."

He had a particularly sweet smile. "You're wrong. Rain is champagne to them."

He was two years older than I, big like Father, with a broad face and skin bronzed by the outdoor life he led. He was a botanist and worked at the seed selection station near Launford. I had been there and seen the testing grounds of giant poppies, red clover and autumn crocuses, on which experiments were made in plant genetics to increase the world's food supply.

Dido was still taunting him. "You wanted to be an artist once. Why don't you paint your silly lilies and hang their pictures round your walls? You might dream of them. Then you'd be happy."

I turned to her, "If you want to be useful you can pass the marmalade."

Dido passed it in silence. I knew all three of us were thinking of the same thing. Dido with mockery, I with regret. Theo . . . ? How did he feel now about Father's rejection of him as a serious artist?

The incident, small perhaps to us, enormously important to Theo, had happened some years ago. Father had been excited when Theo showed an interest in painting and began to take him round the galleries in London.

Absorbed and happy, Theo spent his last year at the university and at home surrounded by paint brushes. He wanted his work to be entirely his own, with no help from Father. He would never show us his paintings. He just said, "Wait until I have something I think good enough. At the moment I'm experimenting."

Then one afternoon he brought a painting for us to see.

Father, who never quite understood Theo's underlying sensitiveness, stared at the propped-up canvas. "I thought you said you intended to be an artist. Don't play jokes. Take it away; do what you like with it but for God's sake don't offer it to the Royal Academy."

Theo took the painting away. We never knew what happened to it.

I remember that after the incident Freda and Father had had their first and only real quarrel—not that it did any good where Theo was concerned. Freda and Nina and I tried to make him see that Father had high standards, that he was tactless but never cruel. We insisted that he wanted to spur Theo on to work harder. Theo must understand, must go on painting. Perhaps he listened to us—we none of us knew, for he said nothing.

But this morning Dido's taunt only made him laugh. "Oh, I often dream of lilies. I create new colors, new blooms. It's like having a secret garden."

"You have a *secret*—" Dido began. And then she stopped.

Polly said, curiously, "What secret?"

Nobody answered her. Dido's head bent over her tea cup—she hated coffee. Theo reached for the toast. The atmosphere was suddenly charged with awkwardness. I said rather loudly, "I'm going to London for the day. Theo, will you drop me at the station on your way?"

He gave me his warm smile. "Of course."

Freda said, "If you decide to stay the night, be home in good time tomorrow. It's the concert at Cypress Mount."

"I'll be here. Don't worry." I turned to Father. "By the way, Luke's back in England. I saw him yesterday. I've asked him to join us for the concert. As Niall won't be here for it, you've got a spare ticket."

Father's eyes glistened. "Luke home. That's fine. Now perhaps I'll get a decent game of chess."

I looked at Freda. She refused to meet my eyes. Father's chess was a case of "Don't think you'll beat me. By fair means or foul, I'll win." I had once, in anger, accused Luke of playing with Father only to make a fool of him. He had replied, "That's not true. It fascinates me to see how many times he can cheat." And we both had laughed.

When Theo dropped me at Launford, the train was already in the station. As I settled myself, the guard's whistle blew and a man came up the platform. He paused when he saw me, leapt on to the train and came and sat down opposite me. He had dark hair brushed off a low forehead and a short straight nose which accentuated his long upper lip. He looked at me through coils of smoke and his eyes were amused, vain and frankly interested.

I remembered now where I had seen him before. He was the osteopath Dido had pointed out to me yesterday. I had a feeling that he had deliberately chosen this compartment and he was going to speak to me. To thwart him, I turned back to my newspaper.

"You are Mrs. Niall Rhodes."

"Yes." I implied: *And what if I am?*

"I know your sister, Nina, quite well. I am Francis Lorian." He said it as if he expected me to recognize the name.

We stared silently at one another. He smiled and said at last, "I see that Nina hasn't told you about me? So you aren't given to girlish confidences?"

"No."

"Then I'll have to introduce myself further. I'm an osteopath, for want of a better word. Actually, I'm unorthodox but very successful."

"Congratulations."

It was like a publicity handout but completely unsubtle, without preamble, without finesse. The train gave a long-drawn-out scream and raced through a tunnel. When we came out into the light again, he said, "Dido Singleton is a very beautiful girl, isn't she?"

I had a feeling I should be on guard. "Yes. But—"

"But have I met her? No. Nina pointed her out to me once when she was in the car with your stepmother. It's a tragedy, Mrs. Rhodes, that she's tied to that chair."

"She won't be for always."

"She shouldn't be now," he said. "She should be walking."

"Doctors can't perform miracles."

"But *I* can."

"Then I'm surprised you don't practice in London, where you could get the recognition you . . . you imagine you deserve."

He said imperturbably, "Oh, I'll get to London later."

He turned to a brief case by his side, deliberately closing the conversation. I was glad, but I was also annoyed. I had a feeling that every move he made was for a purpose. First Nina, now me. What next? Did he expect a concerted effort by both of us to convince Father that he could cure Dido more quickly than the doctors? It seemed obvious, yet he had to be too intelligent to believe that it would be so easy. He had to know what everyone knew, that there were men posing as osteopaths whose qualifications were obtained by some vague correspondence course. This talk of unorthodox methods could hide his own inadequacy. I was glad when he went into the dining car and I didn't see him again on that journey.

I gave up even pretending to read and sat in my corner, regretting the impulse that was sending me to London. My return, even for one day, to the Portland Place apartment gave me no pleasure. Niall's personality was too strongly stamped on it. I felt that it was my home only by his grace and favor.

Niall was a schoolmaster by profession. After his university studies, he had taken teaching posts abroad, in the Near East and Africa. He returned to England after eight years and became assistant headmaster at a school in Sussex. He had been there only a few months when he was asked to participate in an educational debate on television, taking the place of a schoolmaster who was ill.

He appeared and almost overnight was a success. There were no years of plodding for Niall. The general comment was that he had a good mind and he made an obsession of absolute honesty. I often wondered, if a census were taken, how many people would have said they liked Niall Rhodes as they liked other television gods. His image was that of an unpredictable intellectual who had no mercy with humbug. So he intrigued, rather than arousing affection.

Last summer Niall had come to Dorset to arrange a program about Launford abbey. He had known Polly slightly in Africa, and he had telephoned her from his hotel. Looking back, I believe his reason was that he wanted to know Father. Polly, all flutter and excitement, had invited him to dinner at Guinever.

It was the first of many visits during the following two weeks. I would come home from the Launford Art Gallery where I worked, to find that once again Niall Rhodes was expected for dinner at eight. Nina had been in between engagements and was at Guinever so I thought, "Of course it must be Nina."

I was quite unprepared for what happened on the last evening before Niall's return to London. We were in the hall seeing him off and he said to me, "Come out to the car, Sarah."

There, with his hand on the door handle, he asked, "Are you in love?" It came out as matter-of-factly as if he were asking me if I liked roast beef. I said, no, I wasn't in love.

"And you never have been?"

"Of course I have. I'm nineteen." Hurt and remembered anger made my voice hard. "But it's old history."

"We all have our emotional baptisms," he said. Then he got into his car and drove away.

Two evenings later he telephoned me from London. He wanted to take me to a party at the Dorchester for stage and television personalities.

"But I've nothing to wear!" My frantic cry was treated with derision from Father, who thought all women should wear slacks if they were thin, saris if they were fat or, if they were posing for him, nothing at all.

Freda said in response to my protest, "All you want is a new evening dress. I'll meet you in Launford tomorrow lunchtime and we'll go shopping."

Nina lent me her dark green cloak; Freda slipped the velvet case containing her ruby earrings into my suitcase. Thus, I went to London believing that Niall had asked me to the party on an impulse because I had shown such interest in his kind of life. It did not occur to me that there was anything more personal in his invitation. He was outside my orbit, a star from a world I viewed as a novice looks from a London street at the night sky.

Niall telephoned me soon after my arrival at the hotel, and that evening, in the new dark chiffon dress and Freda's ruby earrings, I stepped out of the elevator and into Niall's world.

A disturbing thing happened as I paused in the foyer looking for him. I saw through the weaving mass of visitors a man standing at the window. He had his back to me, and my heart gave a violent jerk.

Luke? Luke Ashton? It couldn't be . . . it mustn't be—not at this moment when a new interest had entered my life. Not Luke . . .

There were thousands of slim, dark men in the world but some small thing gave each of them an individuality—the throw of a head, a certain way of standing, a gesture . . . If it were Luke, then he mustn't see me.

As I prepared to dodge behind a group of people, the man at the window turned.

"Niall!" I said aloud in utter astonishment and wild relief.

I had always been attracted by men older than myself—Niall was thirty-one, and Luke a year younger. And strangely they both looked older than their ages. Quite often during the next two days, I saw again how alike they were in appearance. Alike, and yet so different. Luke, delightful as a companion, a perfect lover—but sidestepping, like a racehorse, if one came too close to him and accepting physical possession but avoiding mental and spiritual intimacy. He had once said, in quiet anger, "You can't talk of loving until you know how to set a man free."

There was no such talk with Niall. In fact there was very little time for private conversation. There was the reception at the Dorchester; a luncheon the following day with his manager, Leon Raphael; a cocktail party at Niall's elegant apartment on Portland Place. Through them all, he was my charming and attentive host.

On the morning of my return to Guinever, when he was driving me to the station, he told me he was going to marry me. His manner was calm, unemotional and confident. I sat by his side in the big car, outwardly as calm as he, my heart doing somersaults. *He can't mean it. You don't ask someone you scarcely know to marry you . . .*

We were early, and Niall had detoured, driving south into Hyde Park. He drew into the side of the road and stopped the car.

"I meant what I said. I want to marry you."

I couldn't speak. I was confused and still unbelieving. I made an involuntary movement and laid my hand over his. Immediately he leaned toward me and kissed me swiftly and without passion.

"Good," he said. "I will come down to Guinever on Sunday and we will make all the arrangements." Then he restarted the car and drove me to Paddington Station.

I sat in the train tightly wedged between a fat man and a woman who smelled of apples. I had a magazine on my lap but I didn't open it. How modern Niall was . . . dismissing sentiment, taking it as a mutually accepted thing that "I want to marry you" was just another way of saying "I love you."

Only by saying aloud to the streets of Launford and the ancient oaks of Guinever: *Niall Rhodes is in love with me* could I convince myself that I had not dreamed the weekend. And I? What else was this heady, bemused sensation? After all, at first, love is a little madness. Niall was infinitely more perceptive than I, more calm, stronger. He had decided for me. So, I walked without a will of my own toward the day of my registry office marriage.

Father said, "For heaven's sake, why? The man has no sense of humor."

I did not want humor. Nor did I want a love affair. I had had that and come out of it wiser about people, but too bruised to bear a repetition. I had buried all that I had felt for Luke and I needed a belonging that was permanent. I was a spendthrift with a purseful of emotion. I was also immature, and, where Nina was coolly adult—knowing what she wanted and where she was going—I had learned precious little about myself. Part of my abysmal ignorance in the days before I married Niall was my acceptance of people at face value. I neither saw nor understood the complicated currents that ran beneath the carnival masks they wore to impress each other.

During our brief engagement I came to London only twice and Niall spent two weekends at Guinever. For the rest of the time, the television studios seemed to swallow him up, and when we did meet, it was usually at some function with others present. "This is Sarah Palfrey." . . . "This is my future wife." I was aware of the long, interested looks, the greetings that were usually warm and welcoming as if a little of

Niall's fame had already rubbed off on me.

At last the emptiness which Luke had left was filled. I belonged. I was needed.

Although we did not meet often, I was quickly aware of the vast difference between us. Once, I said to Niall, "You should marry someone who is your intellectual equal."

He had laughed. "Darling Sarah, I should hate a clever wife, and when you have been married to me for six months, you will be exactly what I want. I wonder if you will recognize yourself?"

I should, of course, have sensed the danger signal, but I did not. His picture of the future Sarah Rhodes intrigued me.

My first and only doubt hit me as I stood in front of the mirror in my bedroom at Guinever in the dress I would wear for my wedding. I said silently to my reflection, "From tomorrow you will begin to change. Niall will change you." And I felt a swift panic rise and choke me. I put my hand to my throat, swallowed and told myself that it was prewedding nerves.

We were married at a registry office in London to a fanfare of cameras. Father gave us a sumptuous reception at the Carlton

Towers Hotel and moved among the guests like a great red giant.

No one's love dies at the flick of a coin. What played the largest part in killing mine was the sense of inequality which, during my brief engagement, I had so happily accepted. Niall could not see me as an equal in anything, even in my judgment of paintings, of which, because of years of training, I had infinitely more knowledge than he. But to Niall, he was, in all respects, the teacher and I, the pupil.

More and more often, as the weeks went by, I found myself waiting for his criticism.

Once, at a reception given for a famous American television star, I went over to speak to a very young girl who sat alone in a corner. Niall found me and led me away. "Leon is asking where you are," he said. "You really mustn't hide in corners."

I said as we wove through the crowds, "You might have waited and let me introduce you. That was Marian Allys, Gordon le Passeur's secretary. He brought her because she's going home with him to do some extra work and when they got here he just dumped her. She was alone and lost."

He said, with his hand firmly on my arm, "That's not your problem. I will tell you whom you must know and not know."

Another time, at a restaurant, I said, looking up from the menu, "Escargots! I've never tasted them." I smiled at the waiter. "I wonder if I'll like them."

I had my escargots. But before they were served to us, Niall said coldly, "My darling Sarah, you do not flaunt your naïveté in front of a waiter."

"But he was very young and it must be dull spending your life serving food to other people. I was just trying to make him feel human, and—"

"—and soft hearts never won respect."

I said indignantly, "Father would have taken one look at him and asked him if he came from Greece. He would have been interested in his background—"

"But I am not"—Niall's voice came with deadly quiet—"so you had better not imitate your father and ask the waiter if he comes from Greece or Albania or farthest India."

"Oh heavens," I cried, "what a bore it is not being able to be oneself!"

Slowly I began to rebel against the efforts to change me. After two months of marriage I was no longer the star-struck pupil. The lessons Niall tried to teach me were too often given. In the end, I answered him back, argued and insisted on a right to think for myself.

The battle that had been threatening for some time between us came into the open one evening. We had been watching a television play and when it was over I crossed the room and switched the set off.

I stood looking down at the blank screen and said, "I want a family."

"Not yet."

I swung round. "Why not?"

When he considered a conversation at an end, Niall had a habit of closing his eyes. "I want you to myself for some time longer. Children will divide your attention; you'll become a fussy, absorbed mother."

"I won't be anything of the sort. I wasn't an over-indulged child in a narrow little household, so why on earth should you imagine I'd be any different with my children? I want a family—boys and girls . . ."

Niall had picked up a newspaper and spread it out like a screen between us. I reached out and whipped it out of his hands. *"Listen to me."*

"I have listened and I have told you: I have no intention of having a family yet. Now, turn that television on again. There's a political discussion—"

"Not until we have talked this thing out."

He got up and put me quietly to one side and switched on the set, "The color isn't quite right tonight."

I leaned against the mantelpiece. "I shall see to it that I become pregnant."

He looked at me over his shoulder, his eyes blank, lusterless. "If you are ever pregnant, I know just where to take you."

The quiet conviction of his voice frightened me. "I don't understand. All you seem to want is to change me, to make me like some ideal you have. But you're failing, aren't you, Niall? Because I can't *be* changed. I am myself." He was twirling the knobs on the television set and my voice rose above the sound of men talking. "Don't you see? You've got to live with the person you married. I don't come up to your standards, but you knew what I was like when you fell in love with me. I didn't play a part in order to try and attract you—I'm a bad actress, anyway. But you loved me . . . or did you?" I felt a sudden, sharp pain as understanding ripped aside all my illusions. "It wasn't love, was it?"

"May I please listen to this program?"

"No. For once I will do the dictating." I pushed his hand away from the controls and switched the set off again. "You didn't love me. You just found, in me, the kind of woman you wanted. Not intellectual—that would have made me your equal—but malleable. You told me so yourself when we were engaged. You told me that after six months I wouldn't recognize myself. Well, I will, because I won't change. I won't be a robot wife."

He was laughing as he bent and kissed me. "Stop arguing—it doesn't impress me, anyway. I can give you violent affirmations of love, if you like. But they would be just a jumble of pretty words. The basic truth is that love between the sexes is desire. Just that. And you must admit that I am a good lover." He walked to the door and switched off the wall lights. Then he came to me and said softly, "Damn the television!" His arms went round me and he carried me to the wide settee and made love to me.

4

I LEFT the train and found a taxi. When it stopped at Portland Place I looked up at the fine stone façade of our third-floor apartment. The windows of the living room where open at the bottom. Our maid, Maria, was on vacation, and I knew I had closed the windows before I left for Guinever in case of a sudden summer storm.

In the entrance hall, Manson, the head porter, was standing by the center table, which always had a splendid display of flowers. His bald head shone so brightly that I often wondered if he polished it.

I said good morning and asked if Maria had come back unexpectedly. Then if anyone had been in the apartment. The window cleaner? No, no one. Of course it was quite simple: I had only imagined I had closed the windows.

I let myself into the apartment and found a pile of letters. Two were from friends of mine who lived abroad. I read them standing by Niall's precious Matisse on the cream-paneled wall. Then I went into his study, put his letters on his desk and went into the living room.

It was large and lit by three tall windows. Bokhara rugs glowed on the floor, the furniture was eighteenth century, the hangings leaf green. When I first saw the apartment, I knew that there was nothing there that, from the stand-point of elegance, should be altered. The place was perfect but, except for Niall's study, impersonal. It had the mark of an expensive interior decorator with nothing added that was gay or quixotic or personal.

I wandered into my bedroom and threw my coat and handbag onto the bed. I had never shared Niall's room. Mine was one of the two guest rooms, cool ice-blue and soft gray walls. One day, when it needed redecorating, I would have a color scheme of yellow and russet and gold. In the meantime I hung two of Father's paintings on the wall—vivid splashes of color depicting the black earth opening onto vast interior fires—turbulent pictures to hang in such a serene room. I also brought my collection of rough gems—onyx and amethyst and rock crystal, jasper and cornelian—my books and my phonograph records. I hesitated over Luke's last gift to me—a small lapis lazuli Kwan Yin, Goddess of Love. It had always seemed to me to have an epitaph, invisibly carved: "Beautiful things, like dreams, never last." But, in the end, I could not leave it behind. Even Niall admired it, picking it up, stroking the cool stone. "This is quite lovely. Where did you get it?" And I had said, "A friend gave it to me a long time ago."

"He had good taste," Niall said, assuming the friend to be a man but asking no more questions.

I ran a comb through my hair and went back to the living room. A small wind stirred the curtains. On the coffee table was a large amber glass ashtray. I remembered cleaning it before I shut up the apartment. Now there were three cigarette stubs in it. Under the table was an envelope. I picked it up. It was addressed to Niall and there was no letter inside. I looked at the postmark. It had been sent the day before.

So someone, taking his time, had sat down, smoked three cigarettes and had opened and read the letter. He must have known that Niall was in New York and I was at Guinever so that he would not be disturbed.

Suddenly the apartment was full of another personality, unknown, unnamed. Perhaps he was still here, hiding behind a heavy curtain.

I got up and with tingling nerves, went from room to room, making a great deal of noise, rattling cupboard doors. I don't know what I would have done if anyone had sprung out at me. But nobody did.

I went into the kitchen last of all. It was orange and white and very tidy. I looked in the sink. It was shining wet, as if someone had run water recently. After that I did a systematic check of jewelry, clothes, silver. Nothing was missing.

There was a sound in the hall. It was so soft that I could have imagined it—just a tiny metallic rattle. I leaped across the room.

An envelope lay on the mat, addressed to me. I took it into the living room and slit it open. Inside was a sheet of gray notepaper, and in a large, untidy handwriting was written: "Ask Niall if he remembers the Italian Doll. Ask him if he dare answer that one on his program." It was signed "Alexandra."

My knees caught the edge of a chair and I sat down with a jerk. The panel program on which Niall appeared was returning in a few weeks, after three months' rest. Only the most erudite questions by listeners were asked and answered by the three experts. I reread the note. It was, of course, quite simple. Someone Niall knew had written to me, knowing that he was away. She wanted a simple question answered. Simple? I had no idea whether the Italian Doll (I noted the capital letters) was a person or a toy owned by someone famous. But Niall would know and would answer—"if he dare." That was the part that held the threat. *And if he dare not*?

I went to the window and looked down into the street. I was too late to see anyone walking away from the glass and wrought iron doors, but Manson would almost certainly have seen any stranger enter or leave the building. When I lifted the receiver, however, there was no answer from the porter's lodge. And that was significant. Someone could have waited until Manson had been sent to get a taxi or to go on some errand and then slipped up the stairs to the apartment. I realized now that I had not heard the elevator gate clang.

I searched for an explanation and came up at last with the one that seemed most obvious. Someone who disliked Niall or was a little deranged had sent that note.

I went restlessly back to the window. People in the limelight, like Niall, had their quota of enemies, of people jealous of their success. When I saw him again he would explain it to me. And perhaps, if he were in a good mood, we would laugh about it. I leaned my head against the cool glass and tried to remember his laughter. I could not.

Healthy hunger drove me at last to look in the refrigerator, knowing that I would find nothing. I picked up my bag, double-locked the door and went out.

Downstairs Manson was sitting reading a newspaper.

I said, leaning on the desk, "About five minutes ago someone put a note through my mail slot. I wondered whether you'd seen a stranger around. The . . . the signature is rather vague."

He looked at the clock behind him. "That would be when I went to get a taxi for Sir Henry Player. I'm sorry—"

"It doesn't matter," I said.

There was a row of little shops in a small back street. I bought a ham roll, some apples and a carton of milk. Mr. Roberly, a miniature John Bull, asked as he buttered the roll, "When are we going to see your husband on television again, Mrs. Rhodes?"

"Soon," I said. "The new series of *In Your View* starts the week after next. And then there is the *Questions and Answers* program."

"I'll tell my wife. We always watch him. It's good the way he shows up the phoneys. He knows so much, too. All those quotations and bits of history."

And the story of the Italian Doll . . .

Back in the apartment, while I waited for the coffee to percolate, I went to the back door and tried the knob. The one thing I was certain of was that I had locked and bolted it before I left. But the bolts were drawn back, and as I turned the knob the door came open onto the fire escape.

I stood by the window, eating the ham roll. It tasted like dust. I watched the traffic stream through the dun-gray afternoon and saw the pigeons wheel round the spire of All Souls' Church.

The coffee was strong and I drank it so hot that it scalded my throat. It was doubtful that whoever had visited the apartment would return. Yet I knew I would not go back to Guinever that night.

I finished the coffee, standing at the

window and looking along the line of parked cars. Was someone sitting in one of them, watching the house? I tried to see into them; those nearest seemed empty.

Freda answered when I put the call through to Guinever, and I told her I was staying overnight in town.

"You'll be back tomorrow. The concert—you remember? And Luke's coming."

I said, "Yes, I'll be back," as if Luke had a right to expect me there.

I walked from room to room like a visitor to a museum who is allowed to touch the precious objects. They were beautiful and I had a reverence for them, too—the collection of white jade, the Chinese carving on the wall, the gilt torchères near the window. Niall's possessions, valued as I was valued, because they were his shop window.

Go home, said my common sense. *Go back to Guinever. You're doing no good by staying.* Except perhaps preventing an unknown caller from returning because he—*she*—knows that I am still here? Anyway, there was no argument. I was going to stay.

The afternoon crawled. I wrote some letters, collected some clothes I would take to Dorset and piled them on the armchair in my bedroom.

By five o'clock I wished I had gone home. I was making a mystery of something that had a perfectly reasonable explanation. All right then, said reason, what is it? *I don't know and I don't care. I want to go home.* There was still time to catch the seven o'clock train. *Then go.*

But my dogged, irrational demon cautioned, "Wait." And like a slave I sat there, obedient and still.

The dun-gray evening closed in. For a few minutes there was one great rift in the clouds and a stormy sun stabbed the sweeping façade of Portland Place. Then the darkness came.

I sat in the chair in the living room and did not turn on the light. I closed my eyes. The clock had just struck the half-hour after nine when I heard the drone of the elevator. I uncurled my legs and sat forward, listening. The gate gave a little metal clang and I knew it had opened on our floor. A key rasped in the lock.

Darkness had painted out everything but the faintest outline of the things in the room. I heard footsteps. Someone stood in the doorway. Then there was a flood of light.

"What the devil are you doing here?" my husband demanded.

Darkish hair, bloodless skin that had sometimes made me wonder in the early days of knowing him if he were ill, eyes pale, without sparkle—his was a face that looked better in a black and white photograph or on a television screen after the make-up department had given him color.

We stared at one another like antagonists across the beautiful room . . . No gesture on either side, no moving toward one another.

I spoke first. "How did you manage to cable me this morning from New York?"

When he was angry he became pedantic.

"I'm no longer a schoolmaster. I haven't time to explain to you the miracles of time and space."

"Oh, for heaven's sake . . ."

"Now I'll do the asking. Why didn't you wait for me at Guinever as I told you?"

"I wanted some clothes. And in any case, I have every right to come here. In case you have forgotten it, this is my home, too."

He began to walk very quietly round the room. A year of marriage, a week of being parted. Yet still no physical contact, not even a perfunctory kiss, and a room quivering with his resentment. *There's nothing left, Niall. Not even friendship* . . . I had reached the bottom of many layers of feeling.

I had to break the silence. "You were here this morning, weren't you?"

The clock on the mantelpiece had stopped. He was giving it his whole attention, winding it with slow, careful fingers. It was very valuable.

I said again, "You were here this morning, weren't you?"

He did not answer me.

Anger seized me. "It doesn't matter whether you admit it or not. I know and you know that I know. You heard me come and you left by the fire escape. I found the back door unlocked. Why did you get someone in New York to send me that cable pretending to be delayed? Because that's what happened, isn't it?"

"Is this an inquisition?"

"If you like."

He opened an onyx box and took out a cigarette. His hand was quite steady as he flicked his lighter.

I shook with fury. "When did you return from the States? Yesterday? The day before? I know you were back here because I found an envelope with yesterday's postmark. But the porter had no idea. You must have come like someone guilty, creeping in when no one was around. And when you heard me enter you slipped out by the fire escape. I know you did because the door was unbolted. You ran off like some damned intruder."

I had no more breath left; I hadn't stopped between sentences. I saw it all quite clearly now. There had been no illicit entry.

"Why did you pretend to be still in New York?"

"Even you can surely solve that one. I wanted the apartment to myself. I like emptiness."

I had known for a long time that Niall was by nature a solitary. I could understand that. Luke had taught me that people needed breathing space. But Niall's need was different. It was an utter and almost violent rejection of companionship, of affection, and I couldn't bear to look at him. Instead, I said to his reflection in the Regency mirror across the room, "I am unnecessary to you. You need a mistress, not a wife."

"Even mistresses have to be carefully chosen. They can obtrude," he answered.

"You play the king. You command; you

dismiss. *I'm real too, Niall.* I want to be reckoned with. But that seems to be too much to ask."

He made a quick impatient gesture with his hand.

A rush of hopelessness welled up in me. "Is this marriage? *Is* it, Niall? If so, it's not for me."

Niall's defense was always a cold logic. "The solution is obvious. You love Guinever; you're happy with your family. All right. Go and live there. I will come to you when I can. And when there is some function we must attend together, you will come up to town for it."

"I'm damned if I will."

"You can't accept the rational, can you?"

"Guinever is Father's house, not ours."

"I hadn't noticed he resents you being there. On the contrary . . ."

I could have said, "But your presence there doesn't give him particular joy." I stood in silence, a finger between my teeth, biting on it in a way I had when I was trying to keep calm.

Niall said, "Don't bite your nails. I've told you, I'll come down and see you when I can."

"So that no one will be able to accuse you in public of deserting your wife."

"I've no intention of deserting you. Face facts, Sarah. A great many men have apartments in London and go down to join their wives when they can. They manage to live very contentedly."

"The weekend wives. We know some. But they have families—children. Their lives are full. And anyway, you wouldn't be down on weekends."

"How can I when I'm at the beck and call of the studio?"

He didn't suggest that he find me a house in the country. For that, I was glad. The idea of living alone, sleeping in an empty house, would make me claustrophobic. I was too used to belonging to a houseful of people. Unlike Niall, I was no solitary.

"What I'm suggesting," he said, "is a good plan."

I passed him and went to the door.

He called me back angrily. "Come here."

"We've said all there is to say. I shall go to Guinever as you suggest. But with this difference—I won't ever come back here. I've tried to learn what you want of me, but the lessons have gone on too long. I'm leaving school, Niall. And don't come down and try to get me back."

He had a way of moving quickly without any apparent rush. His fingers gripped my chin, tilting my head. "Get one thing into your head, my darling." His smile was just a lift of long, thin lips. "You are my one and final wife."

It was like the last line in a drama. The curtain should come down. It didn't. We were not acting and so there was the anticlimax, destroying the artistry of his words. I knocked his hand away from my face. "I shall leave you, and there is nothing you can do about it."

He drew a sharp breath and caught hold of my arms. "I'm not worried. You won't leave me."

Over his shoulder I saw the note lying on the coffee table. I turned and outstared him. "Who is Alexandra?"

His whole body jerked as if I had struck him. His lips mouthed an oath, but whether in shock or puzzlement, I had no idea. His voice was perfectly calm as he asked, "Am I supposed to know?"

"One of us is. And it isn't I."

I picked up the note. The scrawled words

"Italian Doll" seemed especially black, starting out of the paper like ebony fire. I gave it to him and he read it with his back to me. The room became silent until the sheet of gray notepaper fluttered from his hand to the floor with a sound like the faint flapping of a wing.

When he faced me again, he looked quite untroubled. "I'm sorry to disappoint you, but a madwoman's idiotic question doesn't upset me in the least."

"You don't know the name?"

"I may have met someone called Alexandra some time in my life. It's not an uncommon name."

"And the doll?"

"I played with airplanes, not dolls, when I was a boy." He picked up the letter and began tearing it slowly into small pieces. Then he put them tidily into the waste basket. "There are a pile of letters from fans on my desk. You should know that." He turned and considered me. "Are you perhaps jealous of my mail, of people I don't even know?"

"I don't care whom you know, whom you meet. I don't care if you receive dozens of love letters. You can have a horde of mistresses and it would no longer hurt me."

"Now you're being stupid."

I said, "Nothing between us matters any more. What's the use of going on? You are a personality cult, Niall, and being my husband comes far down the list of things that are important to you."

Suddenly he laughed. "Oh, Sarah, what rubbish you sometimes talk—'Nothing between us matters any more,' she says. *Nothing* between us?" He reached to catch hold of me. "You know that's not true—don't you?"

I backed sharply and hit my shoulder against the mantelpiece.

Niall said with amusement, "Don't go up the chimney, my darling. I know of a better place." He caught at the neck of my dress and I heard the stitching rip.

"You're so small, I could carry you." He picked me up in his arms.

I pummeled him with my fists, but I wasn't hurting him. He carried me into the bedroom, laid me on the bed and flung himself over me. "*Now* say that you are unnecessary to me." He undressed me, pulling my dress over my head, ruffling my hair and then gathering it in his hands and hiding his face in it. "Your hair is like silk." He lifted his head. "Don't you know, Sarah, that desire is the one undoubted thing, the only thing that can't lie?"

The sole light came from the living room. It poured obliquely across the bedroom floor. I was glad I couldn't see his face. I could not fault him as a lover, and in the darkness his passion had power to rouse response in me, blotting out memory of resentment, making of the moments an oasis in the desert of disillusion.

Afterward when he got up and left me I lay appalled at the weakness of my own participation. But then, desire is a curious, unreasonable thing that is not concerned with love. I heard him in the living room pouring himself a drink. A heavy despair seized me. This was all it ever was, a physical taking in the darkness.

5

I GOT up at six o'clock the next morning after the longest night I had known. I crept into the kitchen, made myself some coffee and drank it while I searched for two suitcases. I pushed as many of my clothes as I could into them. The thick pile of the wall-to-wall carpets and the growing stream of traffic outside muffled the sounds I made. Even so, I kept giving anxious glances at Niall's closed door.

He usually slept until eight o'clock and did not stir from his room until Maria took in his toast and coffee. But Maria was on vacation and I had no intention of taking her place. He would have to get his own breakfast this morning.

I did not dare ring for the porter to take my suitcases. Instead, I carried them to the elevator and locked the door of the apartment with my key. It was half past seven.

Downstairs, in the lobby, the night porter was vacuuming the plum-colored carpet. He said good morning and took the suitcases from me.

"It won't be easy to get a taxi at this hour," I said and asked him to telephone a limousine service firm nearby.

When the car arrived, I told the driver my train didn't leave until nine o'clock. "Please just drive me around till then."

"Where would you like to go?"

"Hampstead Heath," I said. "It's a lovely morning."

A sense of freedom and the fresh air blowing from the deserted heath into the open window of the car took away the last remnants of my tiredness. As we turned to come back, I saw that we still had too much time. I remembered Father's party tonight after the concert and that he always asked more people than Freda had planned for. There was a favorite shop of hers in Soho where they sold the best smoked salmon in London and tins of guavas.

I leaned forward and gave the driver Giuseppe Cordoni's address. "Greek Street," I said. "I forget the number, but just drive slowly and I'll find it."

Giuseppe was letting down the sun blind as we came to the shop. Cutting slivers of smoked salmon, he asked after Freda. "She is well?"

"She is radiant."

"And opera? She will never come back?" He shook his head. "She sang like Elizabeth Schumann, as if the gods had blessed her. Ah well, she is happy."

"Yes, very." I wandered round the shop, buying far too much, black olives and *carré de l'est*, a cheese which Father adored. Giuseppe carried the carton of goods to the car. "You tell her, I have always loved Freda Linstrom."

I said, "I'll tell her."

"And if she would only sing again, I would buy her a shopful of yellow roses."

"I'll tell her that, too," I said, laughing.

I had a few minutes' panic when I reached the station. Niall must have discovered by now that I was gone and he could have come to intercept me at the train. But the whistle blew and I was alone in the compartment.

Old Connery Badger's taxi was parked outside Launford Station. He was bent over the most gory paperback he could find in the bookstall. But as I approached he looked up, closed the book and smiled.

"Marnin', Mrs. Rhodes. You be 'avin' a lot o' luggage." He opened the trunk and the porter stowed it away.

Whenever the family used Connery's taxi, they always sat in front with him. He loved to chat and it flattered him to drive "the folk from the castle." To everyone of his generation, it was still "the castle."

"They do say," he switched on the engine of the old Austin, "that Miss Nina's playin' her guitar tonight at that there concert."

"She is."

"Like to 'ear 'er, I 'ood."

"When she's in another show in London, I'll send a couple of tickets for you and your wife. How is Betsy, by the way?"

"She's fine now. That osteopath gave her some treatment. And do you know, he wouldn't take no money. 'E just said to 'er, 'Well, you tell 'em up there at the manor that it weren't the doctors as cured you; it was Francis Lorian. You tell 'em, Mrs. Badger.' "

"What have the people at the manor got to do with it?"

"Me wife's working there now as a cook. She started last week. Them's important people—'er ladyship's a countess in 'er own right."

It amused me to hear the pride in his voice. Our village was one of the diminishing pockets of England where titles still had an aura of glory. Then I thought dryly that the significance of Mrs. Badger's working at the manor had not been lost to Lorian. Here was a rich little bit of publicity for him.

Sometimes you meet people you cannot like; it is said to have something to do with chemistry. I knew I was being unfair, but my chemistry couldn't find anything good in Francis Lorian.

The old car trundled through the gates of Guinever and along the avenue of limes. When I got out, the air was full of sounds—children's voices and birds' songs. In daytime the front door was always wide open, and Connery put my suitcase and the carton of food just inside the hall. I paid him and thanked him.

"Lor' bless ye, Missie."

"Missie," just as I had been for twenty years.

On the lawn, Sylvia and Penn's two children, Annalise and Tim, were prancing after Nina, playing follow the leader.

"Hi!"

The children ran toward me and I hugged

them. If I had children would they inherit Father's bright gold hair? Tim had it, and Annalise's hair was soft brown.

"Mummie had to go down to the stables," she said. "Glory has hurt his foot. And Lelani is busy making cakes. So she brought us here to play."

Penn had eight goats. Glory was the white Lucifer of the breed. Lelani was the children's gigantic Jamaican nurse, whose love for them was fierce and total.

Nina had flung herself down on the grass. Her shorts and shirt were multicolored, and she was so slim that she looked like a slender rope of zinnias.

Freda and Polly were in the kitchen. The table was loaded with food to be prepared for tonight's party.

"Ah, Sarah," Freda cried, arms deep in a bowl of pink shrimps. "I'm so glad you came down early. It must be horrid and dusty in town."

So there was no aura of crisis about me at this moment, nothing to make them stop, stare and demand, "What is the matter? What has happened?" And, after all, what *had* happened? I had walked out of Niall's beautiful apartment quietly and without fuss. And I had a feeling that the crisis had not yet begun. Niall would not let me go so easily.

6

LUKE came for drinks and a snack before we all left for the gala concert at Cypress Mount.

Whenever we went as a family to a show there was always maneuvering to sit as far away from Father as possible. He was as extrovert in disapproval as in praise. Like the owner of a dog that steals the meat from the butcher, we tried to pretend Father did not belong to us when he became vociferous. This evening I was the loser in the manipulation. I found myself sitting next to him, with Luke on my right, in the great music room of Cypress Mount.

Father behaved reasonably during a comedy act and shouted enthusiastic applause to a girl who did a marvelous black panther dance act. An opera singer who had retired three times was a different matter. "For God's sake what is she wearing a breast plate for?" . . . "It's a diamond pendant." . . . "Sh-s-h," someone hissed from behind . . . "She's singing flat," said Father, who had an excellent ear.

Fortunately the aria finished on a high note and applause stopped the enraged woman sitting behind him.

Nina came next. Father said, "Dear heaven, she's beautiful. How did I manage her?"

"You're an artist," said Luke and they both laughed.

Nina had the great knack of establishing a relationship with a live audience. She sat on a high stool and seemed to sing personally to everyone.

There was laughter in her voice as she swung her way through three songs, two of which had been specially written for her. The third was a plunge into the past.

She caused a stir in tower and trench
That brawling, boist'rous Scottish wench,
Came I early, came I late,
I found Black Agnes at the gate.

Nina's finger stroked the guitar, singing the song of the defense of the Castle at Dunbar. It was short and catchy, and when she had finished she looked up at her audience. Then, as the two curtains began to swing together she jumped down from the high stool.

Instead of landing on her feet, her ankle turned under her and she crashed to the floor. Someone in the audience gave a startled cry. Nina crouched, a splash of crimson, bronze and emerald, a long black wing of hair hiding her face, her guitar clutched like a sheltered child against her.

She shook her head at the men rushing from the wings to help her, got up and stood on one foot, steadying herself with a hand on the stool. She looked slowly round the audience and grinned.

"Clumsy!" she said loudly and clearly and waved her guitar at them.

The audience loved her.

By my side Luke said, "Come on," and gripped my wrist and dragged me to my feet.

Father rolled round in his seat to make room for us. "She's all right . . ." Then anxiously, "Isn't she?"

"I'm going to find out," said Luke. "She fell heavily and she was in pain, though she tried not to show it."

"Shall I come?"

I said quickly, knowing the way Father fussed if anything was wrong with us, "You stay here. If she's done anything at all, it's probably a sprained ankle."

As I passed Dido's chair, pulled up against the aisle seat, she said, "For heaven's sake, Nina only slipped and that was probably an act. Don't tell me you're calling an ambulance."

"We're going—" I began. But Luke pulled me away into the crowds streaming out for the intermission. We pushed past them into the long gallery, with its mixture of Louis XV furniture and Victorian nudes.

We found Nina in a small anteroom. She was sitting in a yellow chair under an overlarge chandelier. Lady Trenthall, the concert's organizer, loaded with rubies, was with her. Nina was protesting that she had been idiotically careless and if she could just sit still for a few minutes, she'd be fine. No, she didn't want brandy. She didn't want anything. She sat, her shoe thrown to one side, lightly massaging her foot. Then she looked up and saw us.

"Exit Nina Palfrey with a crash."

Lady Trenthall said, "Oh, Doctor Ashton. I'm so glad you've come. May I leave Nina with you? My guests . . ."

"Of course."

"Please do let me know if I can help."

"Thank you, there's nothing," Nina said.

With a harassed-hostess look, Lady Trenthall flashed us an agitated smile, rustled silk and disappeared.

Luke went to Nina, knelt and took her foot between his hands. "Where is the pain? Here? Or here?"

She winced.

"I'm sorry," he said. "But if you'll just keep still—"

"It hurts when you do that."

"Then perhaps we'd better get you to Matthews for an X ray."

She jerked her foot out of his hands. "Really, Luke, I haven't broken my neck. I'll be all right."

He said imperturbably, "I'm sure you will. But you didn't exactly meet the floor like a piece of thistledown."

Someone knocked on the door. I opened it. Francis Lorian looked into the room. "Is Nina all right?"

"Thank you," I said, outstaring him, "but Doctor Ashton is here. We don't need—"

Nina cried over my stiff dismissal, "Come on in. Do you know one another? Luke, this is Francis Lorian . . . Doctor Luke Ashton.

And Francis, do something quickly or Luke will have me whipped off to Matthews and I hate the smell of hospitals."

Luke was slightly taller, but their eyes seemed to meet levelly. Francis smiled. "May I give my opinion?"

I said angrily, "I told you, Doctor Ashton is coping."

Nina looked unduly excited. "Here you are, Francis. Here's your chance to show the medical profession that you have knowledge that doesn't need X rays." Then she said to Luke, "I call him Osteopath Extraordinary," and to Francis, "How do you like your title?"

"It's appropriate," he said.

Nina's attitude was one of defiance. She was violently loyal where I was concerned, and although she had not said so, I was certain that she resented Luke for returning into my life. Also, as Father had once said, "Nina is a champion of lost causes." My elegant, sophisticated sister could not resist helping the lame duck, the betrayed or, like Francis Lorian, one of an unorthodox minority.

None of this, however, prevented me from being angry with her for Luke's sake. When he came quietly and stood with me near the door, letting Francis Lorian take over, my indignation spilled over onto him as well. I wanted Luke to throw him out; I wanted to see the self-opinionated smile wiped from Lorian's narrow face. Instead, we stood by the wall like a couple of humble spectators at a star performance.

Francis drew up a chair, lifted Nina's foot onto his knee and began probing. His hands were large, like a peasant's, and blunt fingered. Yet I could not help noticing the delicacy of his touch. "Lie back," he told Nina. "No, right back. That's it. And don't watch what I'm doing, look across the room—at your sister, if you like. She's very worth looking at."

He was bold and insensitive and blatantly vain. Couldn't Nina see . . . ? I looked at her, then at Luke. "Let's go," I said loudly.

"Oh don't," Nina called from flat on her back in the long chair. "I'm sure Francis would be generous-hearted enough, if he were invited, to watch you perform some intricate operation. Can't you, Luke dear, return the compliment?"

"Put like that," said Luke carefully, "you give me no option," and he leaned against the door, watching.

"*I'm* going." I reached for the door handle.

Luke held me back. I gave him a furious look and stood by his side, willing Francis to fail, to cede the final decision to him. I wanted Nina to be out of pain, but I wanted it Luke's way.

I hated to see those huge hands round the slender, sun-tanned foot, and I looked about me at the portraits and the furniture and the ugly little blackamoor in a corner holding a lamp.

Outside the door was a hum of conversation, footsteps, laughter. Here it was suddenly quiet until Nina's small cry of pain made me start forward.

Francis looked up. "I haven't hurt her. A lot of people do that—they cry out in anticipation . . ." I watched his hands. While he talked, he gave her foot a sudden flick. This time Nina said, "Oh!" sharply and sat up.

Francis laughed and ran his fingers lightly up and down her foot. "Now you can go and do what you like. Dance the Highland fling if you want to. It won't hurt you."

She moved her toes, then her ankle. She stood up and took a few steps forward, then she turned to us in triumph. "You see? All better. And no dreary X ray necessary."

Francis leaned against a carved desk. His smile was insolent. "Lucky I was around."

"Yes, isn't it?" Luke said. "All right, Nina, we'll leave you now. Come, Sarah."

When we were outside, I asked, "What had Nina done?"

"In layman's language she had dislocated a small bone."

We were walking between the nudes. I put out a hand and brushed a cool marble leg as I passed, then I burst out, "Why did you let them behave like that? Brush you aside? In the old days you wouldn't have done it."

"Wouldn't I?"

"Nina rejected *you*," I said furiously, "for that . . . that upstart who isn't even a trained osteopath."

Luke burst out laughing.

"I'm serious," I cried.

He said almost gently, "Save your energy, Sarah. I'm not a cause to be fought for."

Someone brushed past me, pushing me against him. I said childishly, "Well, I'm livid with him—oh, and with Nina."

"Don't be. Who was it said, 'You can't please all the people all the time'?"

I asked in a small voice, "And I'm just 'one of the people'?"

"Aren't you?"

"I hoped I wasn't. I hoped—"

"Don't," he said quietly. "Don't hope anything where you and I are concerned. Just accept."

"What?"

"Oh—friendship," Luke said and stopped outside the door to the hall.

Inside the soprano was singing again. Luke opened the door silently and put a restraining hand on my arm. We stood, close together, listening, waiting until it was over before we went to our seats.

Time telescoped. Once, in the past, I had stood just like this at a door with Luke, waiting to go into a concert hall. I remembered that I had leaned a little against him and laid my fingers on his cheek. He had taken my hand and held it and said, "I love you." I had once made the same gesture to Niall. He had jerked his head away.

While the singer was accepting the applause we moved to our seats.

Father asked, "What was all that excitement about?"

"Overanxiety. We thought Nina had hurt herself. She had, but she's all right." I spoke lightly, wondering, as I took my seat, where

Francis was sitting in the hall or if he came back for the second half of the program.

Nina appeared again halfway through the show and the audience cheered her. She perched on the stool and this time she didn't sing. She played a caprice by Paganini. I thought, as I listened to the chords that seemed to dance like water, how critics had praised her faultless technique. In one of the reviews we collected so greedily, they spoke of Nina's detachment when she played the classics, drawing attention away from herself to the beauty of the music. This evening I could not be so impersonal. Behind the listening I was apprehensive. What was the relationship between Nina and Francis? I had a feeling that the incident in the yellow-damask anteroom had delighted her. Nina had forced us to be witness to Francis Lorian's skill. It had been a common enough orthopedic treatment, yet Nina had made it special. *Like a woman showing off her lover* . . .

I had never known my sister to lose her head over a man, though I had no real idea how involved her affairs became. She lived her life in London and as a family we never intruded . . . "Nina knows her way around the world," we said.

I was aware suddenly of a thunderous noise on my left, of Luke's head turning slightly toward me from the right. Lost in my own thoughts I had sat unaware of the last act. Father was joining in the roaring applause. Luke was clapping. Between them, I was like a dummy. I pulled myself out of my thoughts and banged my hands together.

Lady Trenthall was standing in the front of the stage making a speech about the charity to which the proceeds of the evening were to be donated. Smiles from the stage; a warm, enveloping gesture with her arms; more applause and the evening was over.

Luke said as people began to stir, "I'll drive you back, but I won't be staying for the supper party. I've a long day tomorrow, I explained to your father and he understands."

"You don't need to take me all that way back. I can squeeze in with the family, or Penn and Sylvie can drive me; they're here somewhere."

"I want to take you," said Luke. We had reached the long gallery. He looked through a window and said, "It's pelting with rain. Stay near the entrance and I'll bring the car to the door. It'll probably be a long line, but have patience."

He left me in the circular hall, and Father, charging through the crowds, with the family like the children of Hamlin city behind him, shouted at me, "See you later," and was gone.

"Sarah—" Sylvie came toward me through the crowds. She had probably started the evening by being neat and groomed. But she usually ended, as she had once said of herself, "like someone who has been playing hockey with the girls." Her soft gingery hair flopped round her face, her cheeks were bright pink and she had difficulty with the shoulder strap of her blue dress. But nothing daunted her. She was saying, on laughter, "We came late because there was a slight crisis at the farm. The goats went for a walk and Penn had to saddle the cob and go and look for them. I did ring through to tell you we'd be along as soon as we could, but Niall said—"

"Niall?"

"Yes, why?"

"You spoke to him? . . . All right, go on."

"Well, he said that you'd all left for the concert. He sounded a bit abrupt, but he was probably in a hurry to get here. I haven't seen him, by the way. I suppose you're waiting for him."

"No. Luke is running me home."

"Oh." Whenever Sylvie was trying to puzzle something out she blinked her eyes quickly. I knew she was curious to know why Luke was taking me back to Guinever.

Through the steam of rain beyond the open doorway, I saw Penn's car draw up. Sylvie saw, too, and grinned at me. "Penn has the Palfrey impatience. I'd better go. Be seeing you."

And back at home, Niall was waiting for me . . . A woman in a mauve gown elbowed past me. She wore a bracelet of sharp stones that scratched my arm. I moved nearer the front door.

A clear, carrying voice behind me was saying, "You remember me, don't you? I'm Alexandra. Sorry, I can't stop. I'm in a hurry. I'll call you."

I leaped round and bumped into a man who looked at me as if he thought I were drunk. I murmured, "Sorry," and searched the faces near me. No one gave any indication of an unexpected meeting with an old friend. Groomed heads; jewels, some discreet, some gaudy as Christmas tree decorations; handbags opening, mirrors tilted, reflecting faces . . . And one of them was Alexandra. Or no, she had been in a hurry; she couldn't stop.

Like someone on a jerky pivot I wheeled round again. I was too small to see over the crush of heads round the door. I pushed through the loitering crowd with a kind of swimming movement, good manners forgotten in urgency. Someone called my name. I played at being deaf and dived for the door.

Only one woman was now standing patiently waiting for a car. I saw lights gleam on piled chestnut hair and a pale, clear-cut profile. She paused for a moment, checked by the downpour. One hand went out to a half-pillar that framed the doorway. A bracelet of green stones glittered on a long black glove. The pendant at her throat was a star of grass-green peridots. Then she ducked her head and ran out into the rain.

I followed her, flying down the broad steps and racing along the drive. Quite suddenly I realized that I could see more clearly and that the heavy tattoo of rain no longer beat in my face. The storm had stopped as quickly as if a tap had been turned off.

People were turning on headlights, revving engines. I peered through the sharp contrast of light and darkness and lost her. My left foot plunged into a puddle. I said, "Damn," and pulled up suddenly.

Alexandra must be somewhere nearby. I began to peer into cars and felt that I must look like a rather elegantly dressed thief.

The cars were moving slowly and politely single file toward the steps where people waited.

At the corner of the house, a gravel path led to the stables. Possibly there were cars parked in the yard, too. I could go that way or straight on. I hesitated, looking toward the end of the drive, when suddenly a car came tearing up at race-track speed, passing the slow-moving file. I darted to one side to let it go by.

As the car neared me, the driver turned on the headlights. Dazzled, I flung up my arm. The car swung toward me. Someone behind me shouted as I leaped sideways into the sodden bushes. The car zigzagged and roared on. It had extinguished its lights.

As I fell, one of the cars in the line switched on its headlights. By their light I saw, for an instant, the license plate of the vanishing car. I knew it only too well. It was Niall's black Bentley.

Powerful arms were picking me out of the bush. A man asked, "Are you hurt?"

I must have opened my mouth to cry out as I crashed sideways, for I tasted something hard and tangy. I spat out a laurel leaf. "I . . . I'm . . . all right . . ." And then I did the last thing I felt like doing. I burst into noisy laughter. "Never p-put laurel into a—a salad," I shouted at the strange man. "It tastes l-like bitter mackintosh."

"I wish I'd been quick enough to take that lunatic's car number. He drove straight at you. Of course, he was drunk."

I couldn't stop shivering.

He said slowly, "You're Mrs. Rhodes, aren't you? We met once. But never mind that. I saw your husband in the gallery. I suppose he's fetching the car."

"N—no. He—"

"Here, don't faint."

"I've never fainted in my life," I said in an excessively haughty voice.

"What you want," said the man, "is a brandy. Come on up to the house."

"Thank you, I'm all right. I . . . I'm sorry my t-teeth are chattering. I . . . I'm waiting for someone who is taking me home." I looked down at myself. My dress clung to me like a sodden bathing suit. I pushed whirls of wet hair out of my eyes.

The man was saying, "Then you'd better find the car quickly."

"It'll come . . ."

"Perhaps someone else saw what happened and noted that driver's registration number."

After a show, people have only one absorption, particularly if it's raining, and that is to get away. *The show is over . . . thanks and good night. Hurry . . .* Golden sandals and dark satin pumps stepped around puddles. Nobody even looked at me, and for this I was grateful. I wasn't very decent in my clinging dress.

"Good grief, what on earth have you been doing?" Luke's voice came out of the chaos.

"I . . . I met a very wet bush head on."

The strange man said, "Some damned drunk almost ran her down and didn't stop. She says she's not hurt."

"I'm not. Oh . . ." I hated gigglers but I giggled. "First Nina—and now me . . . accident-prone, that's us!"

I thought Luke was going to put his arm round me. But he seemed to think better of it. I wanted to lean against him, to lower my head on to his shoulder. But I would ruin his suit and that would never do. It flashed through my mind that I was mixing my values. I wanted comfort and Luke's suit would dry. Laughing and crying and shivering, I flung myself at him.

The strange man said, "She's badly shaken."

"I'll take her home," said Luke, and he put his arm round me at last.

In the car, I said, "I want a cigarette."

"You used not to smoke."

"I want one now."

He lit it. I blew out a whirl of smoke, coughed and stubbed the cigarette out. "Sorry to waste it." Then I said, "Niall's here."

"Here?"

"At Guinever."

"Fine. Then when you get home he can plop you in a hot bath and rub you dry. There's nothing like someone else to do the work for you."

Luke had always used flippancy like a defense against his own feelings. And then I wondered what feelings I expected him to have for a dead love. I wanted to tell him that the car had been Niall's, but the words would not come. It was like some horrible secret I had, for some reason I could not explain, to keep for the moment to myself.

Luke switched on the engine. Then, as an afterthought, he looked at me. "You have a very wet face," he said and felt for his handkerchief. "Keep still."

He took his time, as meticulous at drying me as if he were at the operating table. "I can't do anything about that dress you're wearing. I suppose it started out this evening by being rather beautiful."

"Oh, ch-chiffon and c-cats hate the w-wet."

Luke reached back in the car and unfolded a rug. "You look a bit like a water nymph. Like Undine."

The water sprite who saw the reflection of her faithless lover in the mirror. But Luke had never been faithless. He had merely seen a love affair as incidental. He had had other sights. Ambition . . .

I let him wrap the rug round my shoulders, cover my knees. But had it been ambition that had taken him, not to London, but right out of the limelight to work among disease and poverty in India? It occurred to me as I hugged the rug that idealism could sometimes seem as cruel as overambition.

7

THE car moved forward, gathering speed. Lights dimmed as we approached. I was grateful to Luke for not talking. I could think only of Niall, see only, on the black curtain of tree and sky, the headlights bearing down on me like creatures from a science fiction film. I knew what a rabbit must feel like when lights hypnotize it into inaction on a roadway.

Now that I was minutes further away from it, I argued that it couldn't have been Niall's car. In a state of shock, the mind did not relate events with particular accuracy. I said the number of the Bentley slowly to myself. XLM 290K6. And I knew I had made no mistake.

Yet somehow there must be a mistake. Men like Niall—highly intelligent, sophisticated, cautious men whose large incomes depend on their popular image—do not commit murder. The purr of Luke's car beat to a contradiction. Like the rogue tiger, there were killers in all societies—kings and beggars. Kings had royalists to murder for them; the beggars did their own killing. Why should television not have its rogue tiger, too?

Had someone in the line of cars not flashed on his headlights at that moment, I would never have known who had driven at me. Chance? Fate?

Luke asked, "Are you all right?"

"Yes. Just cold."

He switched on the car heater. I said, "No, don't. You'll be boiled."

"And you'll gently simmer. That's the important thing."

We went through the village of Azurstone at a fine speed. Father was at Guinever. I would have to tell him what had happened. Hurry . . . hurry . . . I pressed the floor under my foot as if I were in control of the accelerator.

Father, Niall tried to kill me tonight. He nearly ran me down in his car.

Father would pull out all the stops. He would go into the attack like a fury. I sometimes thought that secretly he believed I had rushed into marriage with Niall because everyone else in the family was gifted and I was not. He thought I had been trying to collect a little reflected glory of my own. But

I was his daughter, and, fool though I had been, he'd mortgage Guinever to bring Niall to justice. That was how it would be when I told Father. Justice . . . police court . . . judge and jury . . . I began shivering again. I didn't want it that way. Yet when a man tried to kill a woman, what other way was there?

We had reached the gates of Guinever. I leaned forward, saying, "Let me out here, Luke, please."

"If you want to get pneumonia, you must choose a time when I'm not with you."

"Please." I threw off the rug. "Niall is at the house."

"Well, what of it?"

"You don't understand."

"No, I don't. Hey, what are you doing?"

The car was moving forward, slowly. I said, unnecessarily, "Getting out."

"From what I hear, you've been nearly killed once already tonight. Has it given you a taste for danger?"

"I want to go up to the house by myself."

"Why?"

"You always did ask too many questions."

He said dryly, "That's my training. Researchers have to keep asking: How? Why? What? Now sit still like a good girl."

"Luke, *stop!*"

"Give me one good reason."

"Thank you for bringing me home. Now I'll walk."

"That's no reason," he said, but he stopped the car.

I said, "I'll run all the way up to the house and fall into a bath." I turned to him suddenly pleading. "I'm not trying to be difficult, but . . . but in the circumstances . . . I want to arrive . . . alone . . ."

I waited for him to ask, "What circumstances?" and knew I wouldn't be able to tell him. But he just put out a hand and twisted a piece of my wet hair. "Undine," he said very softly and let me go.

At the end of the lime avenue, Guinever's uncurtained windows blazed with lights. I climbed out of the car and Luke called after me, "Take the rug."

"I don't want it. I'll be in the house in a minute." I began to run.

He must have watched me for many yards, for the car remained silent. Then I heard the engine start up. I wished I had asked him to stay within sight until I was in the house. As the car's sound receded, I felt panic seize me. For the first time in my life I was frightened of being alone in the long, dark drive.

Rain drips from the trees trickled onto my hair and down my neck. In my haste, I stepped into puddles. Even they were a major disaster to my overstrung nerves.

The night held an uncanny quiet; the sounds from the house party did not reach this far and the sea was silent.

The movement behind me was scarcely more than a twig cracking, but I felt my heart turn over. The sound came again, and I looked round. Someone stood motionless on the grass under the black canopy of the limes. I couldn't see his face. But by the stance, the characteristic immobility with which he often tried to intimidate me, I recognized him. *"Niall."*

He walked toward me, reached out a hand and touched me. "What in God's name have you been doing?"

The avenue, isolated and pitch black with the eerie, dripping trees was no place to tell him. I said, "We'll talk in the house."

"Who brought you home?"

"Luke," I said. "Luke Ashton."

He smiled. "The research doctor at Matthews. The prodigal lover. I'm glad you didn't lie to me."

I tried to move past him. He took my arm, holding me back. "I know all about it, so you needn't run away."

"I'm not running away. I want to get home. I'm cold . . ." Why didn't someone come down the drive, a late arrival, a guest leaving? Why hadn't I let Luke see me right up to the house?

"Your spoiled, pretty Dido told me that Luke Ashton was with you tonight. She's quite a mine of information about your family. She misses nothing."

"Dido probably told you, too, that Nina hurt her foot tonight and Luke and I went round to see what we could do."

"Yes."

"And that Luke came for drinks before the show." I rushed on. "There were too many of us to go in Father's car and Freda drove Dido and had promised to pick up two friends on the way. I went with Luke because there was no room for me anywhere else."

"And on the way home, did he make a pass at you, and, like a loyal little wife, you got out and walked?"

"Luke dropped me at the gates. Now, *let—me—go—*"

He pushed me back so that I stumbled onto

the grass. Anger swept over me. "Why don't you ask me how I managed to fall and get so wet?"

"Why did you?"

"As if you didn't know!" Cold and furious, I cried, "You probably looked in your rear mirror and saw."

"Am I supposed to make sense out of that?"

I managed to fling his hands off me. Freedom gave me a desperate courage. Poised to run, I cried, "You drove your car at me tonight, up at Cypress Mount. You came like a maniac down the drive and—"

"What the hell are you talking about?"

"If I hadn't flung myself into those bushes . . ."

"If you've had too much champagne you'd better admit it."

"It's no use, Niall. Someone else saw what happened, saw you drive at me. XLM 290K6. You recognize the number?"

"Of course I do. Now try to be coherent. Someone nearly ran you down—"

"Deliberately. And then didn't stop—" I pushed myself on shaken legs away from the tree. "I tell you I saw the number. I *saw*—"

"You saw me at the wheel?"

"No. You went too fast."

He drew in his breath, making a small hissing sound. "Suppose I start to work this out logically. Suppose I tell you that you have made this absurd thing up as a kind of revenge for some imagined grievance. Women do; they have devious minds. What do you want?" his voice grew slightly out of control. "What is in your mind, Sarah? A headline in tomorrow's papers: 'Niall Rhodes on a charge of the attempted murder of his wife'?"

I leaned against the tree, feeling sick. "I'm speaking the truth. And there's a witness. The man who saw the car coming, saw me leap for my life. But he was so busy making sure I was unhurt that he didn't notice the number of the car."

He said, "All right. And if I believe you, the fact is that a car nearly ran you down. All that you're making up is the registration number."

"I'm not. I saw. You came straight at me. You had a good long run from the end of the drive to get up speed. I watched you—"

"From the end of the drive?"

"That's what I said."

His reaction was too stunned to be a lie. He

wasn't that good an actor. "Dear God in heaven . . ."

"What—?"

He stared at me and said slowly, as if trying to remember every detail, "When I reached Guinever, you had all left for the concert. I decided I might as well go. What I had to say to you about your dawn exit from the apartment could be said later. When I arrived, the drive was full so I double-parked the car just by the stables. I reached the house after the intermission. The hall was crowded and they brought me a chair right at the back of the hall. When I came out to get my car it was not where I had parked it. I found it down by the gate."

I believed him. "Then . . . Niall . . . who . . . ?"

"How do I know? How can I? But someone moved it."

"After . . . driving at me."

"Using my car," he said.

"Why?"

His face was gray; he was looking at me without seeming to see me, and when he spoke it was as if he were thinking aloud. "Someone wanted me accused of harming you . . . . Someone wanted to break me."

He was by nature so coldly logical that the

melodrama of his words struck a different fear into me. Suddenly we were no longer enemies, we were people caught in an unknown trapper's net.

"Go indoors, Sarah."

"I must tell Father," I said, "and the police."

"No."

"Someone tried to kill me. What am I supposed to do? Give them a second chance?"

"I am involved. Leave it to me. Do you hear? Leave me to deal with it."

"What can you do? Unless you have an idea who drove your car at me."

"I have no idea."

"Why did you come?" I cried. "To fetch me back to London? If so, I'm not coming. You surely don't want—"

He interrupted me. "It's one of the reasons. The other is that I have to go to the Bristol studios tomorrow and it's easier to get over there from here. But that's irrelevant." He made a swift gesture with his hand. "Sarah, listen to me. We're not having the police in on this."

"*I'm* the one to decide. It was my life that was in danger."

"If you go to the police you could easily precipitate something worse for yourself."

I crossed my arms, rubbing them, hot and cold at the same time, like a fever. "Something worse—like what?"

"Whoever drove my car at you could be afraid that you had recognized him and he might try to stop you before you could say too much."

"But how could I? It was dark—whoever tried to run me down . . . must have known he . . . couldn't be identified . . ." I stopped suddenly and gasped, remembering two things: the woman at Gull's Folly and the note at Portland Place. The first a threat to me; the second, to Niall. Somehow we had both incurred a hatred that was hurtling into violence.

"What . . . do we . . . do?" my voice cracked.

Niall ran a hand across his forehead. "Let me think—just let me think."

"In the house," I said and turned, cold right into my heart, and fled up the avenue under the dripping limes, not looking to see if Niall followed. Thoughts ran like shadows by my side. Someone had used Niall's car to try to kill me in a hit-and-run accident. They took a chance that one or two people in the drive would see what had happened and note the Bentley's registration number. It would be traced. Niall would be accused. "Just routine inquiries" . . . "Any statement you wish to make" . . . Niall before a judge . . . headlines in the newspapers—just as somebody had planned.

Then, I heard the voice again, raised, superimposed over the chatter in the hall of Cypress Mount. *I am Alexandra*. Flinging the words perhaps at no one in particular in order that I should hear her name. Nothing was coincidence. Everything was being woven like a pattern in a tapestry. The pattern was Niall's destruction—and incidentally, mine.

Guinever's large double doors were open. The surge of movement, the clink of glasses, the sound of music gave to the past hour a nightmare unreality. I looked for Father and saw him with his back to me, talking to some people. The bright gold of his hair, the gigantic shoulders in the well-cut dinner jacket, the small vanity of his red cummerbund, spread a warmth over me. Father was here and all was well.

"Sarah! . . . What on earth has happened to you?" . . . "Did you go for a midnight swim?" . . . "Are you all right?" . . . Voices came from all round me. They were kind guests. No one even giggled at the sight of me with a chiffon dress stuck to my body like a tissue paper wrapper. I said, "I fell into a wet laurel bush. Silly, wasn't it?" I laughed overloudly and ran past them. To complete my own apparent nonchalance as I passed the buffet table, I reached over and took a smoked salmon sandwich, munching it as I ran upstairs.

If I had had my wits about me, I would have used the back stairs. But my mind had no room for details and so I was in full view of all Father's elegant guests.

He had seen me. "Sarah!" If nobody had noticed me before, his cannon-shot voice brought me into the center of the picture—Luke's Undine, almost as bare as if I wore no clothes, running up a curving staircase under a glittering chandelier.

When I reached the landing I turned and waved to him. "I'm a mermaid," I cried. I sounded too full of champagne.

My bedroom door slammed behind me.

I stripped off my clothes and wrapped myself in a huge towel. As soon as I was dry, I felt too hot. I hadn't realized before that the rain had not refreshed the humidity of the night. I dressed dreamily, senses blurred, no longer even trying to work things out.

I stood at the mirror rough-drying my hair. Except that being wet darkened it and I no longer wore the sea-green dress, I looked no different from when I set out for Cypress Mount. I hoped I would be able to get Father into a quiet corner—perhaps the kitchen—and tell him what had happened.

Dry and made-up, I went to the door. My mind began to function again. Alexandra was beginning to come alive. First, I knew her handwriting; now her face in profile; her hair. Long gloves . . . A voice raised, intending me to hear? *I am Alexandra* . . .

The door opened with a suddenness that startled me. I had not heard anyone outside.

Niall said, "Your Father is asking where you are." He drew me back into the room. "But before you go down—"

I waited.

"Sarah, listen to me. You *must* do as I say."

"Someone tried to kill me. Aren't I supposed to value my life? Well, I do, and—"

"Tell the police, and the story will be everywhere. The clichés. You know how it will go. 'There's no smoke without fire.' "

"Is there any fire, Niall?"

"Of course not."

"So, why do you care?"

He walked past me to the window. "Gossip."

"Evil never hurts the innocent."

"A pretty phrase and entirely untrue. The iconoclasts—"

"You aren't God," I lashed out.

"The public sometimes lifts us precious near it. We're there, on the screen, ready to be—" he stopped, turned and said very quietly, "revered or damned. God—or Lucifer."

"Or just a normal man with a job to do. Like other television personalities." I reeled off a list of the top names with, so far as I knew, happy home lives, accepting their "image" but leaving it behind at the studios.

Niall answered, staring down into the black garden, "My buildup has been different. I'm not a news reader or a reporter. My name has been made in debate. I'm the one with courage, integrity, debunking humbug . . . I didn't build myself up to this. It happened. Dammit, it happened."

The people in the sitting rooms, the hotel lounges, the parlors, with eyes fixed on a magic screen, passing judgment, praising or damning, writing letters to the television companies, making and breaking . . .

But all that applied to a program, not to what a man did when he got in his car and drove away from the studio. I said, "You are obsessed with the idea of your image. You live your private life in public. You magnify it out of all proportion to its importance."

I went to the dressing table, sat down and combed my damp hair again. There was something odd about my face. I leaned forward and looked more closely. I had made up only one eye. Somehow, perhaps because I was still shocked, the unmade-up eye looked nicer than the other. I said, wiping the green shadow off with a tissue, "What are you going to do?"

"Get in touch with a private detective. I'll have them watch."

"Watch whom? You—or me?"

"Both of us, of course. You'll be safe." He moved away from the window and came and stood behind me. With one hand he took the tissue from me and drew me back against him. I could feel how taut he was. It was like leaning against stone. "It'll be all right, Sarah. I promise you . . ." Pleading with me to believe him, almost gentle. *For the sake of an image . . .*

"Unless you know the source of the danger, how can you promise anything?"

"Do what I ask. Please, do what I ask. Do you think I'm going to rest until I've run this lunatic to earth, and of course that's what—he—is. Only leave it to me. Let me handle it. Don't discuss it with anyone . . . not yet."

I hadn't missed the hesitation before the word "he." I said clearly, "I saw Alexandra at the concert."

He gave me a blank stare.

"Oh, no, you haven't forgotten the note she wrote to me at Portland Place. You haven't, have you?"

"There must be a thousand or more Alexandras in Britain. You take a coincidence and make drama out of it."

"The drama is there, Niall. I didn't make it."

I don't think he heard me. When he spoke, I realized that his thoughts were on something I had said earlier. "An obsession? *My* image an obsession? But of course. There's no point in life unless there is one overwhelming ambition to carry you through."

That way, I thought, madness lies. Aloud, I said, "That's not true. Ambition, perhaps. But obsession leaves you no room to care about anything else."

"What else is there?"

I could have said, "You have me; you have a home life." I didn't, because I knew that he spoke for himself and what he said was the truth for him. *What else is there?* For him, nothing. He *was* his obsession. It was almost shocking, like the stripping of a mask, the terrible confession of a man without faith, without feeling. The straw man of *The Wizard of Oz*.

"Go downstairs, Sarah."

"I'm going." (With nothing resolved, not even linked by mutual fear. Nothing.)

Footsteps came running along the passage. I heard laughter. "We'll find Sarah. Sarah?" Someone hammered on the door.

"I'm in here," I said.

"Damn them." When the door opened Niall was at the window.

"Oh." Polly looked at us. "Kester said—where were you. I—we—came to look for you." Behind her I saw Sylvie with her hair on end.

"I had to dry myself," I said. "I got pushed into a very wet laurel bush."

"Pushed?"

"By a car. But I'm all in one piece, and I hope in my right mind."

We went down the stairs, chatting and laughing—theirs natural, mine forced. Niall didn't follow us.

The chandelier in the hall lit up the heads of Father's guests crowded round the buffet table. I saw Theo standing near a table on which stood a bowl of golden-streaked tiger lilies. He had a drink in his hand and his bright head made him look a bit like Apollo—Apollo, I thought, guarding his lilies.

The clock gave a low rumble and began to strike. I glanced up at it and saw that the hands were at midnight. An hour had passed since I had had my brush with death.

Father stood by the french doors opening out onto the terrace. "Ah, there you are. You said Nina was all right but where is she?"

"Probably drinking champagne at Cypress Mount."

He looked me over. "What happened to you? Did you fall into their lake? I've always said it's damned dangerous to have an unguarded lake right on top of the house."

I repeated my line about the laurel bush.

"Another drunk who should be disqualified from driving," he thundered. I saw his head lift, eyes on the door. The last chimes of midnight merged with the buzz of conversation. I looked to where he was looking.

Nina approached. Her hand, trailing behind her, held on to Francis Lorian's fingers.

Father's voice had something of the timbre of Big Ben. "You don't enter, you exit, at midnight," he boomed.

"But I'm not the family Cinderella," said Nina.

Everyone laughed.

Without knowing why, I looked at Dido. Her chair was pulled up beside a settee where three people sat. She was leaning forward as if trying to attract Francis' attention. Her eyes on his face were brilliant and excited.

Nina was saying, "Father, this is a friend of mine, Francis Lorian. I'm sorry we're late. We stayed at the Mount for a drink."

Father acknowledged the introduction. "You didn't hurt yourself when you fell?"

"Oh, I did. Luke came and wanted me to go to hospital for an X ray. But Francis was there and he did some manipulation and I was fine again. He's a special type of osteopath."

Like a dog whose hackles rise at a hated intruder, I said, "Nina fell awkwardly and dislocated a small bone. It could have been put right quite easily at the hospital."

Francis smiled. "But I saved her that inconvenience."

Father took instinctive likes and dislikes to people. I knew by his expression that he wasn't going to take to Nina's new friend any more than he had taken to Niall.

I also felt Francis' eyes on me, amused, mocking, as if we shared some secret. I slipped away before I was drawn into conversation with him and went to talk to Penn, who was standing with a Launford lawyer and his wife.

Everyone was having a wonderful time. A famous artist, a guitarist and a former opera singer. Niall was missing, although I was certain that some of Father's guests must have caught a glimpse of him and wondered where he was. Sooner or later someone would ask, "Where is your husband, Sarah?"

And I would say glibly, "Oh, somewhere around. He may be working in his room.

There's probably some urgent job he has to do." I wished I could escape, too. I was in no mood for a party.

Later, when Freda called for more ice, I went to fetch it. Off the kitchen was a small maid's room we sometimes used for meals in the winter because it was warmer than the dining room. My footsteps were muffled by the rubber flooring of the kitchen so that the people in the little adjoining room did not hear me. Their conversation went on unsuspectingly.

". . . you really do think you could? You *really* think . . . ?" Nobody could mistake Polly's breathy, hesitant voice.

A man laughed. When he spoke, I also recognized his voice. "You'd better ask the hundreds of people who have passed through my hands. There should be a sign by the traffic lights. 'Hospital road barred. Left turn for Lorian's house.' "

He seemed to have an endless supply of advertising slogans. I stood still in the middle of the yellow kitchen, blatantly listening.

"But how can I get Dido to you without—without Kester knowing. I mean . . ."

"Oh, I know what you mean. Caution, because I have no accepted qualifications.

'Show me proof, and I'll believe. Until then, he's a charlatan.' That's what he'd say, isn't it? Because I'm unorthodox in my treatment. There are many who talk like that. But they come round."

"Then how . . . ?"

"Just bring Dido to see me one day when you're supposed to go shopping."

"I can't. I daren't."

"Mothers find a way when they want their children cured. You'll find one. Just ring me when you can get into Launford and I'll make time to see you."

"You're so good."

"Don't you believe it. I'm ambitious."

"You should be practicing in London."

Freda was calling me. "Ice. Ice . . ."

"The ice woman cometh." I ducked my head into the refrigerator.

There was absolute silence in the little maid's room.

8

ON the morning after Father's party, I was the last down to breakfast. The day was cloudy and the round table stood just inside the open terrace doors. Only Theo and Dido were missing; even Nina had appeared, dreamy and still vague with sleep, holding her coffee cup in both hands like a child. It was nine o'clock and Theo would have already left for work. Dido's energy was always at its highest in the morning and her inability to work it off in movement made her mornings a time of frustration and short temper. We understood and did all we could not to cross her, but this morning she was nowhere to be seen.

I asked Nina if her foot hurt. She shook her head and asked me about my laurel bush bath.

"I don't think I'm heading for pneumonia," I said lightly and glanced at Niall.

He was standing and smoking by the open windows. Beyond them the wind chased clouds across the sky so that oyster light and violet shadow played over the Purbeck hills. The delphiniums by the terrace edge swung as the wind pushed them, and down on the lawn the cat, Pepita, lay on her back and played with a leaf.

I had interrupted a conversation. Polly took it up again. "But, Kester, if he really *can* help—"

Father leaned over the table, a curl of bacon poised on a fork. "I'm not having some damned newcomer I know nothing about experimenting with any of my family."

"She's *my* child," Polly said with sudden spirit, "and if I think Francis could help her—"

"He can," Nina said, lazily, "and you're just being bloody-minded, Father. These days everyone goes to osteopaths."

"There you are!" Polly cried.

"Dido may be your child, but it looks as if she has become my responsibility. You're not particularly gifted in that way."

"You're just prejudiced against someone whose work you don't even know."

Father sawed furiously at the bacon on his plate. "I'm perfectly aware of the good these men do. But Lorian is a newcomer, and from what I hear, when it comes to complicated cases he's got some cockeyed form of treatment. You can't remove the child from hospital care on a whim. And you're not going to. There's nothing more to say. Pass the toast."

Nina said, "Nobody appears to think of asking Dido what she wants. Suppose—"

"Suppose nothing," Kester shouted at his favourite daughter. "And now we'll drop the discussion."

Polly turned to Niall. "Please," she said. "Be on our side. After all, you knew Dido in Africa; you used to see her running about."

He was pacing up and down in front of the glass doors that led to the terrace like someone caged. I wished he would sit down at the table until everyone had finished eating. On the few occasions at Portland Place when he joined me for breakfast he would wander about in just the same way as he drank orange juice or smoked a cigarette with his coffee. I was, therefore, used to this restless morning habit. But Father was not and I knew that it irritated him. He crunched toast; Nina stared at her coffee cup and hummed a French song very softly to herself. Except for these two sounds, the room was silent.

Polly fixed Niall with her pleading, protuberant blue eyes, waiting for him to speak. When it seemed that he had no intention of doing so, she raised her voice. "*Niall, did you hear?* I'm trying to persuade Francis Lorian to treat Dido. He believes that with the right kind of manipulation, he can make her walk in a matter of weeks. The hospital is being so noncommittal about it that she's losing heart."

Father said briskly, "I seem to remember you took her to an osteopath once before and he could do nothing for her."

"But this man has an entirely new method of treatment. I'm told it's very advanced. Niall," she pleaded again, "you do agree that Francis should try, don't you?"

"I know nothing about the man, or about Dido's injury, so I can't pass an opinion."

Polly persisted. "But you remember her as she was in Africa before the accident—so gay, so brave . . ."

"What in the world has that got to do with it? If you must argue, keep to the point."

I knew that look of cold impatience on his face and, glancing quickly at Polly, saw the dull red flush spread over her cheeks. Niall was in ill humor this morning. But if, in this discussion, he had disagreed with Father, a plea of a bad morning mood would not have saved him from the whiplash of Father's tongue about rudeness in his house. Polly was often exasperating but only Father was allowed to be impatient with her. However, Niall was remaining carefully neutral and so Father dug into the marmalade and pretended not to hear.

I said loudly, "Niall, what do you think?"

"The choice of treatment for Dido is not my affair."

Polly said again, "But you knew her in Africa—"

"My acquaintance with her was limited to a few brief glimpses. I heard about the accident, of course. Even the smallest piece of news is splashed across the local papers in these towns."

"It wasn't a . . . small . . . piece of news . . . to me."

Niall bent over the table and stubbed out his cigarette. The conversation was obviously boring him.

Father said, "From what Polly tells me there was precious little inquiry into who was responsible. If I'd been there I'd have used third degree on every single rider in Nairobi who had been out that day."

"It might not have been anyone from Nairobi," Polly said. "It could have been someone who had ridden for miles and didn't know the area and . . . and was surprised to find that wall and just . . . jumped. It *was* a high wall, so he probably had no idea there was anyone on the other side."

She had used this argument so often to us, stressing her point that the rider was innocent. Polly could not bear to believe ill of anyone. Then, desperately wanting to be convinced, she turned in her chair to Niall. "You knew the spot, didn't you? When you jumped that wall, you couldn't see if someone was close up on the other side, could you?"

"I only rode that way about twice in all the time I was in Nairobi. I really can't remember."

"And with the noise of a horse's hoofs, you wouldn't be able to hear anything—I mean like a scream—or a cry . . ."

He said, tense with impatience, "Heaven give me strength! That great dog of yours would make enough noise yelping to drown everything else. Whoever jumped that wall that morning must have heard, but was riding too fast to stop."

Polly said sadly, "I suppose so. But MacAdam was a wonderful companion for Dido. We'd had him from a puppy and he adored her . . ."

Father passed his cup to Freda for more coffee. "The point is not what the dog did then, but what I'm doing now and I am not handing Dido over to some nonqualified man who might do her irredeemable damage. Is that the mail?"

Johnny, the village postmistress' son, delivered newspapers and the twice-daily mail. The boy always rang his bicycle bell to announce himself. We continued breakfast, waiting as usual for Dido to bring the letters in. There was no soft swish of her chair wheels.

"She must not have heard him," I said and went to collect the mail.

Four letters for Father, one for Freda and one for Nina. Niall left the window and came to the table for more coffee. I went onto the terrace outside the dining room and looked at the sharp contrast of cloud and blue space in the sky. To my right, where the terrace turned the corner, I saw the edge of Dido's chair and part of her wide pink skirt.

I asked, puzzled, "Why are you hiding there?"

She looked at me with fierce eyes; her mouth was tight and down-drawn.

I tried to ignore the signs of temper and asked, "Didn't you hear the mail?"

"I heard enough."

"Enough of what?"

"You all talk too loudly."

"You heard us discussing you. I'm sorry," I said gently, "but we're all trying to help."

She stared at me in angry disbelief. "A lot you care! Why pretend?"

"All right, if that's what you want to think, I'm not going to argue about it. But at least come into the sun. You're shivering."

"I'll move when I want to. Leave me alone."

I walked to the low terrace wall remembering the old nurse who looked after us when we were very young. "You got out of bed the wrong side this morning, didn't you?" she would demand of our moods. But no one said things like that to Dido.

Besides, I knew the difference between a morning grouch and real unhappiness. Dido had overheard Father's refusal to let Francis treat her and in her characteristic way had resorted to anger rather than hurt tears.

I had no idea how I could comfort her. In this mood she closed herself against everyone.

I stood hesitantly, my hands resting on the rough stone balustrade. The delphiniums were at the height of their blue glory: the lawn was emerald green. But the peace of the garden stopped at the terrace. Dido's tension reached out like some dark aura and I felt depressed and helpless. The only thing to do was to leave her alone. But before I did that, I made one more effort to break through what seemed a wild, unreasonable resentment.

"We care, you know. That's why we discussed you."

"Thank you for nothing. I heard enough—quite enough—to know how much *your* side of the family cares."

Her meaning was not clear. "*My* side? If you mean Father, he only seems difficult because he wants to do the best for you and if you think otherwise then you didn't listen properly."

She slammed her fists on the arms of her chair, and her face was so tight with hatred that I gave up in despair and walked away.

Father left for Wells and his nearly completed ceiling, shouting a reminder over his shoulder to Freda that they would be leaving for London soon after his return late that afternoon. "We won't have much time, so you'd better be ready."

"I always am," Freda sang back.

They were attending an arts dinner at the Dorchester, and Father was to be a guest of honor. Ten minutes after Father, Niall left for Bristol.

I was to be ready and packed, he said, when he returned. Whoever had driven at me could extend the mischief—he called it mischief—and start a rumor that all was not well between us. He said bitterly, "You know how it will go: 'Someone drove a car at his wife and they say that it was his own Bentley.' The rumors, Sarah, the whispers . . . eyes watching us . . . So, you'll return to London with me."

I remained silent. I had left him the previous morning, resolved never to return. But events had drawn us together like reluctant allies against an unknown enemy. I did not know what I was going to do when the evening came.

During the day I telephoned Lady Trenthall ostensibly to congratulate her on the concert. We chatted for a time before I asked her if she knew someone called Alexandra. I had forgotten her surname, I said. I described her. Lady Trenthall said she could not place her, but then the majority of people who had bought tickets for the concert had been unknown to her. Alexandra . . . Alexandra? No, she couldn't remember ever having known anyone of that name. She would ask her husband. A semiaudible conversation was carried on until she returned to the telephone saying that the name meant nothing to him either.

Late that afternoon I went into Theo's room to put his laundry away. On the floor, behind an armchair, I saw a triangle of bright color. I bent and pulled it out. It was a painting of a peony bed that faced the gap in the hedge leading to Theo's lily garden. There was a silvery glow over the canvas. Rain veiling the scene. Yet the vivid colors were slashed on with a kind of frenzy that made me think of Van Gogh's painting against time before madness took over. But there was no madness in Theo. If he had rushed the painting it was for some other reason. A fear, perhaps, that one of us would come along and see what he was doing and tell Father. We thought he had never painted again, but when he was hidden behind the hornbeam hedge of his lily garden the compulsion to touch brush and canvas was stronger than Father's autocratic rejection. Very carefully, I replaced the painting exactly as I had found it, with one corner showing.

Father burst into the house at five o'clock. "Freda? Freda, where are you? Oh Sarah, you'll do. Pour me a stiff Scotch; there's a good girl." He disappeared into the kitchen, came back munching a hunk of cheese and took his drink. "I'll have it upstairs while I'm changing. Get the car out for us. I'll be down in ten minutes."

A newspaper was swept off the table; a hammer he had borrowed for some mysterious purpose that morning appeared from his pocket and was dumped on the settee; a box of matches spilled as he lit a cigarette. Father was home.

Niall had not returned before I took Freda and Father to the station. I waited with them until the train came in, let Father kiss me noisily, told him to be careful not to be too bawdy in his speech and waved them out of sight round the bend of the track.

It was an odd thing, but whenever Father went away it was as if Guinever's backbone was cracked. I drove slowly through the gates and up the lime avenue. Halfway up I braked hard as a rabbit shot out from almost under the car's wheels and dived into the lavender bushes on the other side. I watched its white tail stump disappear and then saw something move by the cliff wall. I caught whatever it was out of the corner of my eye and, when I looked properly, it was gone. "It" was the wrong word. What I had seen was a man—or a woman. I stopped the car and my hand went to the door to open it.

Long before my grandfather's time, someone had hewn a narrow path along the cliff top on the other side of the wall. It ran three hundred yards to where the cliff fell to the pine-girdled ravine. Theo, Penn and I sometimes used it as a shortcut to and from the farm, but nobody else did. It was so narrow that Father forbade Freda to use it. "You'd bulge out over the side and lose your balance." Nina never walked unless she could help it, and Polly was scared to death of the path. There was every possibility that I had seen one of my brothers—Theo, perhaps, going to have a drink with Penn, or Penn himself. Yet, without knowing why, I was certain it was neither.

I got out of the car, leaving the door swinging, and raced across the lawn. I pushed through the tamarisk and looked over the wall. There was no one in sight. The cliff path sloped down to the ravine; the tide was out, and far below the weed-girt rocks gleamed in the sharp, pale sunlight. I had no idea why I had looked down, because no one could reach our treacherous beach except from the low level of the ravine. Whoever had scaled the wall had not wanted to be seen and had gone swiftly out of sight round the bend of the cliffs. Not Theo. Not Penn. They respected the danger too much to hurry. Someone, then, preferring the risk to being seen—and recognized? . . .

There was another possibility. Whoever had been near the wall might not have escaped by the cliff path—might be, in fact, still hiding in the bushes. Watching and waiting for whom? For Niall? . . . For me? My race across the lawn might have plunged me straight into danger. Impulsiveness would be the death of me. The cliché was like a bad joke. I pulled myself together. I had seen no one. It was all in my imagination. Bushes swayed with the wind. A sudden puff of it could have swept across Guinever. No one had escaped; no one had been watching the house. I began to sing aloud one of Nina's songs. But I drove very fast toward the garage.

With a sinking heart I saw that Niall had returned and the Bentley was parked outside, ready for tonight's drive to London. I had just enough room to maneuver Father's car into the garage. As I came out again I passed close to Niall's car. The door on the passenger side was not quite closed. Something lay on the seat—a splash of color—a scarf, perhaps, though I didn't recognize it. I pulled open the door. It was a doll dressed in peasant costume, a red skirt with bands of green round the edge, an embroidered apron and a little white blouse with short puffed sleeves.

As I picked it up, its head fell back, waving like a torn leaf about to fall from a tree. I saw that a piece of fuse wire had been tied so tightly round its neck that it had cut into the doll's stuffing.

In the short time it had taken me to drive to the station and back, Sylvie or Lelani must have brought the children over for a walk before supper. Children sometimes take violent hates to a doll or a toy. Had Annalise played some ghoulish game of garroting and then, afraid that the tender-hearted Lelani would be angry with her, done a casual hop and skip to thrust the doll out of sight in Niall's car? Even as the idea struck me, I knew that it was too farfetched. Neither Annalise nor Tim were destructive. I carried the doll into the house, dangling it by one limp hand.

Polly was on the telephone. She hadn't heard me and she sat huddled over the receiver. When she was excited her voice took on a breathless quality. "Kester is away so I can manage it. No, I'm not going to tell anyone and nor must you, yet. Please, not till . . . everything's all right . . ."

I walked away. I had heard enough. There was a cling as the receiver was replaced.

"Oh, Sarah, there you are. You've been quick." She looked guilty and excited; her hands fluttered ineffectually. "What have you got there?"

"Some child dropped a doll." I held it to my side so that she shouldn't see the dangling had. "Was Annalise here this evening?"

"No. I didn't see her. But sometimes

Lelani brings the children over just for a walk without calling at the house."

"I'll ring Sylvie."

"Do that." She gave me an overbright smile. The doll didn't interest her. She looked as if, for the first time in her life, she was getting away with something, the mistress of a situation.

I sat down by the telephone and dialed the farm number. Sylvie answered. No, she hadn't been near Guinever all day, nor had the children. Lelani had taken them for their walk down to the sandy cove on the other side of the ravine. Tim wanted to look for seashells and it was safe there. Why did I ask?

I said, "I've found a doll and I wondered if Annalise had dropped it."

"What sort of doll?"

"It's got black hair and it's dressed in some kind of European peasant costume."

"Then one of the village children must have left it there. They do trespass sometimes, don't they?"

But village children who might wander into the grounds to look for wild strawberries in the summer would not venture as far as the garage.

Upstairs in my room, I put the doll on the

dressing table and the more I looked at it the more horrible it became.

A doll. Alexandra's note had said, "Ask Niall if he remembers the Italian Doll." I was more than ever certain that the placing of it in Niall's car, the broken neck, was no child's act. Yet because it seemed so childish, it was the more sinister.

I should, of course, show the doll to Niall. But there was a muted sound of talking coming from his room and I guessed he was tape-recording something. One of the lessons I had learned was that I must never disturb him when he was working. So I left the doll where it was and went downstairs.

9

FOR the next hour, I kept thinking of the doll, lying exposed and malevolent near the things I used every day—my brush and comb, powder, scent bottles. It was like a slow contamination, building up as the minutes passed, and at last I could bear it no longer. I rushed upstairs and, picking up the doll by its red skirt, thrust it under some sweaters in a drawer of the bureau.

When it was out of sight, my acute horror eased. I walked round the room, tidying a pile of paperbacks. I picked up a record that lay on the table and put it on the phonograph Father had given me on my sixteenth birthday. Nina's voice drifted round my room, singing a Greek folk song which had been translated for her into English.

The house was abnormally quiet and I was on edge. There was only one way to stop fear and that was by action. I would go and see Luke and tell him of Polly's plan for Dido. Perhaps there was some medical reason why it would be dangerous for Dido to break her treatment at Matthews. Luke would know. He would help me prevent an unholy row when Father heard what Polly had done.

I drove fast into Launford. Luke's car was parked outside his house and Luke himself opened the door to me.

"Why, Sarah—"

With the space of a doorstep between us, I looked up at him and was honest with myself. Dido was an excuse. The longing to see Luke was a personal, paramount thing.

"Come in."

The room was strange to me, but what was in it was only too familiar.

I looked about me and felt the old pain of remembering. I had lain on the olive green settee so many times, enfolded in Luke's arms; I had sat upright on it, my eyes blazing with anger as we quarreled. Father had given Luke that painting of one of his models, a girl in a dark dress and red hair caught in a golden snood. On our last Christmas as lovers I had given him the piece of Bristol glass that gleamed like blood. Long ago, in a different world . . .

"You're just in time for a drink."

I chose a sherry and sat back and watched him pour, thinking again how like Niall he was, how helplessly I seemed to be drawn to slim, dark, arrogant men whose characters contained all the things mine did not—strength and mastery, ambition and, most potent of all, a desire for freedom from the very involvement I craved.

Luke stood over me, holding out my drink. The low sun glittered on the glass, turning the facets to sapphire and emerald. "Is this a purely inquisitive call?" he was laughing. "Did you want to know whether I had remained faithful to all my possessions? Well, you see, I have. Nothing seems to have been harmed by storage."

"It's a beautiful little house. I love Regency architecture."

"It suits me."

I sipped sherry, aware of him standing, glass in hand, leaning against the mantelpiece, and asked, "Are you glad to be in England?"

"I have a conscience about it."

"Why?"

"If you had lived for three years, as I did, in Bihar, you'd know why. And if I'd been made of finer material I'd have stayed. There's so much to be done and so few to do it."

"Research is necessary, too."

"I could have done that sort of work there. But I didn't. I may go back."

I said, "Anyone would think we were overstocked with researchers here. Why go?"

I was not conscious of resentment in my voice—I meant none. But Luke made a small, swift movement of avoidance as if we'd met in the street and were about to collide.

"Perhaps it depends."

"On what?"

"On no one but myself. It's a form of claustrophobia, I suppose. But I must be free to come and go, to people and places. I can't be hedged in. I can't be tied to a home and a hearth."

I said, "No small, encumbered place for Luke Ashton."

I wasn't meaning to mock, only to let him think I understood and it didn't matter. But he lifted his whisky glass, drank and asked, "What did you really come for? Surely not to see how I had arranged my furniture?"

He was deliberately refusing to become too personal with me. I said, "Polly is going to take Dido to Francis Lorian."

He lit a cigarette; then, when he made no comment, I said, "Father is away in London and so she's seizing her opportunity. Luke, we've got to do something to stop her."

"Polly has a right to go where she chooses. If she thinks Lorian can help Dido—"

"But he can't. You know he can't."

"I know no such thing."

"You mean to condone what Polly is doing?"

"I have an open mind."

"*Must* you be so cautious?"

His eyes flashed gray and brilliant at me. "What do you want me to do? Fly off the handle and accuse the man of being a quack? Threaten to expose him? Expose him for what? From what I hear he has done a great deal of good?"

"Dido is a patient at your hospital."

"And Polly is free to stop her daughter's treatment any time she chooses."

I put down my glass and got up. "Then I'm wasting my time."

He burst into laughter. "Thank you very much."

"Oh, Luke. I dislike Francis Lorian. I think I'm afraid of him. He's snaking his way into the family. First Nina—*look* at the way they behaved at the charity show."

Luke laughed again. "I should stop worrying about Nina. She has always been attracted by the unconventional."

"And we can't stop Polly?"

"No."

I watched him, knowing all over again, with an ache in my heart, why I had loved him.

He turned from the mantelpiece, where he was fingering a crystal bird, and looked directly at me. The moment's silence between us became charged with something too fragile to explain yet too strong to ignore. I had to say something, and say it fiercely in order to conceal the real reason for the emotion that swept over me. "You know Polly's making a terrible mistake, yet you do nothing. What has changed you? In the old days you'd have fought for what you thought was right."

He flung back his head. "God forbid I should sound like Sir Galahad. I'd have said that I always fought to get my own way, which is a very different thing."

The sunlight struck his face. As I looked at him, I wondered whether he was having a love affair with anyone. If so, who was she? Would he marry her? If I touched his hand it would be cool, his hair crisp and strong under my fingers. I was trembling and I moved away from him, pretending the sun was blinding me. "I think I'd better go." It sounded so banal.

"Without having said what you came to say?"

He knew me too well. I gave a high, false laugh. "The failure of a mission, Luke. I accept defeat and exit gracefully."

He said, as if he had forgotten our earlier conversation, "Oh, Dido. But that wasn't the real reason for your visit, was it?"

"Why couldn't it be?"

"Because," he said practically, "you know perfectly well, without coming to me to hear it, that Polly is free to take her daughter where she chooses. There's something else on your mind. You may as well tell me."

"It's nothing."

"And that's the understatement of the evening."

He defeated me. I began to play with the clasp of my bag, clicking it open and shut.

I said, without looking at him. "You once accused me of being too possessive."

"Did I? Then I was unfair to you."

His confession touched a tiny oasis of

happiness. I said softly, "All this time, I've been thinking it was my fault."

He turned on me, without anger but with a kind of violence. "All this time? Three years? Heaven forbid I occupied even a corner of your mind that long! I can't believe it. I don't want to believe it. I hope what you've just told me is just an idea, suddenly thought up. I hope you threw me out—memory and all—long ago."

White butterflies danced through the sunlight in the garden. So no one would ever hold him. Now it was in the open—the thing I had known by instinct yet never understood, blaming myself and still blaming myself that I had not let him go gracefully. I said, "Niall wants more breathing space, too. His plan is for me to live at Guinever. He will come down when he can. That's why I asked you about possessiveness. I've been thinking, 'Perhaps it's always my fault.' Now I realize that I just . . . pick the men who want . . . to be free."

Luke looked out into the garden. "I was lucky when I bought this house. The roses came with it, and the old walnut tree."

This was the way in which he was changed. In the old days he would always let me talk out a problem with him. Perhaps now he was afraid that as he and Niall were so clearly alike in this one way, there would be an involvement for him in this obvious similarity. Perhaps he was afraid of having to take Niall's side. But then, he didn't understand that the character likeness was limited. Luke was kind and very strong; he had a wonderful sense of fun which had meant that we had laughed a lot. Niall seldom laughed except to mock.

I said, "I was right. You are different."

"Wrong!" he said. "I've never changed." His eyes were very brilliant and he was laughing as if at a joke. He lifted his glass to me. "I have always been in love with you."

I felt as if I had leaped into a pool of light. Everything that I felt must have shown on my face, for Luke said, "Oh no, that wasn't an opening gambit. The old feeling for you is there, but it is all safely locked away in a bit of me that's as strong as a bank vault."

He could do what I couldn't do: he could laugh at love. His head tilted and the crystal glass in his hand glittered as he drank. Luke, who had lain with me and loved me, who had walked out of my life. And he expected . . .

But he expected nothing. He wanted nothing of me.

A kind of helpless anger seized me. Against both instinct and wisdom, I cried, "Doesn't it mean anything to you that Niall neither gives anything to me nor needs anything from me—anything real . . . deep . . . ?"

"I have no intention of letting it mean anything. I'm not a gambler, Sarah. I won't take risks."

"I'm a risk?"

"Of course. All love is a battle and a fever. Perhaps you win; perhaps you don't. Perhaps it's total; perhaps perfect only for a time with the sadness and bitterness eating it away in the end. It isn't enough just to love." He put down his glass. "But let's not get bogged down." He ran his fingers through my hair and pulled my head back gently. "Thank God, I'm strong." He kissed me lightly, as a friend would. "And now, may I please go and have my dinner?"

"I would hate you to starve on my account."

He chuckled. "I won't."

We walked together in silence into the hall. The front door opened and the scent of roses blew in.

I asked, "Does this mean you won't be coming to Guinever again?"

"Why not? If I'm asked, I'd love to come."

"Of course, come," I said and walked out to my car without looking back.

10

I FORGOT about the doll hidden in the bureau until I saw Niall's car still standing outside the garage.

I had told no one about it. Polly, scared of everything from spiders to thunderstorms, would have seen some terrible significance in it. Nor would I have told Dido. On the other hand, when Nina and I met in the passage, there was no reason why I should not have taken her into my room and shown her the doll. No reason . . . but I did not.

Niall did not come downstairs until we were sitting down to dinner. While we ate salmon sent us by a friend on a fishing holiday in the clear sweet Irish waters, Polly asked Niall about the television series he had been to Bristol to discuss.

He said, "You'll hear about it when they choose to release the news. I'm not at liberty to tell you anything."

Nina laughed. "You make it sound like a Military Intelligence operation. Come on,

Niall, no mysteries. You can at least tell us who is on this panel with you."

He said, "A top-flight novelist, a scientist and an astronomer. And that's all the news I can give you."

The discussions must have gone well, for he smiled at her and then at me.

Dido said, "We saw you this evening, Sarah, coming out of Luke's house."

I stabbed a sliver of tomato. "That's right. I went to see him."

Nina swung her hair from her shoulders. "Luke is a very old friend. It's nice to have him back in England. We've known him for most of our lives."

Niall said with mockery, "The universal uncle."

"Cousin is a more likely word."

Dido said, "But he has always been Sarah's *particular* friend. In the old days—"

"When we were very young."

Niall looked at me with amusement, "You must tell me about him some time."

"There's nothing to tell."

Dido's eyes flashed at me. "Don't believe her, Niall. It was quite something. It really was. A sort of *grande passion*."

"If you want to use French words," Niall

said, "then you must learn the correct pronunciation." His tone and manner were as unperturbed as though Dido had said, "It rained last Friday."

Polly said quickly, aware of the anger in Dido's eyes, "If you've all finished, I'll get the pudding."

She had tried her hand at a soufflé and it had failed. Niall refused it, shook his head at the cheese board and got up from the table. "I'm working on an idea for a documentary. I want to finish it before we start for London."

"Oh, Niall," Polly cried. "You'll be so late. It's nearly eight o'clock now."

"I like driving at night," he said.

When the door closed, Nina said lightly to Dido, "One of these days you may learn the difference between a grand passion and a light love affair."

Dido said sulkily, "Sarah went about looking dazed when Luke left for India. I wouldn't have called that a light affair."

I had managed to eat my portion of the ruined soufflé and I pushed back my chair. "I'm going to get coffee."

In the kitchen, firmly modernized by Freda, I found that the green and white Worcester cups and saucers were already on the tray; the coffee was bubbling gently. Polly had forgotten the spoons. I got them. Dido had had some purpose in saying what she had. *She's jealous of me.* Jealous because of Niall? I put the spoons in the saucers. I doubted if Dido had, or ever would have, any capacity for loving, only desiring. Niall represented for her money and success, and I suspected that a face known to millions on a television screen was her interpretation of glory.

Twilight still clung to the northwestern sky in washes of lavender and yellow. Theo was out somewhere and Niall was shut in his room. It was half past eight. I supposed Polly and Dido were watching television. I could not hear, for the walls were thick, and Father, who hated any noise that he did not make himself, would never allow us to turn the volume up. Even when he was not there the habit of low sound prevailed. The house was silent, and the walls pressed in on me. I felt restless and on edge. I did not want to return to London with Niall, yet paradoxically I knew that I would go. Our strength lay in temporary unity.

I pushed open the french doors and crossed

the terrace, walking aimlessly across the lawn. The lemon afterglow gleamed in a far corner of Theo's lily garden. I went through the gap in the hornbeam hedge and stood at the edge of the pond where the water lilies grew.

In daylight it would be rich in color, vermilion and golden yellow, pink and copper. Now the afterglow scarcely reached down to the garden, and in the near-darkness the flowers had an almost phosphorescent luminousness. Against the hedge were the earth lilies, tall and strong and giving out a scent faint enough to seem only in the imagination.

At the far end of the garden, just out of sight behind the hedge, was Theo's tool shed. The door was open. I went in. My foot touched something soft. I picked it up and saw that it was a paint-stained rag. I knew that it didn't belong to Father. For one thing, he never came near the shed, and for another, his rags remained on his own studio floor.

Theo had been painting. I looked round and could see neither palette nor brushes, but they must be somewhere here, hidden away. I remembered the peony painting behind the chair in his room.

I felt a surge of fury for Father's tactlessness, which had thrown Theo so much into himself that painting had to be a secret thing. Here were two personalities so opposite that, for all their affection for one another, they could not meet on the ground that was closest and most loved by them both.

I could tell no one that Theo painted in secret. The puzzle was how he managed to do so without any of us knowing. I had never seen him leave the house with his equipment. Then I remembered the strange silver-gray film over the peony painting. Of course. Theo painted when he could be assured that we were not around—when it was cold or wet and he was safe from inquisitive eyes. If Father were his son's idol or were less of an artist himself, Theo would not have had this feeling of shame that he was unable to measure up to Father's brilliance.

I closed the door of the hut and walked slowly back round the lily pond. When I came to the gap in the hedge I saw Niall crossing the lawn. This was the first chance I had had to tell him about the doll. He was coming my way although I did not think he had seen me. For a moment he was outlined in the sun's final trail of lemon light. Then he moved into the shadow of the cedar on the lawn. A high thin whistle sounded from somewhere in the distance, carrying clearly on the still air.

The shot came in one swift crack. From somewhere above me a bird stirred and fluttered panic wings. Then there was a moment's petrified silence.

I stood flattened against the hedge. The direction could be deceptive. Penn or one of his farm workers might be shooting rabbits down in the ravine where it was still light. But the direction was not as deceptive as all that. The shot had come from somewhere near me—by the cliff wall.

Niall began to run. He was hunched up as if holding his arms across his chest. Then I saw him stagger.

My shout lifted and became a roar of sound in my ears. I was by no means brave, I just gave no thought to the fact that there is more than one bullet in a gun. I raced across the lawn. I saw Niall, far ahead of me, weaving up the terrace steps, saw Polly running to the door.

By the time I had reached the living room, Niall was half-sitting, half-lying on the settee and Polly was taking off his coat.

I heard Dido's chair wheels hissing frantically along the hall from the side door, where a ramp had been fixed for her to propel herself to and from the garden. As she came, she cried out, "What happened? Mother, what *happened?* I was in the herb garden and I heard a shot . . ." She stopped on the threshold of the room and gave a sharp, high-pitched cry. Her hands made wild, hysterical little slashes at the air. "Niall! Who did it? Who shot at you? Mother . . . someone's out there in the dark, aren't they? And they could be mad. Perhaps he wants to kill us all . . ."

Polly turned from easing Niall's arm from his coat sleeve. "No one is going to harm you, darling. Go into the other room and watch the television play and tell me later what it's all about. Forget what you've seen. Everything is all right." Then she saw me and spoiled the calming effect her words might have had. "Oh, Sarah, it's awful . . . someone shot . . ."

Niall's eyes were half-closed. His skin was clay-colored. Polly was rolling up his shirt sleeve; there was blood on his upper arm.

"Go and fetch a bowl of water and bandages," I said to Polly and turned to Niall. "Let's get the shirt right off—"

He jerked away from me. "I can do it. There's no need to fuss." But his hand was shaking so much that he could not undo the cuff.

"You must let me—" I pushed his fumbling fingers away.

Behind me Dido was giving odd little indrawn breaths, like sobs. I said over my shoulder, "There's something you can do. Go and call Doctor Marshall. His number is in the red book on the telephone table."

Niall jerked himself upright. "You'll do no such thing."

I pulled his shirt over his head. I had always been surprised how the skin on his body was neither warm pink nor suntanned, but alabaster white. The wound on his arm was bleeding.

"Go and do what I ask," I said to Dido. "Tell the doctor—"

"For Christ's sake, I won't have all this fuss made. I don't *want* a doctor," he was shouting. "*Now* do you hear me?"

"Perfectly well." He was shocked and I had to make allowances. "But someone shot at you. I don't know much about bullets and things, but if there's one in your arm, then someone's got to get it out."

"A bullet, embedded in my flesh?" he demanded with a touch of his old mockery. "A serious accident—with just that trickle of blood? Don't be silly."

"This is the first time I've seen a man who has been a target for a bullet," I flashed back, "so perhaps I can be excused for being stupid."

"If you'll look at my coat, you'll see that the bullet went in and out the other side of the sleeve. It has only grazed me."

Dido cried, "All the same, it's horrible. Niall . . . someone tried to kill you . . ." She began to tremble violently. "But who? Why?"

I was waiting for Polly and the bowl of water. "Poachers," I said.

"But we don't get poachers," her voice rose. "There's nothing here to . . . to . . . poach, is there?"

"Rabbits and hares by the thousand," I told her, deliberately exaggerating.

Polly came back, the first-aid box under her arm, a bowl held in front of her. "Here we are. I wasn't long, was I?" She slopped water over the carpet as she scuttled toward me. Her wide, slightly protuberant eyes were scared.

"Where's Nina?" I asked.

"Upstairs. I heard her phonograph. And her car is outside."

I tore off some cotton wool and began to clean Niall's arm. "She must have heard the shot."

"Not with all that noise she's making. She's got one of those Spanish folk songs with a chorus. Shall I call her?"

"What for?" Niall demanded, cringing as I touched the wound. "To make a public spectacle of me?"

Polly hovered at my side. "But we must call Doctor Marshall."

Niall turned on her. "You heard me say no. It's just a graze. If you'd like to crawl through the grass some way from where I was walking, you might find the bullet. Now let's stop making a fuss."

I said quietly, "Polly, dear, go to Dido. She's upset."

"She hates the sight of blood. If you can manage—"

"Of course I can." I finished bandaging the arm.

"It stings," he said and touched the place cautiously.

"Of course it does." I picked up his coat

from the floor. There were two searing holes on the left sleeve where the bullet had passed through.

"Throw it away," Niall said. "Give it to that old man who comes to do the garden. And get me a cigarette."

I found him one and flicked on the table lighter. Cigarette in his mouth, he leaned forward cautiously as if afraid he would break if he relaxed. His fingers twitched. Smoke curled up thinly.

"Would you like a drink?"

"A brandy. A good stiff one."

I poured it out and brought it over to him. He had been calm enough, but the effort had defeated him. In that appalled moment as he took the drink, I saw for the second time in two days the disintegration of his features, as if they had slid away from one another. I turned my head quickly, feeling an interloper prying on a man's fear. "We must report this to the police," I said, "whether you like the idea or not."

"I don't like it, and you won't."

"We can't let some gun-happy poacher loose in the neighborhood. Next time—"

"If there's a next time I shan't be here to experience it. We're leaving tomorrow."

"You had planned to go tonight."

I saw him look past me toward the window. "Tomorrow—in daylight," he said. "Not tonight . . ."

He was afraid of the dark, of the walk from the house to the car, of the drive down the long black lime avenue. He was afraid that someone still waited there. But he was even more afraid of calling the police.

"If you want to go tonight, I'll drive," I said. "It's all right, Niall. Whoever shot at you will be a long way from Guinever by now. Poachers who are rotten shots—"

He interrupted me. "I've yet to hear of a man walking upright being mistaken for a rabbit."

A shiver went through me. "Then, if it wasn't that . . .?"

He got up and walked across the room and drew the curtains over the window. Then he stood with his back to them. His heavy eyelids seemed to lift with difficulty. He moved his hand, like a blind man, over the table by the window, fumbling, brushing the marigolds in Nina's blue luster bowl. "Who hates me enough to stalk me in the dark and shoot?"

I had asked a similar question when the

car nearly ran me down. We stared at one another. Somewhere in a room above us—in another world—I could hear Nina's guitar. Outside and far below, the sea hissed at the rocks. I ran my tongue over my dry lips and tried to speak. My voice was a croak. "I . . . can't . . . believe . . . it was deliberate."

"Then if it wasn't, it was a pretty good imitation."

"But people don't try to kill—not the kind of people we know—not ordinary . . ." The harsh uncompromising lines of his face checked me for a moment. Then in a rush, I cried, "I won't believe that someone intended to harm you."

"Then you'd better overhaul your credulity." Even at this crucial moment he could not resist being heavily pedantic. "Because there's no other explanation. None."

He spoke with emotion. Yet I saw the way his hand continued to brush the table. There was such violent muscular tension in the act that I felt that if anything had been in his way—a flower, a book—he would have torn it apart.

"That car, the one you told me tried to run you down"— He made a queer sound as if he were gulping down air—"I can believe anything, even that story. Murder. For God's sake, it can't be true. Yet that's just what it is. Attempted murder . . ." Cigarette smoke curled between us; his eyes were small pinpoints of light.

I said slowly, "Suppose someone only intended to wound you—some lunatic angered by something you said in one of your programs—or someone who has a grudge against television generally and making us the victims? But it isn't credible, is it?"

"Nothing is more fantastic than the truth. You once said that yourself. Read the newspapers, look into people's lives . . ."

Yes, I thought, our lives. I closed my eyes. You walked the streets; you sat in a beautiful car, smiled and talked; fussed over the color of a lipstick, the line of a dress. And behind it all was yourself . . . full of fears and anxieties and everlasting doubts . . . And for Niall and I, "so blessed by the gods," as one interviewer had put it, the terror of an unknown violence.

"Who wants me dead?"

Suddenly, I was the strong one. I went to Niall and put my arms round him and drew him against me, all bitterness forgotten because in naked fear, he needed me. I said, "We'll go together to the police."

He stirred angrily in my arms. "Must I keep saying no?" He broke away from me. "Your father keeps a couple of guns in that room in the keep, doesn't he? Let's see if they're still there."

"Of course they are."

"One of them could have been fired and replaced."

"Father is the only one here who can shoot."

"Anyone can pull the trigger of a gun," he said.

Polly came running in from the garden. She was panting. "I've been out on the terrace to see—" she addressed Niall and I knew she was wanting him to say how brave she was. When there was no reaction, she added lamely, "There was no one there."

"I doubt if the gunman sat on the lawn and waited for you to find him."

"It's all right, Polly," I said quietly. "Just leave everything to us."

Niall moved to a closed door near the end window. There was a narrow passage beyond, leading to the keep and, at the far end, two small stone rooms, one where we stored everything we seldom needed, the other an empty dark place with archers' slits looking onto the sea. Polly watched Niall cross the room and must have thought he was going into the garden, for she cried, "Oh do be careful. He might be around."

"I'm not going out. And as for still being in the grounds, he didn't take a pot shot at you just now, did he?"

"No, but I—"

"You, what? You're not the one he's after and I am. Is that what you mean?"

"Niall, how can you think that *I* think such a thing? It's just that . . . that I don't know what to say. I mean . . ." She struggled with words and gave up. Her pale blue eyes bulged with horror.

"Whoever fired that shot," I said, "will be back in his cottage, keeping his fingers crossed that nobody saw him."

Polly said, sighing, "I wish Kester were here. He'd know what to do. He'd get the police—"

Niall's voice was like smooth ice. "Lucifer give me strength! You can stop crying for the police, both of you. No one is going to call them. Come, Sarah."

Polly watched me across the room. "Where are you going?"

"Sarah knows."

It was safe. Neither of the guns would have been fired.

The stone passage on the other side of the door struck that chill which emanates from thick, ancient walls. The two doors ahead of us had heavy iron latches. I lifted one and the hinges creaked. I flicked on the light—electricity in a medieval tower. The single bulb threw a garish light over a jumble of old possessions. Tennis rackets and cricket bats, a pitted dart board. There was a tea chest with great brass locks. It was full of Victorian and Edwardian clothes, rotting silks and laces our ancestors had worn. We had kept them, arguing that they might be useful for some fancy-dress affair, but nobody had ever used them so far. Sometimes we took them out and sprayed them with moth repellent, looking at them kindly, wondering about great-grandmothers, and great-great-aunts.

The gun cabinet was against the far curve of the wall. Niall opened it and took down each gun, sniffed it and returned it.

"I told you neither would have been fired,"

I said edgily. "Now whether you like it or not, this has got to be reported."

He said, very quietly, "It is ironical that it is my wife who wants to ruin my career for an impulsive decision. I will not have this kind of publicity."

The pattern was the same as last night, when he had heard of my accident . . . The danger was not to a life, but a career.

I said explosively, "Damn publicity. I'm concerned with lives—yours and mine. And I'd rather act on impulse than be too cautious. Next time—"

"Yes, there could be a next time."

"And still you do nothing! You won't even let me call a doctor. You just talk about some private detective. And between now and when you get him—what happens? Who is going to get hurt next? If—"

He interrupted me again. "I've got other things to think of. Newspapers, reporters, the gossips—"

"You overrate your importance. Come down to earth."

"That is exactly where I am. The whole point of my caution is that I know I am only important so long as it amuses the public to build me up and make me seem worth what

I'm paid. I can be just as quickly knocked down. All right, so you tell the police about the car that nearly ran you down, about the shot fired at me. The newspapers will be on to it. I've been put on a kind of pedestal of honesty and integrity. Topple that and they'll ask, 'What's wrong with Rhodes and his wife? Why have they got violent enemies?' Start those questions and I'm done for. My damned image—"

I cried, "Your 'damned' image? Oh, Niall . . ."

A look that was close to self-hatred crossed his face. "I used the precise word. 'Damned.' I have no love for what I am, but I have to cosset it, because it is all I have." He turned his head away from me and said, "You see, I am a realist. I haven't your charming idealism. Only two things matter—power and sex. When they fail, there is nothing."

"That makes life a façade."

"You're learning. That's what it is."

He was wrong, but I couldn't argue with him. Our values were alien. We had eyes that saw the world so differently that we could have no influence on one another. I thought, "There's another thing. Niall cannot give."

Suddenly he said impatiently, "Have I

taught you nothing? Do you still have pretty ideals?"

The insufferable tension in me snapped. I lost touch with the danger we were in. We were two people at odds with one another, face to face, yet as distant as if we inhabited opposite ends of the earth. "Don't try to teach me your way of looking at life." I picked up a broken table tennis ball and cracked it furiously in my fingers. "Come to that, don't try to teach me at all. All right. So I'm not realistic or, to your way of thinking, even logical. But I'll muddle along. You tell me you hated schoolmastering, but you didn't. Shall I tell you what you really hated? It was youth. You love teaching because it gives you a sense of superiority. And your kind of television technique is only an extension of it. You gave your knowledge to children, now you give it to adults. The medium is the same whether you're sitting at a schoolroom desk or in front of cameras. All right, if you want it that way, have it. But treat me as an adult—and start now." I stopped only because I had no more breath left. "Oh, let's get out of here."

I saw him glance at the window slit that faced the edge of the garden. Was he afraid someone still lurked outside? If so, he wasn't the only one. I was glad when we left the cold room, our footsteps echoing along the stone passage.

The living room was empty. Niall said, "I'm going to bed."

"Is there anything you'd like? A hot drink? Another brandy?"

"To be alone," he said and paused at the door. "We go back tomorrow, both of us. Good night."

I picked up a sweater Father had dropped and began folding it, waiting until Niall was out of hearing. Polly was probably in the next room with Dido, watching television and trying to keep her mind off the accident.

I knew what I was going to do. I ran out of the front door to the garage and got into Father's car. I was going to tell Penn what had happened tonight. Someone other than Niall, who was frantic for secrecy, and Polly, who was quite useless, must know and help me decide what to do.

The car wouldn't start. The engine burred and died on me. Pulling out the choke and bullying and coaxing did no good. There was not a spark of life. It blocked the exit so that I could not get out the station wagon. I could take the Bentley, but it would mean going to Niall for the key and that would have involved an explanation I did not want to give him. Nina's Dauphine was nowhere to be seen. She had probably gone out by the back stairs, which was the quickest way to the garage, and, as yet, knew nothing of what had happened.

I tried Father's car again. It spat and died with a groan. When Theo came home, he would know what was wrong with it. I got out and ran across the lawn to the cliff wall. I pushed through the bushes and, finding the place where the bricks had broken away, climbed over on to the cliff path. Whenever I stood there, I knew that it was only safe for a mountain goat. But it was the quickest way to Penn's farm. It was difficult enough by daylight, when one could see a step ahead. At night, it was little short of suicidal unless you kept your back against the rocks and edged along.

The rising moon gave a certain light. The path, worn and broken by time, dipped sharply to the ravine so that as I went, slow step by slow step downward, the cliffs grew higher above me. The path was jagged and uneven and the rock ledges and crannies were filled with sleeping seabirds. Only a few yards along the dipping path, Guinever was no longer in sight. I was enclosed in a primeval stillness.

There was a sharp bend in the path, and when I had crawled round it, I could see, beyond the dip of the ravine, the steady lights from Penn's farmhouse.

A sound, so faint that I could have imagined it, came from somewhere to my left. I stood for a moment, pressed against the cliff face, my hands clammy, my body tingling with fear. I had, of course, only disturbed a sleeping gull. Or perhaps a fox, high up above me in the bracken, could have been attracted by the sound I made and come, hunting, to the cliff top, dislodging a stone. As I crouched there, straining my ears, the terrible thought struck me that if whoever threatened us was around, I could not escape. This was the impetus I needed to go on.

I did not hear the sound again, but the stillness and the emptiness was slowly undermining my courage. I wished desperately that I hadn't come, yet I didn't dare to turn back. On the beach below, the waves were like tiny dancing ghosts; the moon was like a long, smiling silver mouth. Here and there sharp pieces of rock scraped my hands and I was angry with myself for not having put on thicker-soled shoes.

At last I came to the point in the dipping path where the ravine was easily visible. The drop had become less steep and I would soon be on a level with the sea.

There was a car pulled up under trees. It was so well hidden that if moonlight had not gleamed between the tree branches onto the hood, I would not have noticed it. The ravine was a favorite place for lovers from Launford, and normally I would not have given it another thought. But someone had been in our grounds tonight; someone had shot at Niall and had probably watched me go down the cliff path and was still watching. The place where the car was parked was just below the spot where the great bank of oaks stood sentinel, guarding Guinever.

The last hundred yards of the cliff path was child's play. I could have done it at a run. In my light dress, I must now be clearly visible. Then I saw someone come out of the shadow of the oaks and dive into the car. Just one person—and I was too far away to see if it were a man or a woman wearing slacks. I heard the door slam, the engine start up. The car swung round and made off toward the village. It had not turned its lights on.

11

PENN was standing on the porch. I caught a whiff of the tobacco he smoked before I actually saw him, and I felt safe.

"Hey, Sarah."

I hadn't realized until then that I had been running like a hunted hare across the ravine road, through the gate and up to the house. I almost fell on him, gasping, "I must . . . talk . . . to you . . ."

"That's obvious. What's happened?"

"Nothing—yes, it has—I mean . . ."

"You don't make sense, sweetie, come inside and gather yourself up." His casual tone, his unhurried manner and his arm across my shoulder as he led me through the hall were as comforting as if he had been Father.

The huge living room windows were open and a few moths danced round the lamps. Sylvie was sitting in a low chair. She had a pad on her knee and she was writing a letter. She wore an amber linen dress which matched her sun-gilded skin. Her hair was a tangle over her forehead and she pushed it back with a quick hand and smiled at me. A clumber spaniel had planted its glossy haunches on her sandals. "Did you come with Luke?"

"No."

"He's supposed to be looking in for a drink and he's very late. I thought perhaps he'd called at Guinever first."

"There's his car now," Penn said and went to the door. A moth got caught in the little cloud of smoke from his pipe and began a dizzy dance.

Tires hissed softly on the gravel drive. Sylvie said, "What's the matter, Sarah?"

I turned my head and waited a second while the men entered. Luke looked surprised to see me.

"There's no car outside. Did you walk over? I'd have called for you if I'd known you were coming."

"I took the cliff path."

Sylvie cried, "You—*what*?"

"I took the cliff path."

"At night? Don't you dare tell Father that."

I sat down in one of the deep chintz-covered chairs and said, "Someone shot at Niall this evening."

For a second no one spoke. Then Penn gave a trite, explosive, "Good God."

Their eyes were on me, waiting for me to explain. Sylvie said in a carefully quiet voice, "Penn, pour us all drinks. Is Niall badly hurt?"

"The bullet only grazed him. I wondered," I turned to Penn, "whether it could have been one of your farm workers."

"Where did it happen?"

"At Guinever."

"I don't employ poachers," Penn said.

"I thought perhaps you'd taken on a new man who didn't know . . ."

"I've no new men." Penn handed me a brandy. "That's what you want. Now, have you called the police and the doctor?"

"Niall won't let me."

"To hell with what Niall will and won't let you do. Or course you must report it. Or I will. We can't have a lunatic at large." He crossed to the door. I knew he was making for the telephone in his office.

"No," I shouted at him. "Penn, don't—please, for my sake . . ."

"*Your* sake?"

I said, "All right. If it's the only way to stop you calling the police, you may as well have it. Niall is afraid of the publicity."

Penn said impatiently, "In the name of goodness, what's got into him? And anyway, if Niall doesn't want the poacher found, then I do. I've got valuable animals here."

Sylvie said, "Poachers don't usually shoot. They trap or grab from chicken runs. So, if—"

I said as she paused, "So if someone shot at a man walking, they *meant* to shoot him. But why? Nobody in their right senses would harm a man just because they didn't like his television personality."

"There are crazy people at large. Sometimes you don't *know* they're mad until they do something like this . . . There's always a first time."

We talked round and round the subject and got nowhere.

I sipped my brandy and felt the silken warmth of it curl about my body. Tell them about the boy in Gull's Folly, tell them about the doll . . . I had always been impatient of people in trouble who kept the salient points to themselves. Now, sitting in this sane, easy household, I understood. Without quite knowing how it was done, subtly and insidiously, one could be "conditioned." I argued it to myself while I joined superficially into the conversation around me. When I had finished my drink I said, "I'm sorry to make it such a short visit, but you understand. I must go before I'm missed."

Penn said, above Sylvie's protest, "Let her, if she wants to. I'll run you back, Sarah."

Luke said, "My car is outside, I'll take you."

"And come back," Sylvie called to him.

Penn leaned against the door on the passenger side of Luke's car and said, "If you change your mind about calling the police, telephone me. I'll come and give you moral support."

I nodded at my brother. "Thanks."

"You know," he said impatiently, "it seems to me that you and Niall are behaving like a couple of silly ostriches. If someone did take a pot shot at him, you'd be better advised to do something about it—and pretty quickly. Hiding your heads in the sand doesn't make either of you invisible."

"I know."

When Penn was angry, he was very like Father. "What the hell has that man got that he can change your character? You're a doormat, Sarah."

"I'm not. It's just that I can understand something of Niall's argument."

"I'll bet he saw to it that you did!"

The car moved forward. I stared into the golden track made by the headlights. Penn stuck his head into the window. "Call me tomorrow and tell me you've seen sense."

"Sense," I shouted back, "is all a matter of a point of view."

Beside me, Luke laughed. "At least you had the last word."

We scarcely spoke during the drive to Guinever. When we arrived, slowing down at the curve of the avenue, I lifted my arms like a cat stretching its paws. My fingers touched the windshield and I wrote something on it. "Invisible writing," I said. "Shall I tell you what it is?"

"Well, what is it?" he asked lightly, indulging me.

"I'm writing, 'I would like to stop time.' "

"At which moment?"

"Now. Here with you."

"We'd get very cramped and uncomfortable after the first thousand years."

Again, laughter to combat intimacy. I said

quietly, "Thank you for bringing me home, Luke."

He held me back with a hand on my arm. "Do what Penn says. Go to the police." And then he added, "Advice is so easy when you're not involved. I wish I could help, but I'm not a policeman."

"Penn's right about reporting it. But if I do then Niall—" I stopped suddenly.

"Niall what?"

I didn't want to explain. Instead, I stared ahead of me into the great black arch of the trees, stretching far into the distance. The car's headlights made a golden path under them for just a little way, highlighting the nearest leaves so that the whole scene was like a stage set. The Guinever of medieval days should be at the far end, the minstrels singing and the lord's table weighed down with suckling pig and wine.

Luke was watching me, waiting for a reply. But I couldn't tell him that if I went against Niall's wishes he would take it out on me in some way or other. I said reluctantly, "What I mean is that Niall wants to cope with things his way."

Luke looked down at his hands, square and strongly masculine. "That business the other night outside Cypress Mount. I suppose it *was* a drunk who nearly ran you down?"

"Of . . . course . . ."

"Two people in the space of two days involved in accidents? First the wife, then the husband."

"Coincidence."

"You said when we met at Gull's Folly that you didn't believe in it."

"Touché," I said tritely and more flippantly than the conversation warranted. I didn't want to talk about it any more. He was seeing things too clearly and I had had enough for one night. Besides, a part of me had disengaged itself from the rest and was living this moment here with Luke, wanting it to go on, wanting to cherish this black velvet moment under the lime trees. Above the trees I could just see the outline of the battlements of the tower. I said, "Do you remember when we went up to the top of the keep and you taught me something about the stars?" It was the first thing I could think of to keep him there with me.

He said on laughter, "I taught you kid's stuff. The Plow and the Bear. I pretended to know more than I did."

"You talked about Venus glittering in the afterglow . . ."

"What a one you are for remembering." He lifted my hand and laid it lightly against his cheek.

The small gesture took me back three years. I cried softly, "Oh, Luke."

"Beat it!" he said grinning at me.

"On your orders? Why should I?"

"Because I happen to want to call back at Penn's as I promised, then get home and do some work."

"At this hour."

"Uh-huh."

"There's so much we have to talk about."

He said easily, "Well, I'll be around for a while and some other time we can take up where we left off tonight. Where was it? Something about Venus glittering in the afterglow. Go on, Sarah. Scram."

I was home and halfway up the stairs when someone knocked on the front door. The sound echoed hollowly through the hall.

I stood quite still, holding on to the banisters. Polly put her head round the living room door and said, startled, "Oh, Sarah, where *have* you been? I thought that was you knocking because you'd forgotten your key."

"Someone's at the door," I said unnecessarily.

"I'm scared to open it."

So was I, and without any sensible reason. I walked slowly back down the stairs. The knock came again. Polly's head darted backward and forward, ready for a final dive if a man with a shotgun stood there.

I flung open the door. My eyes traveled upward to the height of the six-foot-two young policeman. Jim Pherson, who guarded our innocuous village, Azurstone, gave me his deceptively shy smile.

"Sorry to disturb you, Mrs. Rhodes, but we had a report that there's been a shooting accident here. Of course, the call could be—"

"Sarah, you mustn't," Polly cried.

"—a hoax," Jim plodded on. "But we have to investigate."

"Do come in." I moved to the carved chest and sat down on it, my hands pressed against the lions' heads on each side of the iron lock.

I kept my face resolutely turned away from Polly. "It wasn't a hoax," I said. "My husband was walking across the lawn. Someone fired a shot. Poachers," I added flatly.

"And you didn't report it?"

"The bullet only grazed his arm. He—we—didn't want a fuss."

"But you should report these things, Mrs. Rhodes." He was like a grave, overgrown schoolboy dressed up for fun. "Is Mr. Palfrey around?"

"No, he's in London with my stepmother. It's all right, really," I said lamely. "My husband . . . took control and he prefers to do nothing about it."

Jim produced pen and notebook with the speed of a magician. "Give me details, please. Time. Place. And I'd like to see your husband."

Polly was leaning against the wall muttering, "Oh dear! Oh dear! He'll be so angry."

Jim twisted his long body around. "Angry? At reporting a shooting accident? Why, Mrs. Singleton?"

"Because . . . well, he's famous, you know, and he dreads bad publicity."

"It doesn't seem to me, ma'am, that he has anything to worry about on that score. He was shot at, so he's the innocent party—"

Polly held her hand to her mouth. Over her splayed fingers, her eyes bulged.

"Now, Mrs Rhodes," Jim turned to me, "if you'll give me the facts."

I said, "Who called you and told you?"

"I don't know. He rang off without giving his name."

"It wasn't my brother—"

"No."

"You remember, we had trouble with poachers two years ago. Perhaps this one stumbled and the gun went off accidentally."

"Perhaps. Now if I could just see your husband."

Polly said, "Oh, but he's gone to bed."

"He wouldn't be able to tell you any more than I can," I said, "He saw no one, nor did I."

"Perhaps in the morning, then, I can have a word with Mr. Rhodes."

I nodded vaguely. In the morning we would be on our way to London.

Jim shut up his notebook. "I'll just take a look round the grounds. If you'll come with me and show me where exactly your husband was walking."

His flashlight raked the lawn as we walked together. The moon had slid behind the turret, lighting it like a film set for *Hamlet* at Elsinore.

I said, "Who could have telephoned you? Who could possibly have known?"

Not Penn. And, I was sure, not Luke. Who else knew? Only the one who had fired the shot. A man's voice, not a woman's. Not Alexandra's . . .

"Jim, do you think you could keep this rather quiet? My husband would hate it if the newspapers made some exaggerated story out of it."

"I'm only the village constable. I'll have to report it to Launford." It could have been by accident—I wasn't certain—but the flashlight lifted and shone for a moment in my face. "Don't worry," Jim said. "We'll try to keep it to ourselves—you and Mr. Rhodes and Launford and me—and the poacher."

I stood quite still. "I think this must be about the spot. The bullet went through my husband's jacket so it could be somewhere in the grass."

He glanced about him. "We'll do something about that in the morning. Now, I'll just have a look round. I won't worry you again tonight."

"Wouldn't you like a cup of tea . . . or . . . something?"

"Not now, thanks. Funny place, isn't it, to

think you see a rabbit? Just a flat stretch of lawn, no bushes, nothing for quite a way round."

"Yes, funny place," I said.

"Good night, Mrs. Rhodes."

"Good night. I'm sorry you were called out. We really didn't want a . . . fuss made." *Sorry you've been troubled because tomorrow Niall won't believe that I didn't call you.*

Polly was hovering in the hall. "Do you think he believes it was a poacher's shot?"

"What else?"

She said in a scared whisper, "Then who telephoned?"

"Perhaps the poacher has a conscience or an odd sense of humor."

"Jim thought it very strange, didn't he?"

"Thought what strange?"

"That no one from here reported the accident. I think he was suspicious."

"You mean that he had an idea who the gunman was?"

"No. That it was one of us who fired the shot."

12

WHEN I went to bed that night, Niall's room was in darkness and I guessed he had taken one of the tranquilizers he always carried with him.

I pulled out a drawer and put away a sweater and immediately felt the hard body of the doll. I grabbed it and, holding it away from me as if it were unclean, crossed to Niall's room. I turned the handle of the communicating door as cautiously as I could and edged it open a couple of inches. I called softly, "Niall?"

I waited a moment and then, as there was no answer, guessed that he was either asleep or pretending to be. Whichever way, it was wise not to disturb him. I would show him the doll in the morning. I pushed it back in the drawer.

I had the kind of night when, every time I slept, a nightmare took over and tore me into waking with a start and a frantic leaping heart. In the end I lay, dreading sleep again, and heard the wind whip the sea and the clock downstairs chime three and then four. At last I fell into a final broken bout of sleep and woke to a red dawn. It glowed on the silver rattle with the bells which I kept on my dressing table, childishly, like a prized toy. I had found it once in a teak box in the Portland Place flat. When I showed it to Niall, he had said in disgust, "Throw the damn thing away." I had refused, shaking it so that the bells jingled. "It's charming. Is it really yours?"

"Some stupid family tradition that it is given to the eldest child at his christening. Get rid of it."

But I hadn't. I had brought it down to Guinever with me.

A gift at a christening . . . And had somebody cast a spell over him as he lay in his cot in the Edinburgh house where he was born? "You shall have three wishes." . . . "I will choose intellect, then, and success and good health." . . . "And with it, for balance, one curse—and that you cannot choose. You shall love only yourself." . . .

I got up unrefreshed, dressed and went into Niall's room. The wound on his arm was so slight that I discarded the bandage and put a Band-Aid over it.

"Did you sleep well?"

"I took a couple of pills."

(And didn't hear Jim Pherson call.)

"Would you like me to bring your breakfast up?"

"What in the world for? I'm not half-dead. And while I don't find the conversation round Guinever's breakfast table particularly stimulating, I have no liking for breakfasts brought from a kitchen miles away and served cold."

Treating Guinever like a hotel where he must be the honored guest.

"Please yourself," I said and left him.

We were all together round the table when the mail came. Dido brought the letters in, and with them, two newspapers. She gave one to her mother and, ignoring my outstretched hand for the other, pushed her chair away from the table and began to read.

I knew it infuriated Niall that he was not allowed first choice of the newspapers. He stood by the french window, tapping his foot and staring out at the oyster-colored clouds.

I said, "Shall I turn on the radio for the eight o'clock news?"

Before I could move, Dido cried, "Oh,

Niall. There's something here about you."

The coffee cup in his hand was slammed into the saucer. Like a cat, he leaped across the room and snatched the paper from Dido.

"Middle column," she said.

Polly said, "It's here too about . . ." She shot a scared look at him and thrust the newspaper at me.

It was a short paragraph at the top of an inside page.

TELEVISION STAR IN SHOOTING ACCIDENT

Last evening, at his wife's home, Guinever Court in Dorset, a shot was fired at Niall Rhodes, the controversial television personality. His injury was superficial. His wife, Mrs. Sarah Rhodes, aged 20, told the police that she suspected poachers whom Mr. Rhodes must have disturbed. The police are investigating.

"Who told the police?" Niall's voice was very quiet, but it filled the room with a vibration of such fury that Polly sat licking her lips in alarm, knife poised unconsciously like a weapon of defense.

Niall flung the newspaper from him. It fell across Dido's face. She put up her hands and tore it down. "All right, tell him, Sarah. You'd better, hadn't you? If you don't, Mother will. You know she can't keep secrets."

"What—secret?"

"Last night," I began, staring out at the silver morning, "when you had gone to bed, Jim Pherson called. Someone must have telephoned him and reported the accident."

"Who?"

"I don't know."

"And the policeman came here and you told him what happened."

"I *had* to. I couldn't say that the call was a hoax."

"Why not?"

I cried exasperatedly, "Because it *wasn't*. Someone knew about the shot and reported it."

"And you hadn't the wit to laugh it off."

"It would only have made the whole thing look suspicious if I'd lied about something that could be proved true."

"So you went against my orders—"

Polly cried, "Sarah only did what she thought was right."

"I wasn't addressing you."

"Polly has a right to speak." My voice rose.

"And so far as Jim was concerned, I didn't even hesitate to tell him. If you're angry, I'm sorry. But it had to be done. If there's a gun-happy poacher around, someone might get killed next time."

Polly reached for Dido's hand. "Next time, it could be my little daughter."

"Oh, Mother, do stop!" She snatched her hand away. "Sarah should have done what Niall told her to. I'm on his side." She looked up at him, her eyes like clear aquamarines.

I said, "I suggest you give a statement to the press as soon as you get to London. Play it lightly. Just say that it's true someone was trespassing and you disturbed them."

"A nice facile explanation." His eyebrows were slightly lifted, his slate-colored eyes dull and full of scorn. "After a year of marriage you still haven't a clue as to the importance of bad publicity, have you?"

I said what I had said before. "You are overrating its importance in your private life."

"And it bores you?"

"If you want the truth, yes."

"Then that justifies my plan for our future, doesn't it?"

Dido asked, eagerly, "What plan?"

Polly silenced her.

I should not have been so frank in front of Polly and Dido. My self-control had been strained enough during the past few days; it could have held a little while longer, until we were alone. Angry with myself, I went to the table and held out my cup to Polly for more coffee.

Behind me, Niall was saying sententiously, "It isn't the gods who destroy; it's the little men and women."

I drank my coffee scalding hot and murmured that I would clear away the breakfast things. I reached for the tray on the serving table. Wash up the china, make the beds, tidy the living room . . . Then pack for London. I began stacking plates.

I was going to London. I would make a show of being seen around with Niall—of all being well between us—and then return quietly to Guinever. Two days, three at the most . . .

Polly stayed my hand with the tray.

"We haven't quite finished, dear. Leave it. I'll see to everything."

Niall said, "We're starting for London in half an hour."

I opened the terrace door and stepped out.

Light rain dripped from the vine that never gave grapes; the sky was as luminous as spun glass and the great oaks made a smoky blanket in the mist.

Polly's voice made me jump. "Are you really going to London this morning?"

"Yes."

"But if the police come and you aren't here, what will I do?"

"Perhaps they won't come." Since we had not sent for them, would it be an invasion of privacy to call? Or would it be their duty? I had no knowledge of police procedure.

"I suppose they'll come and look for the bullet. Oh, Sarah, if they do, I'll have to cope."

"No you won't. Just tell them to wait and then call Penn. He'll be over here in five minutes. Leave it to him."

"I wish Theo were here."

"He'll be home tonight. Then you'll be all right with a man in the house. And Father will be back tomorrow. Now I must go and pack."

"Freda said you were staying down here."

"I'll be back very soon."

"But you didn't mean to go back, did you? Why have you changed your mind?"

(Because, dear simple Polly, there's a saying that you don't hit a man when he's down. And Niall is frightened for the security of the one thing he cares about. And, incidentally, I'm scared, too . . . for my life.) Aloud, I said, "It's quite simple. Niall needs me for a few days."

Dido was calling Polly. She ran back into the house. I stood where I was, wondering if Alexandra had a gun.

From somewhere above me, through an open window, Niall called. I went upstairs and found him standing by the dressing table in my room. My two suitcases lay open on the bed; my clothes had been tossed into them like rubbish into a rag bag, mounds of crumpled yellow and rose and dark brown silk. A white sandal lay on a piece of delicate lace.

I started to say, "What are you doing?" My voice froze. The mirror gave back Niall's reflection so that there were two men holding two dolls with tossed red skirts and sagging necks . . .

I cried, "Oh heavens, the doll!"

He held the horrible thing up by one leg. Its matted hair was like cotton wool, the thin strand of wire round its neck caught the struggling sunlight.

"What is this? Bloody witchcraft?"

The room was full of hate and evil. I reached to snatch the doll from him and he flung up his hand as if to strike me across the face. Almost in the same movement, the hand dropped.

I backed away and he misunderstood. "Oh, no, you don't." He moved swiftly round me, barring my way to the door.

I said quietly, "I'm not going to run away."

"When did you start playing with this mumbo jumbo?"

I couldn't look at it. I said with averted face, "I found that doll in your car last night. I meant to show it to you."

"I don't believe you."

"It's the truth."

He crossed the room and slammed the door with his foot. The loose stopper of a little crystal bottle on the dressing table tinkled as the room shook.

"Now, the truth," he said. "What are you up to, weaving medieval spells with dolls?"

I put my hands to my face. "This is like going round and round the mulberry bush. Every day there have to be questions and answers . . . nothing accepted, nothing resolved. I tell you the truth and you ask for it again. I tell you again . . . All right," tension ripped my patience to shreds, "don't believe me. Accuse me of hoodoo—or whatever they call it. What do you think I did? Bought that horrible doll and tied a bit of wire round its neck and hid it? Am I supposed to believe in witches and the evil eye—or am I as motiveless as a lunatic?" I stopped for breath. "I've told you," I shouted. "I found that damned doll in your car."

"Why didn't you show it to me before?"

"I meant to, but you went straight to your room to work when you came back from Bristol and we were at dinner when you came down."

"And after that?"

"You went to your room again to work and I didn't see you until you were in the garden—"

"Looking for you."

"And someone fired that shot and hit you. You were hurt and shocked and I was too shaken to give the beastly doll a thought at the time. And if I had, I wouldn't have told you—not then."

"Why should you imagine that some

child's plaything would shock me still further?"

I said miserably, "I don't know. I suppose because it was so horrible, with that piece of wire breaking its neck."

I looked down and saw his fingers tearing at the doll. There was a sharp tug and the head came away from the body. Sawdust spilled out. The fuse wire was buried in its throat. I thought, "Do they still use sawdust to stuff dolls?" and shuddered. "It's horrible. Like a moron playing a joke. It's not worth thinking about. Give it to me and I'll throw it away."

He did not seem to be listening. His eyes were strange, glittering darkly in the grayish tinge of his face. His mouth twitched.

The memory of the boy at Gull's Folly flashed through my mind. They were parallel, that incident and this—both of them childish and macabre. Then I remembered the note slipped through the letter slot at Portland Place. Suddenly I heard myself say, "Niall, who *is* Alexandra?"

A shudder went through him. "I told you before, a name—a name given to a thousand women. Why ask me?"

"Because you know one of that thousand women."

"Gather my friends—No! God knows, I have no friends—then gather my acquaintances together. You won't find an . . . Alexandra among them."

I didn't miss the hesitation before the name. I said, "But Alexandra knows you, and she talked of a doll—"

He drew a sharp breath. "What are you trying to do to me?"

Beneath the anger in his tone, I sensed the tension of despair. "I want to help, don't you understand? I . . . want . . . to . . . help." I felt I had almost gotten through to him; surrender was in the way he looked at me, the flicker of doubt on his face. Or so I had thought . . . But as I watched, a swift change came over his features. For the few moments he had been like a courtier at a medieval ball, letting the mask slip. Then, quickly he readjusted it. His mouth hardened.

He lifted his arm and flung the pieces of the doll across the room. They swept through the air close to my face, black elongated eyes, dangling legs. I heard the small thuds over in the corner of the room.

Downstairs the telephone began to ring.

Niall said, "You see? It has begun . . . reporters . . ."

Polly's voice called up the stairs, "You're wanted on the telephone. It's from London."

"I'm coming." He walked past me. At the door he said, "Now the show begins and we are the actors. You know what the play is called? *Happy Families*!" Then he left me.

I flung open the window and leaned out, taking in long gulps of air. The rain had stopped and the lawn shone like green glass. All the flowers were refreshed, and out to sea a white ship was like a toy on the horizon.

A striking clock reminded me that I must pack. I went back to the pile of clothes on the bed and as I did so I knocked against a badly balanced suitcase. It toppled from the bed and everything spilled on to the floor. A blue cardigan fell across the doll. I darted to the corner and snatched it away. In my overstrung state the doll could contaminate. I picked up the two pieces, found some tissue paper, made a bundle and threw it into the waste paper basket.

Niall came back so quietly that he could have been watching me for some moments before I saw him. He said, "You can unpack."

I said exasperatedly, "Pack and unpack—you make me feel bounced about like a tennis ball. If I unpack now, it's for good."

I don't think he was even listening. "That was Leon Raphael on the telephone. He's coming down with a cameraman to interview both of us. He wants plenty of publicity about us as a united family—enjoying the country together. It's a pity Kester and Freda are in London, but it can't be helped. Nina and Polly and Dido will have to do for the complete family picture."

"But why send people all this way to Dorset?"

He looked at me as if I had asked a stupid question. "To prove the completeness of our marriage."

"Nobody has challenged the point yet."

"On the contrary, someone is damned well challenging it with violence."

I didn't know that I sighed, but he said, "Two more days here won't hurt you, Sarah."

But it will hurt Father, I thought. And if it hadn't been that he would suffer anything rather than cause unhappiness to any one of his family, I know he would have long ago reminded Niall that Guinever belonged to the Palfreys and was not run for the convenience of Niall Rhodes.

He turned away from me toward the window. "God, what a mess." His fists beat on the sill. "Can't you guess what the program planners might say? 'Too bad, Rhodes, but there you are, you know how you've been built up. Adverse gossip will destroy the balance, slant it too much one way; too much controversy . . . Your contract has almost expired. Take a break, Rhodes. Come back later. Or bloody well don't come back at all.' "

I had done with arguing.

I began putting my clothes away in drawers. A suspicion had crept into my mind that Niall himself could have suggested the press interview here at Guinever.

He was standing now in front of the mirror, adjusting his tie. Tall, slim, in the immaculate charcoal-colored suit he had put on for the journey back to London, he looked over his reflected shoulder at me. "If more proof is needed that our marriage is successful, then we'll give them proof."

"How?"

"We will have children."

The shudder inside me seemed to start in my stomach and spread all over me. A lump of ice weighed down my chest.

Niall was studying his nails. "It's what you've always wanted."

"Not that way—not as a prop to your image." I loathed the word, but there was no other I could think of.

I doubted if he heard me. He was looking into his own eyes. "I may even like myself as a family man. I shall come down here to see the children, bringing them gifts. They will be brought up beautifully—no fairy tales, no pretty-pretty illusions that have to be wiped off their minds later . . ."

I picked up a plastic bag that held nylons, put them away in the bureau and slammed the drawer.

"But none of this will happen," I said, "I'll see that it doesn't." I threw a handful of clothes across the bed in a burst of anger. "Anything—*anything* for the sake of an image, even something you hate, like having children. Because you're afraid that a hint that you disliked them or . . . or couldn't have them would blot your popularity. You're so afraid, Niall. Underneath, you're so uncertain, without faith in anything. You're even afraid of me."

"My dear Sarah, that will be the day!"

"You're afraid I might leave you. That

would destroy the careful portrait that's been built up of your happy domestic life. You can't face the slightest shadow of a doubt on that, can you?"

He said, looking away from me, "If you think I am afraid of you, then you're fostering an illusion. I call the tune, and you obey. Shall I tell you why?"

"No."

"I'll tell you just the same. You're soft. You like the sweet luxuries my money provides. You'd do anything for comfort. Well, most women would—it's natural and you're very much a woman."

I laughed with a kind of frozen bitterness. "And so, for the sake of the sweet life, as you call it, I am to have children you don't want and will never love. You may consider yourself an intellectual, but you aren't particularly perceptive, are you? Comfort? I've had comfort all my life—if you think differently, look around you. I'm no beggar girl who married the king!"

His voice softened. "Please understand, Sarah. I'm fighting to keep what we have, and only a humbug would decry fame and fortune. It's quite something. Help me, Sarah—just help me."

I said unhappily, "I've told you, I want to. But it can't be at the expense of everything else. Fame and fortune are only a part of living." I reached for his hand and the contact lasted a few moments.

Then he gave a short dry laugh. "And where do dreams and high principles get you?"

I said soberly, "I was thinking of the importance of just *living*. It seems that we've both been in danger of losing it."

13

AT lunch, Nina told us that she had been offered a place in a new intimate review. She said, "Francis and I are going to celebrate tonight."

Polly and Dido tried hard not to look at one another. They were like bad actors playing a role of conspiracy they could not quite manage. Polly's eyes darted in a way they had when she was nervous. Dido was pushing her food round her plate. She wore her new Wedgwood blue dress. Polly had washed her hair that morning and it lay in curling petals all over her head. The aura of excitement was all too obvious. Polly said, "Oh Nina, how thrilling for you. But it means you'll have to go back to London."

"At the end of the week to sign the contract, then at the end of the month to start rehearsal."

Polly said, "Is there anything—er—significant in your celebrating with Francis?"

"Everything. He introduced me to John Davenham when he came to talent-scout at the repertory theater here. There was a party." She turned to me. "You remember."

"No, I don't. I can't keep up with all your activities if you never write to me." I looked with laughing reproof round the table. "You're an awful family for keeping in touch."

"I know." Nina hunched her shoulders. "But never mind, it's all quite simple—my going out with Francis, I mean. He has a party of friends for dinner and dancing at the Westmore and he has invited me along."

Niall said, "But you'll be here tomorrow afternoon—all of you? I've got the press coming down from London. Leon Raphael wants a few family groups; they're good for publicity."

Nina said charmingly, "Count me out. Sorry, but I'm meeting some friends from town. We're going sailing."

Niall gave her an impatient look, was about to make some comment, then changed his mind and said to Polly, "You and Dido, then?"

Dido looked at her mother and asked quickly, "Tomorrow afternoon?"

"Yes, darling, we'll be here."

But this afternoon? The new dress, the

washed hair, the barely subdued excitement, the half-eaten meal. I knew where they were going this afternoon.

After lunch Niall went to his room to work. I took scissors and a basket and went to the lily garden. Theo was generous; he let us cut his flowers for the house, although we were always careful to take only random blooms so that the garden did not seem denuded.

The sun lay on the pool and the water lilies gleamed—sunrise and copper-tinted Sioux; the beautiful albinos, white as paper; nymphaeas, garnet-red and yellow. And round, in crescent-shaped beds, the earth lilies stood up strongly: arum, tiger and calla.

There was a cluster of rose-red blooms growing in the water just near the bank. Theo would not mind one being cut for Freda's room. I could just reach it by kneeling on the Minerva stone. As I did so, it moved, tilting sideways. I flung myself backward and went sprawling onto the path. Gravel clung to my arms. I brushed it away and crawled gingerly onto the stone again. It took me a few minutes to cut the fiercely resisting bloom, and all the time the stone swayed under me. With the flower in one hand, I felt cautiously under the stone with the other. The earth beneath its edges had been loosened, perhaps by recent storms or perhaps by Theo's weight, which was not much less than Father's.

Theo had better be careful. If he tipped up he'd pitch into the lake and the lovely nymphaeas would be swamped, with the blooms mangled by his weight.

Beyond the quiet garden, a car revved. I heard the swish of tires on gravel. I flung down the secateurs, pushed the basket into the shade of bushes and began to run. As I neared the house I heard the lifting and falling cadences of Nina singing to her guitar. My racing footsteps made a scratchy accompaniment, spoiling the clarity of her lovely liquid voice. I looked up at Niall's window and saw his dark head bent over his desk. I raced to the garage. The doors stood wide open and the station wagon, which was fitted to take Dido's wheel chair, was gone.

I ran into the house calling. Nobody answered me. For Polly to drive a car was an act of courage. She sat behind a wheel looking as if any moment was her last on earth. She would only dare the main roads for Dido. And in the Regency house with the green window boxes, Francis Lorian would be waiting for them.

I don't know what I expected to achieve by going after them. Father could have stopped them. I could not. All I knew was that fear made Polly a frightening driver and that she wasn't safe on the road.

I rescued the basket of flowers from the lily garden and raced to the garage. Theo must have repaired Father's car, for this afternoon it leaped into life at the first pressure of the starter. I roared down the drive. The sky was dark blue. The sun's whitish brilliance washed out its own shape so that there was light without form.

I hated Francis for the way he had insinuated himself into our lives. I thought, "He works like some door-to-door salesman: one foot on the threshold and he's in." Then I thought, "But suppose he can help Dido? Suppose Father and Freda and I are prejudiced just because he has no recognized qualifications? What were we doing but damning without trial?" Then the amused, conceited face floated into my mind and my distrust returned.

To those who knew the district, there was a shortcut through the lanes into Launford. Polly would take this way to avoid a few miles of main road. Over the high hedges, the

Purbeck hills lay like amethyst lions; insects hit the windshield and died. I slowed down to take a narrow turn.

And then I saw the car. It had swerved into a hawthorn hedge, and little broken branches were scattered on the hood. Polly was standing by it and the tears were running down her face. I saw her raise her head in a wild hope as she heard a car approach. Recognizing it—and me—she put her hands to her face.

Inside, Dido was shouting something at her mother.

I drew up behind the station wagon, got out and walked toward her. "You're lucky it was only a hedge and not another car."

"I swerved to avoid one. It was driven by one of those men who want the whole road. I couldn't help it. I—Oh, Sarah, what will Kester say?"

I pushed back the branches and looked at the hood. Apart from some scratches, the car didn't seem to me to have suffered. I said again, "You're lucky."

Dido hurled at us, "Don't stand there talking. Get us on the road."

Polly added, "Please, Sarah . . ."

Without a word, I got in behind the wheel.

"Watch for anything coming," I said. "I'm going to back out."

I edged the car onto the road, straightened out and said, "Now I suggest you drive to the next corner of the lane, turn around and go back home."

"I can't. I have . . . I have an appointment."

"With Francis."

"How did you guess . . . ?"

"It's the only thing that would get you behind a wheel," I said. "And I came in when you were on the telephone making an appointment with someone. You don't hide things very well, Polly. I guessed!"

"Oh, dear—"

"Come *on*," Dido cried.

I almost said, "What do you think Father is going to say?" Then I thought better of it. This was Polly's affair; I had interfered enough. She took my place at the wheel and moved forward in a series of jerks. I wondered how she had passed her driving test. But she had been much younger then and perhaps, during her life with Tom Singleton on the lonely African roads, she had acquired a little self-confidence. If she had, it was gone now.

I let her get ahead of me. Then I drove after her, keeping so far behind that she probably thought I had gone home.

When I reached Gordon Terrace the car was parked crookedly outside Francis' house and there was no one in it. I drove on past the next house and the next two—past Luke's. I wanted to stop there, but he would be at the hospital and he wouldn't be thinking of me. The tips of the pyramids of Gull's Folly rose above the trees. I went past the hospital gates and into Launford's main streets, where I bought half a dozen paperback novels, two baskets of raspberries and a small white alabaster bowl for the water lily for Freda's room.

When I drove past Gordon Terrace again, the station wagon was still there. The door of the house was open and a girl in a white coat was pushing Dido's chair down the path. Polly got out the ramp and they wheeled the chair into the car.

Polly turned the car round in a series of twists, and half the traffic in the street hooted protests at her. I had meant to follow her home, but the traffic lights changed and held me up. I sat and watched Francis' house. I thought I saw someone move in the downstairs room. The nurse, probably. Then the door opened again and a woman came out. Slim and not very tall, hair like a helmet of bronze. Alexandra.

Alexandra in Francis' house. A patient? A friend? I felt a surge of excitement, of an unexpected piece fitting into the jigsaw. I watched her get into a Jaguar parked at the curb and sit waiting for the light to change.

My first impulse was to call on Francis. Perhaps he had no appointment after Dido and would see me, intrigued by a visit from someone who made no pretense of liking him. I could quite imagine that it would amuse him. I would say, "You know a woman called Alexandra—I'm not certain of her surname." Then I would describe her. "Who is she? Where does she live?"

It would be like trying to open an oyster with a feather. I could imagine the gleam in his eyes. "I'm a professional man. I can't give you information about my patients." No, I would get nowhere with Francis Lorian. The alternative was obvious. I would follow Alexandra.

The lights changed and we moved forward with the stream of traffic. I let her get ahead of me, much to the annoyance of a truck driver behind. Then I followed her. She took a road to the right that led away toward the hills. We sped along the miles, between woods and fields dotted with sad-eyed cows, through hamlets where all the houses had marigolds in their gardens. I had just begun to have one desperate thought that Alexandra was heading somewhere too far away for me to follow—Bournemouth, or perhaps a roundabout route to London—when she turned right again and I knew that this was the road that led to the river. Willow Lane was bordered by the gardens of fine old houses built of Dorset stone with the teasing view of clematis dipping over high walls.

The lane snaked, bumpy and rutted, for about a quarter of a mile. Because of the turns, I lost the car, but I knew that there was no entrance down here to any of the houses and that I would find Alexandra when I came to the river. I was familiar with this part of Dorset because once Penn had kept a small cruiser here. Just before I reached the end of the lane, I stopped the car, got out and walked to the clearing.

Ahead of me the river danced with sequins of golden sunlight. There was a small motor yacht moored to the left. It gleamed whitely, the blue fringed awning hanging still in the windless afternoon. Past the bend of the river, there was a colony of houseboats, but in this backwater there was only the yacht and the trailing fronds of willow. I walked through the grass to the planks stretched from the bank to the boat. There was a lounging chair on the foredeck but both that and the pilothouse were empty. The door to the cabin was closed.

I looked about me and then I saw the Jaguar drawn up under some trees. There was no one in it. The riverbank stretched to the right and left, with no hiding place. If Alexandra was not just a figment of my imagination, then she must be on this boat. If she had left the car and walked along the path that curved toward the colony of houseboats she would still be visible.

I had no plan except to get aboard that boat. And when I did, I had no idea what I was going to say to her. The whole thing could be a monstrous mistake. But except for making a fool of myself I had nothing to lose by talking to her, saying what? "Do you know my husband?" And if she said, "Yes," then I would ask, "Why do you hate him?" And if she said, "I don't know what you are talking about," I would have to apologize for intruding and leave. But I would not believe her . . .

The planks gave a little with my weight as I crossed them. Even the river had not the energy to flow on this blazing afternoon. It was as static as glass. I stepped onto the deck.

"Is anybody there?"

A bird swooped past me. I heard the flap of wings as it breasted the water. Then there was silence again. I knocked on the closed door.

"Is anybody there?"

("Is there anybody there?" said the Traveler . . .)

The quiet was making me nervous. A car had driven at me; a shot had been fired at Niall. I looked over my shoulder into the sunlit emptiness. The compulsion to find Alexandra was still dominant, but now I began to be a little frightened. My movements were melodramatic. I put my hand on the door handle and turned it slowly. I planned to fling it open with a suddenness that would startle anyone lurking behind it. I would be watchful for a gun pointing at me. I gave the door a violent push. It swung back and I let out a long, heavy breath. The pilothouse was empty. I walked forward as noisily as I could and looked down into the cabin. Everything was tidy, charming, innocent. ("There is nobody there," said the Traveler.)

At the far end was a closed door. Or perhaps it was just pulled to. Did someone watch me from there? I still had time to turn and run. I didn't. Without one iota of courage, I went like someone with a gun in my back down the stairs and into the cabin. I passed the empty gallery, walked to the closed door and pushed that open also. There was a bed, neatly made up with a sky-blue quilt, a shelf with a sweater flung on it and a cupboard.

I turned and looked about me in the cabin. The decor was jade green and white; there were fresh flowers—golden roses and Iceland poppies in a black Wedgwood jar; a portable TV set; paperbacks on one of the seats; a Martini bottle and some papers on the ledge by the porthole. I crossed and looked at them. A few bills and a small pad with some writing on it. The writing was the same as that on the note pushed through the letter slot at Portland Place.

So now I knew her handwriting, what she looked like and where she lived. The acquaintanceship was deepening. The next thing was to learn her surname. Perhaps the gun that had been fired at Niall was here. I could open the drawers and search. My hand went out and then withdrew. However much I longed for information, there was something nasty about opening drawers in other people's places.

I had a strong sense of presence as if somebody stood behind me. I glanced over my shoulder. I was alone, yet I could have believed in ghosts—a colorful ghost who gave a boy half a crown to play the whispering game at Gull's Folly, who ran into the streaming night at Cypress Mount.

Outside a car started up. I rushed to the pilothouse. The Jaguar had turned and was being driven fast up the lane.

Alexandra had watched me from somewhere. Where? From behind a tree? Or perhaps she had lain under the water like a mermaid.

Had she seen the car crawling past Francis' house? Had she known I was following her—and led me here to discover . . . what? Merely the place where she lived? To make herself more real to me?

I heard a church clock chime in the

stillness, and, defeated, I left Alexandra's boat.

When I returned home, Polly said, "Niall's out. I don't know where." She was bent over a basin of loganberries, picking out the squashed ones. "Oh dear, I let Annalise and Tim pick these. I think they must have sat on the basket."

I perched on the edge of the kitchen table. "What did Francis say about Dido?"

"He examined her and some man who was there with him took X rays." She looked at me over her shoulder. "We're going again next Tuesday, and if you tell Kester—"

"I won't." I ate a loganberry and it was sour. "While you were there, did you see a tall woman, young with copper-colored hair?"

"No."

"No one came out of the consulting room before you went in?"

"I don't know. The waiting room door was closed and with the noise of the traffic outside I didn't hear anyone. Why?"

"Oh," I said vaguely, "Never mind."

Polly insisted, "But you must have a reason for wanting to know."

"I think this woman is a patient of Francis'."

"But what's that got to do with—"

"With me? I'm not quite certain. When I am, I'll tell you."

"Now you're being mysterious."

"I don't mean to be." I sauntered across the kitchen and peered into a cooling pot. "Iced soup," I said. "Lovely."

Suppose this woman were not a patient but a friend of Francis'? Suppose all this time Nina, who must know some of Francis' friends, had met her, talked to her?

I found Nina in her room. She wore a dress of jungle colors—crimson and peacock and green. Her black hair fell in twists over her shoulders, and her sandals were just straps of green leather. She was making up her mouth. "Do you think it's going to rain tonight?"

"No, why?"

"I'm going to that new club with the open-air dance floor."

"That's a very optimistic thing to have in our climate."

"There's a roof that can be rolled across when it's wet or cold. But dancing under the stars on a hot night is so very Continental. I love it."

I walked round the pretty, cluttered room. "Does Francis know someone called Alexandra?"

"Alexandra who?"

"I don't know. But will you ask him?"

"And say you want to know?"

"If you like. He'll probably say that he has never heard of her. Just watch his reaction."

She stood looking at me, frowning. "What do you think she is? Has Niall got another woman—and after only a year of marriage?"

"It's not that."

"Then what else can it be?"

"I'll explain it all one day."

She said sadly, "You're shutting me out, Sarah. You never used to."

I had nothing to say. It was true. In the past we had had no important secrets from one another.

"Let's change the subject," Nina said suddenly and put down her lipstick. "Whenever you mention Francis' name your voice goes cold. I'd have thought you would have been the last person to condemn a man because his methods are unorthodox. Francis won't harm Dido."

"She's attending the hospital. You can't mix treatments."

"There's no law against changing your medical adviser."

"I wouldn't call Francis exactly that."

She said, "You don't like him and I do. It's just a matter of temperament, I suppose, or different wavelengths or something. There are faults in people I don't mind and you do, and others that I hate and you don't. But, Sarah, that doesn't give you the right to be unjust."

"I know," I said bleakly.

"I like Francis. He has valuable contacts and he has helped me—and with no strings attached." Nina stroked her flawless throat. "And if it weren't for Luke, I think you'd be as keen as any of us to have Polly try anything that would help Dido."

"What has Luke got to do with it?"

"You think what Polly is planning is a slight on him. It isn't. Luke isn't treating her; he just happens to be attached to the hospital where she is having treatment."

"Luke has nothing to do with how I feel."

She was fastening thick gold bangles round each wrist. "You aren't the changeable type, Sarah. And if Luke hadn't gone away—"

"But he did," I said too loudly, "and anything between us is now old history."

Nina stretched her arms above her head, looking at her bracelets, turning her head right and left, her hair swinging.

"What *is* it all about—the shot at Niall . . . your interest in someone called Alexandra? I might not be able to help but I'm a good listener."

My hands slid over the glass top of her dressing table. I touched a scent bottle. Joie by Patou. I pressed the gold top and little drops spattered my hand. I held it to my nose, eyes closed.

"I'm persistent, aren't I?" she said unoffended. "All right, I won't press you." She picked up her coat from the bed and put an arm around me. Her lips touched my cheek. "You're still Sarah," she said softly and then she was gone.

14

LEON RAPHAEL was a small man with stringy gray hair, a concave face and avid eyes; he wore superlatively tailored suits. His asset was his tirelessness. He was with us on the lawn, directing everything—interviews, photographs, the lot.

Niall had collected Polly and Dido. Sylvie also happened to come over with the children. Niall didn't want them included, and when Leon insisted, he complained.

"It'll be like some damned Victorian family picture. You're overdoing it."

"Victorian it may be, but people don't change that much," Leon said, fussing the children, pushing them into position. *Stand here . . . kneel there . . .*

Niall said with soft sarcasm, "Perhaps we could bring over the farm dogs and a cow or two."

Leon shouted, "Family. That's what they want. You, as a family man. Of course, when you have kids of your own—"

"Ah!" said Niall.

I looked the other way, pretending that I hadn't heard.

Dido was loving the admiration of the men: eyes sparkling, her voice pitched to the low, soft note she used for social occasions. I knew she saw herself specially mentioned in magazine interviews. "The beautiful Dido Singleton." . . . Nina was not home and so there was no rival.

When the photographers had finished, Niall and I stayed on the lawn with the press, and the family were dismissed.

Niall did all the talking at first. Yes, he enjoyed coming down to Guinever to be with his wife's family. Wonderful house . . . that old part built on the cliff was medieval. Legend had it that its name had a connection with Queen Guinevere, wife of King Arthur of the Round Table. Interesting, wasn't it? . . . Country pleasures? Oh, walking with his wife. But he had so little time for leisure—not that he minded; he loved his work. It was a challenge; he liked challenges. Gardening? No, he didn't know much about flowers, except to love them. That was his brother-in-law Theo's job. He was working at the botanical gardens this afternoon. He was an expert on seed selection. And Nina, his sister-in-law, the guitarist and folk singer. And of course, Kester Palfrey . . . Yes, a remarkable family . . . So it went on and on, with Leon watching, listening, nodding his head, approving of Niall's offstage performance.

The question we had been dreading came at last. "And that shot the other night? The story is that you disturbed poachers?"

"That's right."

"Were they caught?"

"Not yet, but they will be. The police are keeping watch."

"Oh, Niall—" Dido's voice came from behind.

We all turned. She propelled her chair swiftly toward us. She had done her hair and made up her lips again. Across her knees was a shawl of yellow silk. She held the stage as she intended to, her eyes on the visitors. "Please don't make him stay out here any longer." She paused, her face lifted pleading—the velvet bloom of sunlight on her skin. "It's . . . so . . . dangerous."

Niall snapped, "Don't be so silly!"

"I'm scared." She turned to him. "I'm scared for you, Niall dear. They tried to kill you once and . . ."

"You're talking utter nonsense. No one tried to kill me."

"But they did; you *know* they did. Two nights ago . . ." Her eyes, wide and innocent and very blue, moved slowly round us. It could have been her petulant beauty that held the men. Or again, it could have been the horrifying inference of her words. "They *did* . . ." she repeated in a whisper.

One of the newsmen asked, " 'They'? Who?"

Niall said in a frozen voice, "Go indoors, Dido, and stop play-acting."

She hesitated and gave him a look at once terrified and exasperated. "Why won't you *listen*? Don't you *care* what happens to you?"

No one spoke.

"Well, I mind for you," she cried.

"Then you must go and mind all by yourself. I'm busy. Run along." Niall spoke to her as he would to an obstreperous child.

She played up to it. "You're angry with me because I'm afraid for you. You—"

Niall said in a voice that dared anyone to disobey, "Sarah, take that child indoors and keep her there."

"You needn't," she snapped at me. "I'll go on my own."

The tires of the chair made no noise as she swung it round and propelled it with speed over the gravel path.

I knew that at some time or other during Dido's small scene, every man had glanced my way, missing neither the gripping of my hands in my lap nor the alarm in my eyes.

Just as they were leaving, Leon went to the wall and looked over. "This is what I call living." He rubbed his hands together, his monkey face grinning with false jocularity. "All this sea—all this sky . . . Space. Peace . . ."

He didn't mean a word of it. His sudden enthusiasm for the simple life of rural England was an effort to soften the impact of Dido's outburst upon the press. Leon loved the familiar: the paved streets, the diesel fumes and people, always people.

He was saying to the newsmen, "That was a good session. Now you chaps can go to the pub if you like for an hour. I'm off to the beach."

Niall said, "The cove immediately below us isn't safe. Stick to the beach around the ravine." He had held on to his self control, courteous, unperturbed. But I could read the minds of our cynical, hard-boiled visitors.

"Happy families? You can plan that game, chum, but we didn't believe a word of it. Well, boys what'll we report? The truth or the lie? Nurse the popular idol or break the image?"

As the two cars, one bearing Leon, the other the interviewers, the photographers and their cameras, disappeared round the curve of the drive, Niall turned on me in fury. "For God's sake, what did Dido think she was doing?"

"She was genuinely scared for you."

"She's scared for no one. She's wrapped up in a kind of cotton wool cocoon, loving herself."

I thought, *"And wanting you. And hating me . . . She's not a child; she's a woman. Maybe she can't give love, but she wants to take it. You are becoming an obsession with her"* . . .

Pepita came up and rubbed against my legs. I picked her up and held her sun-heated fur against my face. I said lamely, "Don't take any notice of Dido."

"I'd like to be able to tan the hide off her."

"You mind so much?"

"In my job I have to mind everything." He walked away from me. As he climbed the terrace steps I had a sudden sense of his aloneness. He didn't belong here—he didn't want to belong here. Yet Guinever was useful to him, if only because it would house me when he could do without me.

As if at a given signal, Pepita leaped from my arms and bounded toward the keep. Once, she had managed, by a feat of mountaineering which staggered us, to climb around the cliffs and through the archer's slit into the tower. We lost her for two days. Then Father heard her mewing for help, courageous enough to bound into the keep, but not brave enough to climb back.

I had no idea what fascination she found among the gloomy stones. But I had no intention of leaving her there until it was dark and we would have to grope around by flashlight for her. I went through the door in the living room, along the cold passage to the keep and into the room facing the sea. The slits in the wall gave scarcely any light. Something glimmered at me in the darkness. Pinpoints of phosphorescence moved.

We always kept a flashlight on a stone ledge. I felt my way to it and flashed it. Pepita sat in the middle of the floor and watched me with unblinking eyes. I wondered why she came here and supposed that from the slitted windows she was nearer to the sea birds she could never catch.

I hoisted myself up onto the ledge and climbed along the alcove leading to a slitted opening. When I reached it I leaned on my hands and looked out. The rounded wall of the keep blocked the view to my right. To the left, the coast stretched away, the tall golden cliffs falling gradually toward Launford. A shimmering gauze screen lay over the distance so that the masts and funnels of the ships in the harbor were like a stage set for a sea ballet. At first I thought the beach was empty. The tide was in and our cove was covered with boiling gray-green water. To the left, where high rocks resisted the encroaching sea, there was a cove with a beach of fine white sand and dry gray boulders. Here two people stood talking. I recognized them immediately. One was Leon Raphael; the other, Alexandra.

Quite suddenly the two on the beach turned their heads like people aware that they were being watched. I had a feeling that they were looking straight at me.

"For heaven's sake, what are you doing here?"

I looked over my shoulder. Niall walked into the room.

"I came to find Pepita."

"She's behind you," he said.

"I know."

"I wondered, when I saw that the door to the keep was open, what was going on."

"Come here," I said.

I crawled back into the room to make way for him. "There are two people down on the beach. I think you know them both."

"The press," he said disinterestedly. "I've seen enough of them for one day."

"Go and look for yourself."

He gave a bored sigh and hoisted himself into the deep stone embrasure. "I'm not interested—"

"Look to the left," I said.

Niall turned his head. His body, wedged in the long, deep archer's slit, made no movement. My hands were at my sides, nails cutting into my palms. The silence seemed to go on and on into an unbearable eternity. I could stand it no longer.

"You see them, don't you? Leon and a woman. You know her, too."

Niall didn't move. I went up to him and

pulled at his arm. It was like dragging at a rock.

"Who is she? Niall—*who is she?*"

He twisted himself round and leaped to the ground, pushing me aside and making for the door.

"Damn her. Oh God, damn her . . ." He moved like an arrow from a bow. He was in the room; then suddenly he was gone. I flew after him down the stone passage and into the living room. It was empty. I ran onto the terrace. Dido sat in the shade, painting opal pink on her nails.

"Have you seen Niall?"

"No, why?"

I raced down the terrace steps without answering her. Halfway round the house, I heard a car start up. There was the crunch of wheels on gravel. The roar of an engine. Then silence.

I swung round and ran to the old wall. I leaned over and looked down. Sea birds swooped round me. The beach was now empty.

They couldn't have gotten far, for walking over the soft sand would be slow. Their cars would be parked in the ravine. Niall would get there before they did. And so, they would meet—Alexandra and Niall. And Leon—with his sharp, perceptive eyes. The newsmen, too, would be somewhere around, smelling out a story that even Leon would not be able to prevent if it were juicy enough for publication. *A story? Let's have it . . .*

And I had a right, also, to know. I was involved.

The quickest way down to the ravine would be along the cliff path. Once again I climbed it at the place where the bricks had broken away. In daylight the path seemed even narrower and the cliff drop more forbidding because the dangers were highlighted by the sun and the menacing teeth of the rocks.

When I came to the place where the path curved, two brown shoes barred my way. They moved swiftly, swinging round to make room for me. At the same moment a hand went out to steady me. "It's not exactly a promenade, is it?" said Luke.

"And your feet don't particularly help progress."

He still had hold of my hand and he was laughing. "You look like someone who has just stolen an heirloom and is escaping by the back way."

"What are you doing here?"

He got up from his perch of rock. "Just taking time off to stare."

I looked down the dipping path and saw his car parked in the shade of trees.

He said, "There's a place just along there where we can sit down."

"I can't. I haven't time."

"This isn't quite the route to take if you're in a hurry," Luke said. And because it was too narrow for me to pass him, he led the way down to where the path widened.

From here I could see the whole length of the ravine. There was no one in sight. The tall pines cast their mauve shadows across an empty road.

I said, "Have you seen Niall?"

"How would I know? I haven't met him yet."

"He's medium height, dark, like you . . . *is* rather like you."

"That's nice for him."

"Luke, I'm serious."

"Well then, I haven't seen him; I've seen no one. This place is like a primeval pocket in an overpopulated world."

"Luke, where *are* they?"

"I haven't any idea who 'they' are, but if

it's important for you to find 'them' shall we go and look?"

"You mustn't be involved in this. I can't . . . I mean, I don't . . ."

He said gently, "Suppose you sit down and begin again."

"A short time ago I'm sure there were three cars down there." I pushed my hair back from my damp forehead and swung round, looking all ways like a despairing weathercock. "Three cars—one Leon's, one Niall's and . . . another. I must find them."

"If you can follow three cars on your own two feet," Luke said lightly, "then you must have solved the problem of human flight. Come off it, Sarah. Sit down and tell me—or don't tell me. But for heaven's sake relax." He drew me onto the coarse, patchy grass. "Sit," he said as if I were a recalcitrant puppy.

I obeyed and sat clasping my hands round my hunched knees. It was so quiet that I could hear my own heart beating. I looked at Luke. He was staring out to sea and the sunlight struck his face. The years had made him gentler, less arrogant. He was more still than he used to be. These things I noticed with what began by being irrelevant at this particular moment and then suddenly became important. Whatever else had changed in him, he would still be a good listener. And I had to talk to someone.

I began hesitantly, uncertain as to what to leave out. In the end it was easy. I left nothing out, from the beginning at Gull's Folly to the moment, ten minutes ago, when Niall had looked through the archer's slit and seen Alexandra on the beach below.

With the sunlight on our faces and the cormorants clustering round a shoal of fish just off the coast, I told Luke everything.

When I finished, my throat was dry. Luke remained silent, looking out to sea, his hands quite still on his hunched knees. I said at last, "So, what do I do?"

"Your father knows nothing?"

"No."

Luke flung back his head. "Dear sweet heaven!"

"You know Father's not the one I could tell. He'd bluster and shout—he loves us too much to be sane about us if things go wrong."

"I don't know that I feel particularly sane at the moment, either. What does Niall expect you to do, go through life always looking over your shoulder? And what did you think you were doing, keeping it to yourself? All right, let Kester rave. If what you say is true—and I don't doubt it—your life is in danger. Niall talks about a private detective. What's the matter with the man? Damn his publicity, good or bad. This is a matter for the police."

"The consequences—"

Luke picked up a large stone and flung it over the cliff. "Sarah, don't be a fool. Publicity be damned! 'Men say, let them say.' I've yet to be convinced that any human being is less important than his career."

And I couldn't tell him that Niall was the one person to prove that it was sometimes so. Nothing but the image . . . the man of straw.

I avoided the issue and put it another way. I said, "We are never entirely uninvolved with those we have once loved. Something remains—"

Luke gave me a brief glance. "Don't I know it! But let's keep away from ourselves. I'd say the whole of your story is fantastic except that experience has taught me nothing is impossible in the world. This is happening to you. I am an outsider—I can do nothing. *But tell Kester—tell your father.*"

"And make everything worse between Niall and myself. That's why I told you, because you *are* an outsider. If Niall knew that I'd talked—"

"Then don't tell him," Luke said matter-of-factly. "On the other hand, don't play the fool with danger."

I stared at the gulls lazing on the sea. "I don't want to keep it to myself. For heaven's sake, you should know me well enough to realize that I'm not secretive. But there's something I've got to contend with."

"What?"

"Pity," I said. "Pity for Niall. I can't help it. When you have cared for someone—even though it's all over—and you see that he's not what you thought him, not strong, not fearless . . . when you see the awful disintegration, the sheer . . . terror of loss . . . of the one thing he lives for . . ."

"Don't plead your cause so desperately, my dear. If that's what is influencing you, then you can forget it. Men hate pity."

"Niall doesn't know. But it's there, and the thing he dreads is the very thing that would happen if I told Father."

Luke said violently, "For God's sake,

Sarah, stop thinking with your emotions and use your head."

"All head and no heart," I said. "Yes, life would be much more comfortable that way. Strong, ruthless . . . without compassion."

He put up his hand and pulled gently at my hair. "There's a place somewhere in the middle called balance, my little goof. Find it."

"Oh, Luke—"

"And saying, 'Oh, Luke,' isn't helping anyone. You're in danger, yet you are acting in exactly the same way as you act over everything else in life. You let yourself be fooled by feeling. Pity for Niall isn't going to help you if the next car coming at you really runs you down or the next shot finds Niall's heart."

I turned away from the sun.

Luke got to his feet, holding out his hands to pull me up. "So, you'd better go and find Niall, hadn't you? Tell him what you intend to do and then *do* it. Tell Kester."

"Come with me."

"Oh no. I'm an onlooker, the doctor, the listener, the noninvolved."

How wrong you are, I thought. Because you were once part of me, you are involved.

The past never dies, it attaches itself to us forever. But if I told you that, you'd shy away from me like a wild horse. You would escape even from the casual friendship that is all you will allow between us. So, I shall not argue with you. I said aloud, "Thank you for listening. I feel better." I gave him a warm smile and left him, going back the way I had come because there was now no point in going down to the ravine.

15

POLLY and Dido were in the garden, near the cedar. They had the remains of tea between them.

"Oh, Sarah, we waited, but you didn't come. The tea must be cold now." Polly threw down the magazine she had been reading and scrambled out of the deck chair. "I'll get you some more."

"No tea, thanks," I said. "Has Niall come back?"

"No." She sat down again and the canvas bounced with her weight so that her chubby legs went into the air. She said, "I called you both. I thought you were out somewhere together." She gave me a sideways look. "Kester will be back some time this evening. You won't . . . say anything . . . will you?"

It took me a moment to remember her problem.

"About your visit to Francis? But Dido's due at the hospital tomorrow."

"I'll ring up and say she's not coming. I

must give her this chance. *You* understand—and you won't tell."

"No, I won't. But—"

Dido interrupted the protest I was about to make. Her voice had a ring of triumph. "And you can tell your dear Luke that people don't go on a slow boat to China when they can take a plane. And if you don't get my meaning—"

"I do," I said and walked away.

I didn't want to sit with them in the bright garden and perhaps be forced to argue. I wanted no cross currents of tension, no deliberate incursion of Luke's name.

I walked across the lawn and turned left to the garage. I had no formed plan when I opened the door of Father's Rover, sat behind the steering wheel and started the engine. Something propelled me and I obeyed. The car purred down the drive and through the open gates. Sunlight flashed on the wrought-iron lettering: "GUINEVER COURT."

I turned toward Launford, but I wasn't heading for the city. I was going to the river, though I had not given clear thought as to why. Like Omar Khayyám's Moving Finger, something outside myself wrote its instructions in my brain and I obeyed. I was nearly there when I began to feel afraid. My hands became tight on the wheel; my foot lost its sensitive touch on the accelerator. The shadows of the bushes closed in on me like sable troops menacing my approach, waiting for a signal to attack. Every time I looked in the rear mirror I was amazed to find that I was not being followed. I was forgetting that it was I who pursued, going after Alexandra.

I drove too near a bank and the branches of an overhanging bush scraped the side windows of the car. The sound, above the purring engine, made me start. The sensitive wheel swung in my hands. I just managed to prevent the car from mounting the bank. The moment of near-accident sobered me.

A small brown dog with a large tail leaped out of a farm gate barking at me. A little girl in a yellow dress waved at me from a five-barred gate. I waved back as though I hadn't a care in the world.

The lane that led to the river was full of swallows darting in play before the night. Gold dust lay over the tops of the trees; the sky's serenity mocked me. How much wiser would I be in fifteen minutes, in ten, in five . . . ?

When I reached the clearing and the river

where the white boat lay, I pulled the car up close to a clump of bushes, got out and looked about me. Alexandra's car was there, but the Bentley was nowhere to be seen. I had no idea whether Niall had tried to follow Alexandra and lost her in the traffic or whether he fled from Guinever, afraid that she would come to find him. I did not know whether I was relieved or sorry that he was not here. I walked through the grass and stepped onto the boards. As before they rocked gently with my weight.

The door to the pilothouse was open. In pale gray linen Alexandra waited for me.

"This time," she said, "you can come on board by invitation."

"Thank you." I was proud of my own outward serenity. I followed her down the steps, wondering what scent she wore, noting the perfect line of her neck, the rich springy glory of her beautiful chestnut hair. Her gloves were soft gray silk, reaching to her elbows.

In the cabin she waved me to a seat. "I suppose you know who I am."

"It's one of the things I came to find out."

"Of course, Niall never told you."

"Told me—what?"

"That you aren't the first Mrs. Rhodes."

I sat down because my legs wouldn't hold me up.

She leaned against the cupboard, watching me. "He has no courage."

"But on my marriage certificate–"

"He chose to forget me. But then he's a man whose memory can reject the unpleasant."

I ran my tongue over my dry lips. "When?"

"Eight years ago."

"There was a divorce?"

Her eyes were gray, lifting at the corners. She would look charming when she laughed. But her face now was grave. "Niall divorced me."

I said, "Oh," and nodded. "I—see—"

"No, you don't. There was no other man. I disappeared. He waited seven years and—"

"And so I am not really married."

"Oh, yes, you are."

"Why didn't he tell me? Did he think I would be jealous of you? Oh no, he couldn't . . ."

"Niall had a very strong reason for playing the bachelor," she said.

"If you chose to leave him, why did you come back?"

"I suppose you're thinking that it could be a matter of money. It isn't. I have my own."

"Then—?"

"Do you smoke?"

"No."

She took a cigarette from a red leather case and lit it. "Niall and I married in Rome. When it was all over, I went to the States." She paused, looking past me, her mouth bitter. "I was there some time. Then I went to live in South America—São Paulo."

Brief and to the point, a précis of a life . . . But behind that short history—what?

I asked, "Why come back—why, after all these years?"

She shrugged. "What had Niall to lose while he was just a schoolmaster? They're never exactly rich or important."

"You have just said that it was not a question of money."

"The paramount thing for Niall is his own importance. That's what I came back to break."

"You dropped a note through the letter slot at Portland Place. It asked if Niall remembered an Italian Doll. And you left a doll with a broken neck in his car."

"That must have seemed childish to you, but Niall would have gotten the message. I found the doll in an old suitcase. It had belonged to my grandmother when she was a little girl. It's neck was already broken—Niall did that once in Rome when he was in a temper. I tied the piece of wire round it." Her eyes held bitter mockery. "You see, I could not think up any subtle way of scaring him. I'm not highly intelligent. If I had been, Niall would never have married me. I'm sorry if that sounds like a slight on you, too, as his second wife, but it's true. In my case he wanted my money, but not intellectual competition. So, you see, I was incapable of thinking up brilliant ways of revenge on him. The things I did were spontaneous. But they were effective. He has been badly frightened, hasn't he?"

"Yes—"

"Niall gave up teaching when we married," Alexandra continued. "He had always hated it. I had money and we opened an antique shop on the Via del Babuino in Rome. But we knew too little about antiques and it failed. Niall argued that we hadn't enough stock. He wanted extra money from me to buy more things." She tapped her cigarette against an ashtray. Then, suddenly, she crushed it. The tobacco fell out like brown seeds from a pod, like sawdust from a doll's broken neck . . .

The silence was too tense for me. "You left Niall because the business failed."

"Do you think I am playing a slow torture game with him because of that? Or even because he forged my signature to a check for a large sum of money? I'd have counted him well out of my life for those." She moved a little toward the light. "Come here."

I went nearer. The scent she wore intrigued me. It was like something dimly remembered, hinting of incense, sandalwood. She was peeling off her gloves slowly, first one, then the other. I held my breath in case the cry "Oh God!" should escape. I managed to look at the hands and the awful forearms without flinching. The brown withered skin with the puckered seams of great scars was thrust at me. I instinctively reached out and touched one of the wrists gently, feeling the ridges of the scars under the tips of my fingers. "I'm so sorry."

It is the way things are said, not the words,

that matter. I knew immediately that I had done and said the right thing.

"The result of burns," Alexandra said. "That is why I call myself a revengeful woman." She picked up the gloves and put them on, smoothing them over the dreadful scars. Outside, the water lay like glass; the trees were still. A warm and gentle evening . . .

"Now you know," Alexandra said, "why, when I discovered how successful Niall had become, I returned to England to find him."

"The . . . burns . . . on your . . . arms?"

She shut her eyes. "When we had our last quarrel I threatened to take him to court for forging my signature. He stood there, cold and scornful. Then, without warning, he hit me. I fell, stumbled against a table, which overturned and knocked me onto an electric heater. I know I screamed before I lost consciousness. I suppose when he saw what he had done he thought the house would catch fire, that I would die. I didn't. When I came to I was in a hospital. A woman who lived in an apartment above the shop had heard the noise and saved me. I told no one what had actually happened—I said I slipped and fell. Niall did not come near me and I did not try to find him. At that time, in my state of shock, I couldn't bear to see him again—even on the witness stand at a police court. I told the doctors that we were separated. I was very ill for a long time. There were operations—skin grafts—but the burns were too deep. I left Rome—I wanted to be free of anything that was a memory. But you can see that every hour of every day I had to remember." She looked down at her hands. "After years of hate, I heard that Niall had become a television personality in England. The more I thought about it, the more I knew that I was past not wanting to see him. I wanted him to suffer. I came to England and set about finding out all I could about him. I learned that he was married. I watched your apartment in London; I watched you at Guinever Court." She broke off and looked at me as if waiting for me to say something.

My body, like my mind, was heavy with shock.

Alexandra said, "It had to be a slow terror for him. One sudden shock is so much easier to bear. What I have to do must be *un*bearable."

"You've—achieved—that."

"Oh no, not yet."

"Surely it makes a difference that I know?"

"How? What can you do to stop me?"

"The police—"

"You won't go to them."

"Why not? You weren't content with little things—the note to me, the doll, the boy in the whispering gallery—"

"Oh, that last was an idea on the spur of the moment. I was caught in the storm and ran into the Folly doorway for shelter. When the rain stopped I just walked around—it was so fresh after the heat. That's when I saw you go in—I had made it my business to know what you looked like."

"And the boy?"

"He was kicking a stone around and looking bored. I thought I'd give him a little job to do."

"Trying to scare me? But that's a children's game—playing at threats in Gull's Folly."

"I know. But I figured you would be puzzled and tell Niall. Husbands and wives do tell each other about odd things. You probably said to him, 'A small boy played a silly game with me today' . . . the sort of game we used to play and Niall might wonder about it and start to get a bit uncomfortable. It was really just the prelude before the act."

"And then," I said, "the play itself began and you became more ambitious. In the end you were prepared to kill . . ."

She gasped at the words. "Kill? What are you talking about?"

"You drove Niall's car at me at Cypress Mount."

"Did I?" she asked without surprise. She lifted her shoulders in a gesture of acquiescence. "All right. So I failed to convince you that it was Niall. But let's get one thing straight. Do you really think if I had intended to kill you—if I were that sort of person—I couldn't have done so? I'm an expert driver. All that I intended to do was to frighten you into thinking Niall was making an attempt on your life. I could have driven even nearer and then avoided you at the last second."

"So you tell me now."

"You'd better remember that I needn't have admitted just now to driving the car at all. You could never had proved it—even by calling in the police." She held out her hands. "Gloves on the steering wheel," she looked at them with a curious, impersonal bitterness.

"And I suppose you didn't mean to kill Niall when you shot at him in our garden."

"Shoot—at Niall?" She raised her head and

stared at me. "But my dear Sarah, I don't own a gun. I wouldn't know how to use one."

"Oh, no?"

"I heard about it, of course, but that night I was at the theater," she said. "It was the opening night of the new production of *The Tempest*. Francis should have been with me, only he had a last-minute call from a patient who had fallen and hurt her back. He was coming along later, but he didn't. The patient was alone in her house and he stayed with her until her son returned from some political meeting." She had been looking away as she spoke. Suddenly she turned her head. Her golden brown eyes were defiant. "If you still don't believe me, I'm sorry. Perhaps the theater can confirm that Francis called for the tickets. But even that wouldn't prove I was there, would it?"

"If you didn't fire that shot—"

"Who did? That's your problem. I don't know. Violence isn't my way. All I know is that all Launford talked about it for days. A man as famous as Niall is news even if he only cuts his finger."

I let the remark go. Something she had said earlier stuck in my mind. I said, "You told me there was a woman in Rome who found you and saved your life."

"That's right. And she's probably still living over the shop we had there. One word from me and she'll corroborate my story of that night in the apartment. Do you want proof that I told you the truth?"

I shook my head—and in doing so, I accused Niall.

She said, "He has no reserves. He'll break. I'm sorry if it affects you. It needn't. Unless the money he makes is of greatest importance to you, you can leave him."

"You think it's that easy?"

"You mean because what he did to me is no concern of yours?"

"No, because you've trapped him. He's so alone, without friends, without anything but a superficial public popularity. Nothing else. You can't abandon someone who is utterly lost."

"If you stay with him, then you must be involved." An expression very near gentleness crossed her face. "It would be better for you if you left him *now*. Believe me, I don't care whether you are on my side or not. I'll break him without your help. But your pity is wasted. Niall has no love for you, for anyone. He has nothing to love with."

Luke had once said, "You live on impulse. You don't stop to think." But I was trying to think now, quickly, while Alexandra watched me. In spite of her protest that she was not interested in how I was reacting to what she had told me, I wondered if she were trying in a seemingly disinterested way to maneuver an ally. I had admitted no love for Niall, and I had to guard against being caught in Alexandra's web. I had to be strong, to refuse to be grist for her destructive mill. I knew the dreadful truth and now I had to find Niall.

Alexandra said, "I met Niall's manager this afternoon. I saw him come from your house and I followed him to the beach. I told him nothing, but I got into conversation with him, casually—two people on a deserted beach admiring the view. He found me interesting enough to make a date with me in town."

Slowly, inexorably, the twist of the dagger an inch at a time . . . I felt a little sick.

Alexandra echoed my thoughts. "And when we meet in town I'll feed him a bit more of the story. There's no stalemate; but there's no swift death, either."

Without another word, I swung away from her and walked up the steps to the pilothouse. A breeze had sprung up and the blue awning flapped gently, the white fringe swinging.

My low heels clip-clapped along the planks. The grass whipped round my ankles like tiny punishing lashes. Foremost in my mind, taking precedence even over the horror of her personal story, was the fact that Alexandra had not fired the shot that had struck Niall. So there was someone else who hated him.

I had parked the car just round the bend of the lane, out of sight of the river. I was seldom untouched emotionally by my beloved Dorset—the savage heath and the lilac hills, the trees bent by the prevailing southwest winds, their branches burned by the harsh salt in the air . . . Thomas Hardy's country of *Tess of the D'Urbervilles*. But, this evening I was blind to the blaze of the sky, the sweep of heather, the scent of honeysuckle in the hedgerow. Fog or rain or snow or tempest, it would have been all the same to me. The black wing of the immediate future blotted out everything.

Except Niall's face.

My own turmoil gave a fantastic reality to

his features. I stood quite still, staring. It was imagination, it had to be. What I saw was a twisted caricature. But the lips in the face moved, spoke. The face was real.

Niall stood in my way. "Where have you been?" He bore down on me, larger than life. "*Where have you been?*" he said again.

My own voice came from a distance. "To see Alexandra." My hand brushed a stinging nettle and my palm began to burn. "She is living on a boat. Did you know that? Did you follow her here?"

He ignored my questions. "What did she say to you?" His voice had a hollowness, like a sound in an empty shell.

I couldn't speak. I made a small movement, stretching out my arms, and looked down at my hands.

He knew what I meant. "So you know everything . . . the truth according to the version given by Alexandra Rhodes." His voice rose shrilly. "I suppose she told you I was responsible for the accident in Rome."

"Why did you keep your first marriage a secret?"

"Because I refuse to accept the fact that a man's past has anything to do with anyone else."

"It's all tied up," I said, "past and present and future."

"I might have expected you to listen to a woman obsessed with finding some scapegoat because a bit of her beauty has been destroyed. You are too easily convinced." He reached out and broke off a long tendril of honeysuckle, sliding it through his fingers like a necklace of pale amber. "She tried to kill me. Do you call that being sane?"

I breathed in the scent of the honeysuckle. "She denied it. She admitted to everything else. But she didn't fire the shot in the garden."

"And you believed her?"

"Yes."

"That presupposes that there are two lunatics at large."

I did not speak. The silence was broken by the sound of children playing in a hidden garden.

Niall said, "So Alexandra thought she was safe in accusing me of causing her injuries because no one can disprove it. But she is too optimistic. What cannot be disproved cannot be proved, either. No one can state on oath that I was there, except my accuser—and it is her word against mine."

"There is a woman in Rome, in the Via del Babuino, who heard you both quarreling—who found Alexandra."

He dropped the honeysuckle. "Even so, it is her word, also, against mine, her version of a story too old now to be verified. Oh, no, Sarah, I can't be frightened by that one."

"Then why were you frightened?"

"For the same reason that you were. Our lives were in danger."

"Perhaps they still are."

He said very quietly, "Not now that I have found Alexandra."

"I think you were even more afraid for your job than for your life—and that's still in the balance—now that Leon and the press and the studios know about Alexandra."

He was looking over my shoulder. I wondered if there was someone he could see on the boat at the end of the lane, but I didn't turn round. I wondered, too, why he was so calm now. Was there a story he would tell to Leon, something released to the press, that could make everything right for him again? The dreadful disintegration of his features that had been visible when he was so afraid was gone. He was completely in control of himself, like a man who knew what he had to do. It filled me with a new alarm. What *was* he going to do?

Out of the corner of my eye, something dazzled me. I turned and saw the sunlight gleam on the hood of the Bentley drawn up under the trees.

"Can't you understand?" Niall asked impatiently. "I'm telling you the truth. I did hit Alexandra. But I was in an rage. I hit her and walked out of the room."

"That's not her story."

"Of course she's lying."

"But you must have known that she fell—you would have heard her. And with burns like that, she would have screamed with pain. Yet you didn't go back."

He outstared me. "I heard nothing."

"That isn't possible. She fell when you hit her—she screamed. You couldn't have been out of hearing in that short time."

"She can say what she likes; there is no longer any proof one way or the other."

I still couldn't understand his unnatural serenity in the face of all that he was losing. Desperation seized me. "What are we going to do? Niall . . . What will be the end of it?"

He moved a step toward me and reaching out, took my hand.

"Poor Sarah. I tried so hard to make a beautiful, sophisticated woman out of you, but you wouldn't change. And now it's too late." He dropped my hand, but I could still feel the strange coldness where his fingers had touched my palm. "I must go."

"Where?" I asked.

"You know perfectly well, to the boat."

His manner was so strange, so calm and at variance with his burning eyes, that I was afraid. "Niall, don't—" I began and then stopped.

"Don't what?"

It was useless for me to beg him to understand Alexandra's bitterness; useless for me to request or advise. We were too far from each other.

I heard myself saying in a flat voice, "It's over, Niall. We must be free of one another. But if you should need me—"

He shook his head. "No, I don't need you."

Without another word I crossed to the car, got in and sat for a few minutes without turning on the engine. I had made another discovery about Niall. If Alexandra's story was correct, how incredible that over the years he had persuaded himself that he had not seen her fall, that the accident had happened after he had walked out of the room. He had willed himself to believe a lie. But how deep could that belief possibly go? How far could a man of intelligence fool himself?

I sat huddled in the driver's seat and stared at the twisting lane. It was useless to tell myself that intelligent men like Niall could not fool themselves. No combination of brilliance and quirks was impossible in the human brain. Madness and genius sometimes went together, strength and weakness, scholarship and superstition. In Niall I was having a kind of private view of this phenomenon. And now he had gone, calmly and coldly, to the boat . . . to Alexandra.

I drove up the lane and the low sun dazzled me, turning the tears on my lashes to dancing emerald and gold. But behind the compulsive weeping was still the question. Who had fired the shot in the garden at Guinever?

16

I HAD to slow down at our gates to let some people cross the road. At the same time, I heard a shrill, tuneless whistling. It was familiar and I switched off the engine of the car. It was the same tune and the same unmusical whistle that I had heard at the time Niall had been shot. It came from somewhere inside the drive, drawing swiftly nearer as if someone were approaching at a run. I leaned forward.

The tall, wrought-iron gates were open and Johnny, our freckled newspaper boy, swung into sight. His head was tilted upward staring at the sky so that he didn't see the car until he almost touched it. He made a wild swerve and fell sprawling in the roadway.

I ran to him but he picked himself up with a grin and grabbed his bicycle. "Lor, Missus, that be a near'un."

"Are you all right?"

"I be fine."

"Then I suggest that in future you leave plane spotting or whatever you were doing to moments when you are not on a bicycle, or next time you'll be a dead duck."

He was still grinning. "I were looking at that bird—it be an eagle."

"A hawk more likely. We don't see eagles round here. Tell me, were you anywhere near the house on the night my husband was shot at?"

The grin vanished. "Me, Missus? No, Missus."

"I'll lay a bet that you were. I remember that tune you were whistling and the way you whistled. You can't do the high notes, can you? Well? You *were* here, weren't you? Why?"

He gave me a sideways look.

"Come on," I said. "Come clean, Johnny."

"You won't tell me mother?"

"Not unless you were up to something you shouldn't have been."

"It were me girl," he said.

"Your—girl—?"

He was nearly fourteen but he looked about twelve, and he was so intensely serious that I said gently, "What about her?"

"You won't tell me mum?"

"No."

"We meet sometimes in the evening, she

and me. And we can't meet down in the ravine because me two sisters meet their boys there, and they'd laugh. So, we meet up in your wood. But it's so dark she don't know where I am 'nless I whistle."

I said, slowly, "And that night you were there and heard the shot?"

"Yes. 'Twere awful, weren't it? I thought it was one o' you from t'house after me with a gun. Then I 'eard you runnin' and I knew I was all right. Then I thought I 'eard me girl and I whistled."

I said, "And so it was you who told the police?"

"I thought someone was dead . . . bein' shot at like them spy tales on the TV. So me girl—Lana's her name—an' me went to report it." His voice was clear and proud. He had participated in a drama and he felt important.

"But surely they asked for your name."

He said proudly, "I didn't give it. In them murder films, they start suspectin' you if you call up. Besides the one as shot Mr. Rhodes could a' thought I saw 'im—an' might be after me."

"*Did* you see anyone in the garden—apart from Mr. Rhodes and myself?"

"No, Missus."

"Honest?"

"Well, I didn't *see* no one, but there was a bit of light in the sky. I saw them bushes down by the wall move—and there weren't no wind."

"I suppose after you had telephoned the police, you told your friends all about it."

"No, only me mum. I didn't tell 'er about Lana—just that I went for a walk and 'eard the shot in your garden."

"I see."

He said, "Mum went to the White Horse for a drink or two like she sometimes does. She could a' told folks there, but she wouldn't 'ave said 'twas me as told 'er 'cos she knew I'd be scared to 'ave the murderer know. She's good to me, me mum is."

"There was no murder," I said. "All right, Johnny." I let him go with another warning to stop and look before he came like a bat out of hell into a main road. He thought that very funny.

So whoever had shot at Niall had hidden in the bushes by the wall and must have escaped along the cliff path. One disturbing point, however, had been cleared up. I knew now who had called Jim Pherson to Guinever.

The first thing I saw when I came within

sight of the house was Theo's car by the front steps. Father and Freda had returned from London and Theo had gone to meet them. As I neared the house I realized, with dismay, that it was not to be a serene homecoming.

Father's voice shouted at someone in the living room. "Then why in the name of blazes didn't he tell me? Hadn't I a right to know? Good grief, what's going on in this house—some damned conspiracy? . . . 'Don't tell Father.' . . . As if I were some monster who terrified my family."

Freda said in her quiet but carrying voice, "Nobody's afraid of you, Kester dear. How could I tell you, anyway, before I knew myself? I only found out on the day we left to go to London. I had no intention of telling you then—I had a feeling you'd behave just as you are behaving, and I wasn't going to spoil our visit to town."

Father heard me enter from the terrace and swung round. "Did *you* know about it?"

"About what?"

"Those." Father stabbed a finger at two paintings propped up on chairs.

"Oh," I said weakly. "Theo's. Who found them?"

"I did," Freda said. She was calmly working at her patchwork.

"Well?" Father demanded of me. "You don't look particularly surprised to see those canvases."

"I'm not. I saw one of them once in Theo's room." Then I asked Freda, "He didn't show them to you, did he?"

She shook her head. "I found them. Theo asked me to send a suit of his to the cleaner's and then forgot to give it to me. So I went and fetched it. The lock on his wardrobe door is very stiff and I had to pull and push it to get it open. Something inside fell with a thud and I reached in to prop it up again—and found these. Did you think I was going to keep them a secret from your father?"

The clock in the hall struck, and at the same time I heard Theo's voice saying something to Dido. Father was crouched before the two paintings; Freda sat, head bent, sewing sapphire silk to emerald. I might have known she would tell Father.

Theo strode across the hall. Cowardlike, I wanted to run from the room, but Freda's calm shamed me into remaining where I was. Theo was in the doorway. The colors of the canvases had drawn his eye before he had looked to see who was in the room.

For a moment he did not speak, but his dismay was such an overwhelming and tangible thing that I was suddenly angry with Freda. I would have liked to have torn the brilliant silks from her and demanded what right she had to do this to Theo. He found his voice at last, flat and hollow, saying, "I suppose Dido told you. She saw me once, putting my painting things in the hollow under the Minerva stone."

"Among the ants? Oh Theo . . ."

He looked at me. "There was nowhere else."

The remark was forlorn in its starkness. *There was nowhere else.* Nowhere in this house of extroverts where something could be hidden, safe from our quick, inquiring eyes.

Theo said in the same flat voice, "I kept everything in tins and wrapped them in polythene." He walked across the room and stood in front of the paintings, shielding them from Father's eyes.

Freda said, "Dido told us nothing. I found those two in your wardrobe."

"They were right at the back, out of sight."

"I wasn't prying, Theo dear. One of the

canvases slid to the floor as I opened your wardrobe to get out your suit. When I saw what had fallen, I took it to the light and it seemed good to me. Then I found the second one."

"I might have guessed someone would."

Freda said, "You painted in secret—"

"Behind the hornbeam hedge in my garden," he said bitterly. "Is there anything else you want to know?"

"Yes," said Father. "Are there any more?"

Theo said, like someone caught in a crime and confessing to more, "Plenty. Stacked in the cupboard in the conservatory."

"I've seen nothing there."

"I don't mean the big conservatory. I've got a locked cupboard in the one I use behind the lily garden."

"Then unlock it and bring me all you've got . . . Go on . . . ," Father ordered, as Theo did not move.

"I'd rather not."

"Oh, don't be a fool, man! Listen to me. These are good. *Good*, do you hear? Line, color, perspective—the lot. That's why I want to see the rest."

Theo swallowed twice. "When I showed you some a few years ago, you more or less told me to forget painting. You made it quite clear that I was no good."

"Yet you went on painting, didn't you?"

"I couldn't help myself. It was a kind of compulsion."

"And now you're turning out good work. You were very young and there was ample time to improve and you've done it."

"Oh, Theo!" I said softly. Nobody took any notice of me.

Father swung a chair round and sat astride it. "You went on painting without a word to me? Without even asking my help . . ."

"You don't expect help from someone who accuses you of playing jokes with paint."

Freda calmed the atmosphere. "Go and get the rest, Theo. Please."

When he had gone, Father said gloomily, "How in the world did I produce a secretive son?"

"There are people you can shout at and who just let it drift over them, like Penn. You should know your own children by now. Theo is different; he is intensely sensitive. He needs praise and a little gentleness."

"Well, I've just given him praise," Father said plaintively.

"And if I hadn't found those canvases,

you'd never have known, would you, Kester? And perhaps a very good artist might have been lost."

Elbow on the chair back, Father bit his knuckles and stared at the far wall. "There's that exhibition of paintings at the Launford Art Gallery. If Theo is quick about it, he could send in a couple of canvases."

Theo must have done a record racing sprint across the garden, for he returned out of breath, canvases gripped in his hands, clutched under his arms. Father took one and propped it on a third chair. Eyes narrowed, he studied it for a full minute while we stood silently, watching him.

"Better. Better still," he said. "That luminous, wet-day light is nearly perfect."

Freda said, "Kester wants you to submit a couple of the best for hanging at the Exhibition in Launford."

"And you'd better get them in quickly," Father said. "The judging is tomorrow."

Theo made a swift selection and, carrying three of his pictures, strode to the door.

Father said, "Now where are you going?"

"To take these into Launford."

Freda said, "Couldn't you wait? Dinner will be in an hour . . ."

"Wait?" boomed Father. "Of course he can't wait. He's only twenty-three years old. It won't hurt him to have an empty stomach for a few hours."

I had never seen such happiness on Theo's quiet face.

"I'll go and set the table for dinner," I said.

Freda stopped me. She piled the silks onto her special side table, put away her needle and rose with a lovely, single movement which the stage must have taught her. "Kurt is on his way to dinner and he's bringing Shesu."

I said quickly to Father, "If they're staying the night, I'd better get the beds ready."

"They aren't. Kurt is over at Mayduke's place in Wells and Shesu is staying there, too. She's modeling for the bronze he's doing for the new Overseas Hall."

Kurt Sorel was the art critic whom Father alternately clapped on the shoulder as his friend and quarreled with, accusing him of never having progressed beyond the Post-impressionists. Shesu was a half-Formosan girl with an enchanting, plaintive face and the body of a child. She was gentle and given to hero-worshiping Father, who often used her as a model. Her manners were perfect and only Dido disliked her.

Polly entered and asked Father what time his guests were arriving. She looked flustered, and Freda laid a hand across her shoulders.

"They may not be here for an hour. Don't worry. Everything is cold except the lamb chops, and we can cook those while the men are having drinks."

Freda leaned toward me as I passed her. "Luke is coming to dinner, too. We met him in Launford when Kester stopped at the art shop for another supply of pencils."

I said vaguely, "Luke? Oh . . . good," and thought, "They'll meet at last, Luke and Niall . . . ," and then a shiver ran through me. I had left Niall down by Alexandra's boat. My delight at Theo's happiness had brought temporary forgetfulness. Now memory flooded back. "Tell Kester," Luke had said. I would; I must. But not until I had warned Niall of what I intended to do.

"Did you hear, Sarah?" Freda was asking. "We need some raspberries to top the mousse. Dido can set the table if you'll pick the fruit."

The raspberry canes were behind the hedge where Polly grew herbs. I picked steadily, pushing aside the leaves and finding the soft crimson berries. But every movement was mechanical—something I had done so many times. All the while, against the background of the rich, thick canes, I saw the cabin of the white boat, sunlight shafting onto hands bare of gloves. Withered skin . . . scars too deep for plastic surgery . . . Niall's face . . .

Johnny came spinning up the drive. He saw me in the distance and waved a letter. There was a plane tree by the herb garden. I picked a large leaf, filled it with raspberries and called Johnny. He gave me the letter and went back to where he had left his bicycle, happily stuffing raspberries into his wide, pale mouth. I looked at the envelope in my hand. It was addressed to "Mr. or Mrs. Niall Rhodes."

I slit the envelope. Inside was a cutting from a local paper we did not subscribe to. I unfolded it and looked at Alexandra's strange, compelling face.

The caption read: "Mrs. Alexandra Rhodes, ex-wife of the television personality Niall Rhodes, has returned to England. She is seen here with Mr. Francis Lorian, whose unorthodox treatment for spinal and other injuries was the subject of an article in this newspaper a few weeks ago."

I pushed the envelope into the azalea bushes to throw away later and slid the cutting down the front of my dress. Alexandra next to my heart . . .

Then I went back to picking raspberries. I was only dimly aware of the roar of Kurt Sorel's supercharged Riley, which startled the birds. I wondered how much Francis knew—had known all along. Surely if Alexandra had told him the whole story, he would have stopped her frantic revenge. He was far too ambitious, too jealous of his reputation to be implicated in something that might, at any moment, explode into real violence. Alexandra had said, "I hate violence." But, like a car with failed brakes, revenge could get out of hand.

I had finished picking raspberries and walked slowly, dragging my feet, back to the house.

A second car was turning in at the gates. I recognized it at once and turned back down the drive to meet it. Luke pulled up at my side. He looked at the basket I carried. "Raspberries! I could eat the lot. You look happy."

"I'm screwing up my eyes against the sun," I said, and to my own dismay, I burst into tears.

Luke turned off the engine, got out of the car and drew me down onto the grass. We sat with our backs against a lime tree and I, who hadn't cried for years, felt the helpless tidal wave of weeping sweep over me.

"You'd better get up to the house." I hiccuped with my head turned away. "Father's expecting you. Kurt is there and Shesu—she's one of Father's new models and lovely. Go on . . . I'm . . . all . . . right . . ."

"You're choosing a very odd way of showing it."

"It's over," I said and swallowed hard. "I'm sorry."

"Why? Crying is as natural as laughter. It's merely the other side of the coin. Now, tell me."

I felt inside my dress and brought out the newspaper cutting. Luke watched me and shouted with laughter. "That's where women have the edge on men. We can't very well stuff things down our collars." He took the cutting from me, unfolded the crumpled paper and read quickly, then gave it back to me without a word.

I said, "This is only the beginning of what she's going to let the press know. One move at a time, like the old Chinese water torture, slow destruction . . . She told me so."

"Where is Niall?"

"I don't know. But I know where he went this afternoon."

"Where?"

"To see Alexandra," I said and told him of my own visit, told him what I'd heard and then, painfully, what I'd seen.

Luke said gently, "They can do wonderful things these days with graftings—plastic surgery."

"Then why didn't she have it done?"

"The burns could possibly be too deep." He touched the piece of paper I was folding over and over. "When are you going to tell your father?"

"As soon as he's alone," I said. "Tonight, if possible."

"And now," said Luke, "it needs no more talking out. Come on, we'll go and listen to your father arguing with Kurt Sorel about things we don't understand."

I said, "You'll meet Niall at dinner."

Luke did not answer me. But, as we neared the house, he took my hand.

Polly was protesting as we entered the living room, "But Niall isn't home yet. Shouldn't we hold dinner back?"

"No," said Father and there was a gleam of triumph in his eyes. He was delighted at the opportunity to demonstrate that this was Kester Palfrey's house. Niall could conform or go without.

I looked at my crumpled dress. "I must go and change. Start dinner; I won't be long."

Niall did not come. One lyre-backed chair stood empty across the table from where I sat, plate and napkin and silver unused.

At nine o'clock, Leon telephoned. Where the hell was Niall? He was supposed to be following him to London but there was no one at our apartment. Leon had left messages with the porter, had rung up Niall's club. Was Niall still there at Guinever? No? He coughed and spluttered into the telephone. "And that's not all. I've had a letter—anonymous, so it may be some jerk's idea of a bad joke. But if so, it 'ud better be denied right away."

"What did the letter say?"

"That Niall has been married before."

I said faintly, "That's right. The local

paper has already gotten hold of the story. You've met his wife."

"*I* have? What in the name of . . ."

"You talked to her on the beach here."

He was silent for a moment. Then he burst out, "Good God. I remember. There was a rather beautiful young woman—we got talking; at least she started talking to me." I could imagine the surprise on his dark, Levantine face. "You don't mean that she's the one?"

"Yes."

He swore softly. "And she could have written that note."

"Yes."

"Damn it, it's possible. The note said that some years ago Niall forged his wife's signature to get money. It said, 'This is the first instalment. There's more news of Niall Rhodes to follow.' " He sucked air sharply through his teeth. "I've got to contact him and get the lowdown on that first wife. She could be a cheap little blackmailer. But if what's in this letter is true, it'll cause a hell of a lot of trouble. The things she hints at cut right through all that we've carefully built up."

I answered swiftly, knowing the speed with

which Leon consulted his legal advisers.

"Whatever you do, don't contact the lawyers until you've found Niall and talked to him."

"That's the obvious thing to do if he'll come out of his blasted hiding place."

"He will. He may even now be on his way to London. But I don't know for certain. Leon, I don't know!"

He sensed my distress for the first time. "It's bad for you, too, Sarah. All right, we'll wait a bit, though time's getting short. There's a meeting in my office tomorrow at three with the producer and director of the new show. If Niall's not there"—he broke off and I heard the heavy breath that hissed across the wires—"God help him, I'll break his neck."

I must have been sitting so long by the telephone that Freda became worried. I heard her at my elbow. "What is it? Niall?"

I nodded.

"Don't worry. He's probably got a mood on and is staying away until he works it off." She slid an arm round my shoulders. "Come along in with us."

17

THE hall clock had struck eleven. Voices came drifting up from the living room, where only Father and Kurt were left to argue the case for and against hard-edged abstraction. Isolated words, broken sentences came, Kurt's voice organlike, reverberating: ". . . symmetry . . . deep sense of color . . . You've blocked your mind not to accept it . . ." And Father, yelling back about "shut-in emotions . . . symmetry be damned . . . wall-paper art."

It was the usual pattern of conversation when these two came together, clashes over late-night brandies, ending always in roars of laughter.

I stood in my room with my arms folded tightly, listening for the sound of a car, for Niall's return, for Father to be alone so that I could talk to him, for something to happen. I went down for the third time and telephoned the London apartment. There was no answer.

The living-room door opened and Kurt came out.

"Why, Sarah." His small eyes in his square face looked me over. "You're like a pretty ghost in that white dress. When is Kester going to paint you?"

I said lightly, "When he pays me a model's wage."

He laughed and went up the stairs, still talking, his legs spread-eagled as if he were walking a ship's deck. Father laid an elephantine arm round my shoulders and bore me back into the living room. "You and Niall had a quarrel?"

"Sort of, and I don't know where he is."

"Oh, caught up with some fans somewhere—showing off, I shouldn't wonder."

"I don't think so. This is serious."

"Is it?" His eyes brightened. "Really serious? You mean there's a chance of you and he splitting up?"

"Father, I've got to talk to you. But will you promise not to be furious with me for not telling you before?"

He said, "What's been going on, Sarah?" and sat down, stuck out his legs and waited.

In the vast medieval room made warm and beloved by three generations of close-knit Palfreys, the story of revenge and attack seemed too outrageous. As I talked about it, it was like a tall tale told in a nightmare—a macabre joke, an Alice-through-the-looking-glass fantasia, a toy car driven at me made to look large by trick mirrors, a bullet that would never penetrate flesh, brown streaks horribly painted on unblemished arms, a story told on a boat to mock my gullibility . . . But I left out no detail, and when I had finished, Father strode around the room giving little snorts, cracking his knuckles as if he longed to punch something or someone. I sat curled up on the settee and waited. Father picked up a straight-backed chair, swung it round and straddled it in his favorite attitude, glaring at me. The long red hairs of his eyebrows stood up like hackles over his brilliant eyes.

"I don't care what time of day or night he gets back, I'll be waiting for him and I'll knock—"

"No, Father, you won't. You'll go to bed and sleep on the story. Tomorrow when . . . if . . . Niall returns, we'll cope with it together."

"He's nothing but a bloody crook."

"What Alexandra told me might not be quite the truth. It's the old saying about waiting until you get both sides of a story."

He banged the chair's back with his fist. "And you've been going around as if nothing had happened, telling no one."

"Until today I only knew a small bit of the story, and Niall wanted me to keep it to myself. He was going to employ detectives—"

"Huh! So he tells you. And you believed him."

"Yes. It seemed the only way to cope, since he felt he had to avoid the kind of publicity he dreaded."

"Avoid the truth coming out, you mean. Detectives! I'll lay even money he had no such plan. He was just fooling you—" Father got up and almost slung the chair across the room. "All this has been going on and I've known nothing about it."

I said gently, "I'm sorry. When everything reached a climax—when the shot was fired at Niall—you and Freda were in London."

"There's a telephone in the house."

"I know," I said unhappily. "But you were enjoying yourselves in London, and, anyway, you knew about that. We told you."

"The explanation given to me was that Niall disturbed poachers. My daughter goes in danger of her life and Father mustn't know—"

"Don't," I cried. "Please, Father. I can't take trouble from you, too." I got up and leaned against him. "I'm tired. Drained. I've told you. Now let's leave everything for tonight?"

He sighed, relaxed and held me close. "All right, my little one. We'll cope with it all tomorrow."

We walked together up the stairs. On the landing he said, "Pity you and Luke didn't get together. Though, I don't know . . . perhaps not. With the way he ups and goes off just when he seems to have settled down, he wouldn't be much of a husband."

"He only went away once."

"This is the second time."

"This?"

"Didn't he tell you? He's off to India again in a few weeks. I heard it in the bar of the White Horse just before I went to London. Funny that he hasn't mentioned it to us."

"Perhaps it's just a rumor."

"Oh no, it's true all right. They say this time he's going to start a research unit in Kerala. So, that being considered, I can't see he'd make much of a home for a woman. He's too footloose."

My huge, lovable father, my tactless, bull-in-a-china-shop father . . . I said, "Oh, really?" and walked blindly to my room.

I think Father called after me something to the effect that I was to sleep well and not to worry, that he'd take control of everything in the morning. In my room, I pushed up the window, pulled a chair toward me and sat down with my arms on the window sill and my face in my hands. The cool night air played round my head, but I felt no comfort.

Luke would go away again and this time he would go lightly, without my bitter reproaches, my adolescent desire to hold him back with the old, old line "If you loved me you wouldn't want to leave me." Doctor Luke Ashton, the research worker, the man who had to be free.

Long ago, when we were very small, an old fisherman of Launford had once said of his son, "Keep 'im by me? Larks alive, this comin' and goin's the perfect life for 'im. Don't 'e know? There's them that 'as slept with a goose feather under their pillows and they baint for stayin' at home." Someone had put a goose feather under Luke's pillow.

I raised my head and looked into the blackness of the garden. Then I got up and began to walk round the room. For the first time in my life, the rhythmic crashing of the sea irritated me and I shut the window, but the sound was still there, as if my ears were hollow shells. I went downstairs. There was just one light in the hall. Father had left a note on the table for Theo. "Don't lock up. Niall not in." I crossed the sitting room and opened the door that led to the long stone passage. Ahead of me were the two doors of the tower rooms. To the right, the worn steps that wound spirally upward to the top of the keep. I was as mindless as a sleepwalker, obeying no conscious urge.

The steps were dark. I clung to the side rope and climbed to the top. I pushed open the door, stepped out and leaned against the crenellated stone. The moon had risen, a half-inflated balloon over the black oaks. The west wind blew my hair across my face. The sea swayed and glittered. Something moved by the bushes and it was not the wind. Again secret people were in our garden, walkers among the sable shadows. Alexandra—Francis—or the unknown third enemy who had tried to kill Niall . . . On the other hand, it could be Niall, aware that I knew the truth and afraid to come into the house. I turned and clambered down the twisting steps from the tower, and because I forgot to close the door, the moonlight lit the first half of my way. After that I scrambled in darkness to the landing, ran across the sitting room, along the hall and tore open the front door.

The thick blackness of the garden hit me like a wall. "Niall . . . Niall . . ."

No one answered me. I was too vulnerable, standing there open to attack on any side. A target for a shot, a stone aimed with deadly accuracy, an arm from behind, catching me round the throat . . . On that last fear, I leaped into action and fled back to the house. As soon I could touch Guinever's walls, I felt brave again. With my hand keeping contact with the wall, I moved round to the front of the house. Neatly parked in front of the garage stood the Bentley.

I called Niall's name again and my voice startled a hare or a rabbit in the undergrowth. It scuttled away. I edged toward the car. It was empty. The perfume Alexandra used had been distinctive. I opened the door, leaned in and sniffed. The car smelled faintly of warm leather—and not at all of a woman's perfume.

Someone had brought the car back. Niall himself? Or someone who knew where he was?

I walked up and down my room, wondering if I should rouse Father and tell him. But morning would be soon enough. And Niall could still come back.

I lay in bed for two hours, listening, and heard only the sea and the striking of a clock. Somewhere between two and three I fell asleep. When I awoke it was morning. The sky was an unbroken pearl; it had rained in the night and the grass sparkled. The house was full of the sounds of morning vitality—footsteps; a radio giving the news; doors opening, slamming; the smell of coffee.

Once, I got up from the breakfast table and telephoned Portland Place. Nobody answered. I telephoned Leon at his home.

"But hell take it, Niall's on live TV tonight. What the devil can have happened?"

Perhaps only the devil knows.

"What did you say, Sarah?"

"Nothing."

"We'll have to find him. So start thinking. Think. *Think.*"

"I know exactly what to do," I said. "I'm going to the police. Father says—"

"No," he exploded into low, violent swearing. Then, as I sat waiting for him to calm down, he said, "Sarah, are you there? *Are you there?*"

"Yes. I'm just trying to make sense, at this stage, of keeping away from the police. Niall's missing—he could have gone for a walk and have been taken ill, lying anywhere . . . on the moors or at the foot of cliffs. And you say, 'Don't tell the police.' "

"Scandal—"

"Who said anything about scandal?"

"For Pete's sake, the anonymous letter to me wasn't written in fun. Niall knows that someone's out for his blood and he's hiding. We've got to play hounds to his hare . . . we've got to scent him out. And I will. Dammit, I will." He hung up abruptly and I knew that he would spend the morning on the telephone.

I wandered round the house, half-heartedly polishing the Queen Anne bureau in the living room, dusting, throwing away old newspapers and magazines. And when I had done all these jobs, it was still only eleven o'clock.

We had midmorning coffee, and after it Freda presented me with a list and a shopping basket. "I've got a busy morning here. Will you go into Launford for me, Sarah?"

I looked at the penciled list and knew perfectly well that she had ample supplies of all the things she had written down. She was making a job for me and I was grateful to her.

The Launford Art Gallery was just off Market Square. After I had shopped, I paid my two shillings and went through the turnstile into the first of the three fine rooms. The paintings were all by artists living within a hundred-mile radius of Launford, some of them established, others young and just starting their careers.

I found three of Theo's paintings hung in the second room and stood quietly listening to comments by visitors as they consulted their catalogs.

"That must be Kester Palfrey's son." . . . "He hasn't got his father's flare, has he?" . . . "That study of peonies is good. You can see how the rain was falling when it was painted. It has a luminous quality." . . . "He's a gentler painter than his father."

I moved into the third room, where paintings were displayed under the heading "Launford Past and Present." There were some eighteenth- and nineteenth-century originals loaned by private collectors and hung side by side with modern artists.

Under the printed words "First Night" were a set of Victorian prints entitled "Launford Theater." They showed a cramped stage and a restless audience. Next to them were three very recent black and white sketches of the new theater, also entitled "First Night." The first sketch was of a stage and the actors; in the second the artist had drawn the audience in the stalls. The third was of the foyer, which had been judged, at the time of the building of the new theater, the finest in southern England. I went back to the first sketch and recognized the costumes and scenery for *The Tempest*, which had had its opening night only a matter of days ago. I moved on again to the second sketch. The people in the audience were not defined by faces, but by characteristics—a particularly high hair style, a lavish white stole, a man on an end seat wearing espadrilles, a woman with long dark gloves. I went closer to the drawing. This woman's face was, like them all, a deliberate blur—the artist had not intended any identification—but I had seen that plain dark dress before and the jewel at the woman's throat. I recognized the lovely sweep of hair, the long dark gloves . . .

I turned away and sat down on a red plush seat in the middle of the room.

Father's voice came in a huge, disembodied boom. "There you are, Sarah. I've been looking for you." The crowds round a huge chiaroscuro parted and I saw him. He was standing with Mason Gluck, director of the galleries and a close friend of ours.

I greeted Mason, "Congratulations. It's an exciting show and beautifully hung."

Mason looked pleased.

I went on, "Those black and white sketches of Launford Theater are rather fine."

"When the Victorian paintings were offered to us for the exhibition," Mason said, "someone on the board of selectors suggested that it would be a good idea to have some sketches of the modern theater hung with them. It was a late decision so we commissioned Con Weldon to do three sketches. He's a very quick worker and he sat up for two days and two nights drawing from the roughs he had made at the theater. I think he's a brilliant young artist." Mason turned to Father. "You agree?"

"He'll do," Father said largely, "when he's

older and takes more time over his work. At the moment he draws and paints as if there's no tomorrow."

I said, "He really did those sketches on the first night of *The Tempest?*"

"We chose it because it's usually the best audience of the run of a play."

Father said, "Want me to take you round, Sarah?"

I knew from experience what it was like to go through an art gallery with Father. Praise and criticism spilled out in an unbroken stream and wherever he stopped, a crowd gathered. It was sometimes embarrassing. "I've seen it all," I said. "You go. I'll wait for you here."

Someone came up to speak to Mason. Father said, "Since I was on the selection committee, I know every picture and there's nothing I want to see again. I came to find you. Freda said she guessed you wouldn't be able to resist coming here."

I knew that Father would not have bothered to drive all this way into Launford to find me unless he had something important to tell me. News of Niall . . . ? I said sharply, "What has happened?"

"Nothing, except that I have decided that

you and I are going to the police. Niall has disappeared and it's no longer just a family matter." He added more gently, "We've got to do it, Sarah."

He was right of course. I let him lead me, his arm heavy around my shoulder, out to the courtyard. I left the runabout where I had parked it and got into Father's car.

"When we get there," he said, "you can let me do the talking. All you need do is answer the particular questions they put to you. And if any journalist's eye spots us, you're dumb. You understand?"

"I'm dumb," I said gratefully.

I sat with my eyes riveted on the road ahead as we crawled toward police headquarters. So Alexandra had spoken the truth to me. I had believed her at the time; now I had proof. She had been nowhere near Guinever when Niall was shot. The fact posed an even more alarming question. Who, then, hid in the bushes and watched us coming and going?

At the station, Father and I gave the sergeant all we could.

Father said, "There's been a lot of funny business . . ."

We were too much under the sergeant's eye for me to give Father a warning kick. I said quickly, "My husband has been very overworked lately. He could have suffered a kind of—breakdown. Amnesia . . ."

The policeman nodded in polite disbelief. He must have heard so many anxious relatives suggest amnesia as an explanation for a disappearance. He said, "There was some bother the other night, wasn't there? A shot fired in your grounds?"

"Poachers," I said, too quickly.

"Could be, Mrs. Rhodes. But in view of what you now report, we must investigate. The bullet is probably embedded in your lawn."

Father exploded. "Why the devil didn't you look for it immediately?"

"Because Mr. Rhodes called on us the morning after the incident and said he remembered seeing a couple of rabbits on the lawn just before the shot. He said, 'It was one of the villagers and we are not charging him.' He said the matter was closed."

Father looked at me. I shook my head. "I knew nothing about that."

"It's my house!" Father shouted. "If I'd been there, not even my son-in-law would have given orders. I'd have had that bullet found, if it took the whole police force of Launford."

"Quite so, sir."

More questions, more answers. Father tried hard, but patience and tact were not in his make-up.

When we left, I said, "Niall could have returned while we were with the police. If he has, he'll be mad—"

"That makes two of us," said Father, and he slammed the car into gear.

When we reached Guinever, Niall had not returned, but Luke was there. He was sitting on the terrace with Freda, and he said to me, "Hasn't it occurred to you that you should go to London?"

"To the apartment?"

"Yes. You may find that some of Niall's clothes and a suitcase are missing."

A voluntary disappearance, escape from the final disgrace of the truth . . . I said, "Yes, I'll go. Saturday trains are slow but there's one, I think, about half past twelve. I'll catch that."

"We'll catch it," said Luke.

"You mean you'll come with me?"

"That's the idea."

He smiled and I had a swift, irrelevant thought. He could enslave a woman by just smiling at her. And then I thought, as I went upstairs to fetch my coat, "And much good that would do her, my once-upon-a-time elusive lover."

We had lunch on an almost deserted train. People were crowding out of London, seeking the sea and the woods and the hills. The clouds had swung away and the sun was hot. Luke brought newspapers. "Read or talk or sleep. I don't mind. Oh, and by the way, I drove down to the river this morning. There is no boat moored opposite Willow Lane."

"There must be!" I stared at him.

Luke said dryly, "Boats are built to be mobile. They can weigh anchor and go away at any time."

"You don't think Niall could have been on it? You don't think he and Alexandra are together?"

"You mean that she has taken him on a pleasant Saturday cruise? That would be saintly after what he did to her, and does she strike you as being the forgiving type?"

"No. But he could have been forced to stay."

"Bound and gagged . . . tied to the mast . . . fed to the dolphins . . ."

"Don't laugh at me. Violence *is* possible."

"Anything is possible in this world—even miracles," Luke said quietly. "Now suppose you stop seeing Niall as someone's helpless prisoner and concentrate on the fact that he's in a devil of a mess and has chosen to disappear? Right?"

"Right," I said in a small voice.

Halfway to London, I asked him the question that had been at the back of my mind since I had talked to Father the previous evening.

"I hear you are going back to India."

He looked at me over the top of his newspaper. "Yes. Some time in September. I volunteered."

"Then going to the trouble of getting a home in Launford was rather a waste, wasn't it?"

He said, "Oh no, my housekeeper will live there till I come back."

"This year, next year . . ."

"Sometime," he said.

"Do you think you could write to me?"

"I'll send you lots of postcards, from the Taj Mahal to the Himalayas."

Crumbs from the rich man's table. I wouldn't be satisfied, but I was a beggar at the feast Luke made of his life. I envied him. The world was rich for people such as he.

"Come and let's have lunch," he said. And I knew he had already forgotten that he was leaving England again so soon. This was one thing I had always known about him—he gave time to the everlasting present and wasted no energy on contemplating the future.

All during lunch the wheels were like accompanying drums to the pictures that flashed into my mind. I still believed that Niall might be on the boat; this could be where revenge had burst through the flood gates that held it in check and turned at last to actual violence. Had the white yacht sailed safely out to where the sea was deep, avoiding the fishing banks, the shipping lanes—was this the place where he had been taken? I drank down the last of the wine, hoping to dull my mind, to become sleepy, heavy, thoughtless. It had the desired effect. Back at our seats I drowsed as the train flew past the fields and suburbs and finally into London.

At Portland Place, Manson was signing for a parcel. He looked up. "I've got some calls for Mr. Rhodes." He gave me a sheaf of telephone notes. "Some of them are urgent." He had read the newspapers; he knew Niall was missing. "There's no news yet, Mrs. Rhodes?"

"No, no news."

Letters were scattered on the carpet inside the door. I picked them up. Maria had cleaned up, and the place had a polished, expectant look. I went into the living room. The envelope which had contained Alexandra's note to me had been carefully picked up from the floor and replaced on the coffee table. On the desk in Niall's study was another pile of letters. I went carefully through his clothes. Nothing was missing. Our suitcases, too, were all stacked neatly in the cupboard.

When the telephone rang, I guessed it was Leon. He asked without preamble, "Where the hell is your husband?"

"I don't know."

"You don't know. I don't know. Nobody knows! But a man doesn't suddenly disappear. Not when he's got an important job to do. For God's sake, is he going to turn up tonight?"

"I'd have thought you'd have realized by now that I can't tell you anything."

"But you know all the places where he might be. His friends . . . relatives. Think,

Sarah. It's the first of the new series tonight. *Think.*"

I shouted over his shout, "And in case you don't remember it, I'm his wife and it's equally important to me to find him. What do you imagine *I'm* up in London for, a joy ride?"

"But you should have some idea—"

"I'm not clairvoyant," I said and slammed down the receiver.

At three o'clock we sat in the quiet apartment and drank tea with dried milk. Neither of us could say what we were waiting for. Outside, the wide and splendid street was quiet, the elegant façades dove gray in the muted light. At four o'clock we knew there was nothing to keep us at the apartment. But when we left and I stood waiting while Luke signaled to an approaching taxi, I wondered whether anyone watched us from a parked car, from a window, from the shadows of Broadcasting House.

In the train, returning to Dorset, we didn't mention Niall's name. Guessing had become fruitless.

We picked Luke's car up at Launford Station and I said, "I wonder if Francis is home?"

"Do you think it would help if you knew?"

"He could have been on the boat. I'm going to find out."

"And then what?"

"If he is at home, there are questions I can ask that the police can't because they don't know all the circumstances."

"Then I suggest you tell them pretty fast."

"I will. But later."

He pulled the car up outside his house. "You'll go and see Lorian whether I warn you its foolish or not, but come in and rest first." He touched my cheek. "Women with white, drawn faces need a pick-me-up."

"I—"

"Don't argue. I'll prescribe and then I'll get a meal. Something not too heavy. Digestions play tricks when one is emotionally drained."

"As a doctor, you're marvelous."

He laughed.

While Luke mixed a drink for me, I telephoned Guinever. Freda answered. "The police called," she said. "Kester had a long talk with them. They're combing the garden for the bullet that hit Niall. They can't rule out that there's a connection between that and his disappearance, though one day's disappearance doesn't call for a concerted search."

Just one day? One day and a bit since we had disturbed Pepita in the keep?

Luke had gone into the kitchen to see what there was to eat. I stood at the window, a martini in my hand, watching Lorian's house. I saw the red car draw up. I gulped down the rest of the drink and rushed to the door. Luke was in the hall. His hands stayed me. "And where do you think you're going?"

"Francis has just come home."

"He'll keep. Would you like omelet and salad? And there are some fresh peaches."

"Lovely," I said and raced down the path and along the street. When I rang the bell, Francis opened the door.

"Why, Sarah . . ."

I took a leap inside the house in case he closed the door in my face. "Where is Niall?"

"Why should I know? But do come in."

I walked into a comfortable, unexciting room and faced Francis. "I know everything," I said, "and so, now, do the police."

He was unperturbed. "And what does 'everything' imply?"

"Yesterday Niall went to the boat, the one

moored at the end of Willow Lane. You know about it, don't you?"

"Will you have a drink?"

"No."

"Then if you'll excuse me, I will. I've been driving a long way and I'm rather tired."

"What happened on that boat?"

I thought that he was going to deny that he knew what I was talking about. But after a pause, while he poured his drink, he said, "If you mean when Niall went to see Alexandra, I wasn't there."

"Why did it leave the mooring?"

He lifted his brows in amusement. "Because the period for which it was hired had expired. It was rented in my name."

"Alexandra lived there?"

"She wanted somewhere quiet and I offered her the boat. After renting it, I found I was too busy to use it myself."

"And now that you no longer have the yacht, I suppose Alexandra is living in Launford? Or is it London? Will it be easier for her to hunt Niall from there?"

He was silent.

"You know about it, don't you?"

He answered me gravely, "She told me."

"So you've been involved from the beginning."

"No." He saw my disbelief and a glimmer of amusement shone in his eyes. "You really enjoy disliking me, don't you, Sarah? Well, you can go on doing so. I'm indifferent. But I'm not indifferent to anyone believing that I am a liar. So you're going to know what happened."

"I know . . . what happened."

"You don't know the picture from my angle, and since you are accusing me of involvement, you're going to hear it."

Outside in the street a heavy truck rumbled by and shook the house.

"In the beginning, Alexandra was just a beautiful woman who came to me for treatment for a shoulder injury. The name she gave was Alexandra Gilson—I learned afterward that it was her maiden name."

"She told you—"

"On the day some wandering reporter photographed us. I like publicity—I asked for it—and I got more than I bargained for. The reporter asked for Alexandra's name and she gave it. Mrs. Niall Rhodes."

"She was a patient, yet she was out with you when the reporter saw you?"

"Why not? Many of my patients end up as my friends. And there are some who come to Launford, as Alexandra said she had done, because they had heard of my work." Again, the mockery danced in his eyes. "Of course I believed her—you would have expected me to, wouldn't you? I'm a devil for believing in myself."

"But you now know the real reason why she came to Launford."

"Yes."

"Giving her married name to the reporter was deliberate—it was like the vital piece of a crossword being filled in," I said. "She sent me a copy of the photograph. You know where she is living, don't you? You know everything."

He nodded.

"Then tell me." I watched him. "Please—where is Alexandra?"

Waiting, scrutinizing his face, I saw that he was less sure of himself. What Alexandra had told him had shaken a little of his brilliant self-esteem. Either he was afraid for his own sake or he was afraid for her—a patient and now a friend.

I said desperately, "Niall has disappeared and Alexandra may know where he is."

"If you think they're together, then you're quite wrong."

"I think she could know where he is. And I want to find her before the police do. They will be looking for her, too."

"Ah, so we've got to the root of it. Now that the pedestal has publicly broken and Niall has been found to have feet of mud, the police are his enemies, aren't they?" He looked at me incredulously. "And you are still, in spite of everything you know, the loyal wife. Good grief . . ."

I stared at the three wise monkeys carved in ivory on the mantelpiece and did not answer.

He said, "She's not on the boat; that's one thing I'll tell you. The owners came to get it this morning. Alexandra went with them to its mooring place in Poole Harbor, because she enjoys the sea. I drove over and we came back together to Launford. Does that satisfy you?"

"No. Where can I find her?"

"That's the third time you've asked. I didn't tell you before. Do you think you've said anything to make me change my mind?"

"You're shielding her."

"That's obvious. She made a wild and pathetic mistake. But now it's over . . ."

"Over?" I asked bitterly. "Because she has achieved her object and destroyed Niall?"

"He destroyed himself; she was only the instrument."

"A fine phrase," I said angrily, "meaning that you condone."

"No, but neither do I condemn. When I said it was over, I meant it. She has shut the door on the past. She is going to marry me."

We stared at one another.

I said, "So I suppose you love her, since you are marrying her, and whatever I say won't make you change your mind and tell me where to find her?"

"No."

"And you weren't involved at all in Alexandra's attempt to ruin Niall."

"Not unless you include running his car back to Guinever as participation."

"So it was you I saw from the keep. Why did you bring it back?"

He made a swift gesture of impatience. "Why? Sweet heaven, I thought that was obvious. Alexandra has done with trouble."

"Why should . . . you imagine there would be . . . more trouble? They'd met on the boat. They must have talked, argued, even quarreled—I don't know. But at least they met."

"You're so right, they met! But he hadn't done with her. And we figured that he would be hanging around until it was quiet—it's a very isolated part of the river. He would be waiting for night, very late night when even the lovers had gone home. He must have seen me arrive soon after he left Alexandra. He probably thought that when I was on the point of leaving her, I would tell her that she would be perfectly safe for the night if she locked the doors to the pilothouse and the cabin. But I stayed . . . and he waited. His car would have been his easy way of escape. That's why I drove it back to Guinever."

"What happened . . . the first time . . . they met? What could have happened for Niall to make . . . you both . . . think he was dangerous?"

Francis looked at me through cold eyes. "He went on board, burst open the door of the cabin and threatened her. He dragged her up on deck. In that lonely place there could so easily have been an accident—a drowning, for instance—and no one would hear cries for help—"

My sharp cry interrupted him. "Oh no . . .

not Niall." My protest was weak and pointless because I knew that it could be true. Desperate men's minds didn't function clearly; they so often gambled on a last terrible throw of the dice.

Francis went on without comment, "Niall had so little to say to Alexandra. He was in a hurry. Action, self-protection, was all that he thought about. The harbormaster, coming along the river path at that moment, saved Alexandra's life. Niall saw him for that one instant before he laid hands on her. And in that moment, sanity must have returned to him, for he walked off the boat and disappeared."

I put my hands to my face. Every part of me burned as if a fire were consuming me. "So you think . . . Niall was . . . waiting for . . . the night. But he didn't come back, did he?"

"That I don't know. He may have been watching and may have known that I stayed all night on the boat. He may have been afraid that if he came, I would have broken his damned neck."

"Yet you left Alexandra alone when you drove the car to Guinever."

"I didn't. She came too, following in my car. Then we returned together. When we got there, I went first onto the boat while Alexandra drew attention away from me to herself by pretending to have difficulty in closing the car door. We hoped he might not have noticed me and returned to the boat expecting to find Alexandra alone. So, we waited with all the lights on in the cabin. It's a pity he never came. I'd have enjoyed meeting him. You see, I've learned karate."

"Perhaps," I said, "when Niall realized what he had so nearly done to Alexandra the first time, the shock brought on some sort of amnesia. Perhaps he's wandering somewhere . . . his memory gone. Perhaps . . ."

He said exasperatedly, "My good girl, amnesia doesn't occur at expedient moments to explain away a mystery." He watched me, rubbing his chin. His eyes held curiosity. "Tell me, was Niall ever physically violent with you?"

"No."

"Then you were lucky. How did you manage to avoid it?"

I was silent.

Francis said mercilessly, "Perhaps I can tell you. Maybe you never withheld anything from Niall that he wanted. After all, at the stage of his life when you met him, he didn't need money from you, and his vanity was being well-fed by his fans. No, Sarah"—his smile was cold and unfriendly—"you were never up against it, were you, where Niall was concerned? That's why I can forgive you, just a little, for sending him to Alexandra on the boat and exposing her to danger." He lifted his hands and dropped them to his side in a final gesture. I knew that he had said everything and that now he wanted me to go.

Without another word, without being aware of a single step I took, I walked out of the room and out of Francis Lorian's house. I went back to Luke and sat like a robot, eating the omelet he had cooked, the fruit, the cheese. If I had thought about the food, it would have choked me, so I just swallowed it mechanically and tasted nothing.

Luke asked me only one question: "Did you find out where Alexandra lives?"

I said, "No," and he didn't press me to tell him any more.

18

THE day passed and the long, waiting night. The next day the police came twice to the house, questioning, asking for names of relatives and friends to whom Niall might have gone. The newspapers carried the story. TELEVISION PERSONALITY DISAPPEARS. NIALL RHODES MISSING."

The paragraph recapped his success, his happy home life—and then raised its subtle questions. A man did not disappear for no reason unless he was ill. His doctor reported that he had had a checkup recently and was in excellent health. His wife had no idea where he was. I was said to be "frantic with anxiety." The reports were subtle and discreet. But the facts were there behind the careful words. A publicity stunt . . . a rift in the apparently happy domestic life? Which?

Polly and Dido had watched *Questions and Answers* on television the previous night. They told me who had taken Niall's place. It was a man he detested.

The telephone kept ringing. Freda answered it every time. "You keep away," she said to me. "You'll just be hounded otherwise. I'll cope."

We learned one thing during that morning. The police had not had to look for Alexandra. She had called on them. She had told them who she was and that Niall had visited her on the boat and had left after an angry scene. She had no idea where he was.

That morning I was very aware of Dido, wheeling herself restlessly from living room to terrace and back again. She had already reduced Polly to tears twice. Polly had said, in her defense, "She's fretting over Niall. She has so little in her life, and he represents glamour to her." All the time she spoke, she kept her head cocked a little to one side in case her own voice should drown the sound of the telephone. I knew why. At some time today, Francis was going to telephone to make an appointment for Dido's first treatment. And Father, shut in his studio, knew nothing of the wild gamble she was taking for her daughter's sake.

The tall gates of Guinever were locked for the first time in my memory, to keep reporters away. Freda found me jobs to do, teased me, overworked me in order to keep my mind off the everlasting telephone calls. Yet I still found odd, unbearable moments when I would go into the keep, climb to the turret and lean against the ancient stones. Free from people and the questions in their eyes, free from the sound of the telephone, I was also free to ask myself if I really believed Alexandra and Francis when they said they did not know where Niall was.

Perhaps I was being gullible and somewhere, secretly, they were laughing their heads off. With the wind coming off the sea, blowing my hair back, cooling my face, I tried to think, as Leon had shouted at me to do. But my tired mind could no longer sort the facts, clarify and assess. I stood and heard the sea sighing and saw a tanker, like a dark diadem on the horizon.

Theo arrived home at five o'clock. A little later, Freda asked me where he was, for she wanted him to do some small electrical job for her in the kitchen. If Theo was missing there was only one place to look. The lily garden.

The late afternoon was so quiet that the sounds I heard from the other side of the hornbeam hedge shot me into swift action.

Someone was crying sharply, hysterically. I raced across the lawn and into the garden.

Dido lay on the ground, struggling to reach her chair. Her green dress fanned around her, her helpless legs were sprawled inelegantly, her fingers clawed at the Minerva stone, which lay at an angle.

She saw me and screamed, "Go away."

"Of course I'm not going away." I bent down and put my arms round her to ease her twisted body. "Try to straighten up . . . I'll help you."

She jerked herself away from me, sobbing.

"Don't be silly," I said sharply. "You can't lie there. What happened. Did you fall?"

"Yes . . . No . . ." She was hysterical. *"Get out. Get out—"* She grabbed the arm of the chair to try to hoist herself back into it, but it slid away from her. I retrieved it before it crashed into the hedge. Dido was still screaming at me. "If you don't go away, I'll tell everyone how you drove Niall to do what he has done."

"What has he done?"

"*You* know. You know whether he's alive or dead. You do—don't you? Oh—" she stopped on a shuddering cry as I gripped her shoulders. "Sarah, don't! You're hurting me.

All right . . . go and get help. You can't lift me . . . on your own. Go *on!*"

As I rose, knowing that she was right and that I could not have lifted her by myself, she gave me a queer look, sliding her eyes round to watch me. I knew her so well. She wanted to get rid of me because there was something she had to do, something she did not want me to know. I saw her swift, involuntary glance at her hands. Her beautiful oval nails were black with earth.

I looked at the Minerva stone. It lay at an angle. I said, "How did you fall?"

"I . . . don't know. I just came here to look at Theo's lily garden, that's all. And the chair . . . tipped me up."

I nearly said, "What a perfect little liar you are." But there was no time for argument. Heaven knew what damage she might do to herself by struggling. "Don't move," I said. "Stay just were you are." I left her and, running across the lawn, saw Freda on the terrace.

"Dido has fallen. Come and help me get her back into her chair."

Freda began to run toward me. "How on earth did she do that?"

"I'd like to know, too."

"Did she faint?"

"No." I didn't tell her that I was certain she had been trying to move the stone. That could come later.

"My little love, what *did* happen?" Freda's strong arms, with my help, got Dido back into the chair. She was very white, but she was no longer hysterical. She even managed a slight smile. "I jerked the chair on this stone, that's all."

"Are you hurt?"

"I . . . I fell forward on my arms." Plaintive and charming and helpless, she pointed her grazed elbows at us.

"You've probably bruised them, darling."

But why was there dirt wedged tightly under her nails?

Freda settled her and turned the chair round. Dido strained back, looking at me. "You're coming, too, aren't you, Sarah?"

I'd like to have said, "Why this sudden desire for my company?" All I managed was a vague "Presently."

"Sarah please . . . *now* . . ."

What was she afraid I would find if I were left on my own in Theo's garden?

"Sarah."

I said, "Go along, Dido. You don't want a retinue."

She beat her fists in impotent temper on the arms of her chair. Freda said with unusual sharpness, "That's enough. You're not a child, and you're not hurt. Your mother's in the house."

"I don't want my mother. I want—"

When she chose, Freda could lose her slow Valkyrie dignity. She began to push the chair fiercely through the gap in the hedge and was gone before I heard the rest of Dido's sentence.

I stood looking down at the stone. Loose earth had spilled over the wording "SEMPER. MINERVA." And beneath it . . . what? I glanced about me and saw Theo's spade flung near the hedge. But he was fussy about his gardening tools. Someone else had got it from the shed and used it. Dido?

I knelt by the stone. It rocked, as it had the other day when I had leaned on it. I lay full length, trying to see underneath it. Where the earth had been scraped away was a hole. I reached in and touched something hard and metallic. I dragged it out, covered with earth. It was a small caliber automatic. I had never fired a gun in my life and I sat back on my heels, holding it in my two hands, careful not to let my fingers touch the trigger. Was this the gun that was fired at Niall? Dido had known it was there, so she could have seen who had hidden it. She knew, then, who was Niall's other enemy. I went back to the house carrying the gun, like the lethal weapon it was, pointed carefully away from my body.

I didn't even knock on the door of Dido's room; I walked straight in. Across the pretty pale green room, Polly and her daughter looked at me and then at the thing in my hands. Polly cried, "What . . . ?"

"A gun," I said. "Dido will tell you where I found it."

Polly snatched it from me and began brushing clinging earth from the barrel. Her words came jerkily, a puppet voice . . . "It's mine. *It's . . . my . . . gun.*"

My first thought was "Polly with a gun? That's almost funny. Who is she protecting?" Aloud, I said, "You are sure—really sure?"

White faced, she stared at it. "Tom gave it to me out in Africa. He said I should keep it by me in case . . . of trouble. I never used it. I'd have been terrified."

"And you brought it to England? I suppose you haven't a license."

She ignored the question. "I kept it—I don't know why. But it was locked away in my bureau. Nobody knew I had it . . ." She stopped abruptly and looked at her daughter.

I looked at her, too. "Except you," I said to Dido.

Polly bridled, saying too quickly, "Of course she didn't know. And even if she did, it would be of no interest to her."

"On the contrary, it's of such interest that she fell out of her chair in her effort to get at it. Why?"

Dido sat rigid. Bitterness and envy flashed in her eyes. She drew a breath and opened her mouth, and words of pure hatred lashed out at me. "You hate Niall, don't you? You wanted to kill him, only you weren't clever enough to shoot straight. Perhaps you tried again, some other way, and that's why he's missing."

I refused to let her see the effect her deep, overwhelming envy had on me. My voice was hard, to cover hurt. "Now that you've got that ridiculous bit of guesswork off your chest, suppose you talk sense. How did you know the gun was under the stone?"

"I didn't."

"Then what were you doing there?"

"I told you, I just went to the lily garden and my chair tipped and I fell. You know how uneven that stone has been since Theo scooped the earth out underneath to hide his painting things."

"Who hid the gun there?"

"How should I know?"

I went up to her and took both her hands. "You went into the garden to get something from under that stone, only you couldn't reach it from your chair, so you deliberately tipped it up."

"I don't know what you're talking about."

I shook the fingers she was trying to drag from my grasp. "Earth under your nails. You should have scrubbed all that away before you began to tell lies."

"I'm not lying. I did fall."

"What you mean is that when you tried to get back into your chair, you couldn't. I suppose the chair slid away from you. What was it you had to do at the Minerva stone?"

"Nothing."

"You didn't tear away underneath it to look for Theo's painting materials, because they aren't there any longer and you know it. But the hollow is, and you had a use for it."

"No . . . No . . . ," Dido screamed at me.

Polly sent the gun spinning across the dressing table. She was no more safe with lethal weapons than she was with a car. "Don't, Sarah, don't cross-examine Dido like that. I won't have it . . ."

"Oh, Mother, do stop. I can cope with Sarah." Dido's words drowned her mother's protest. She turned to me. "If I choose to wheel myself round the grounds, I shall. And without your snooping. Dear Sarah, what are you trying to do? Fasten your own guilt on to me? Where were you when Niall was shot at? Why has he disappeared? Are you just pretending to be ignorant about it all? So, let's have the truth. *What happened to him?*"

"Be quiet, both of you." Polly took small, agitated steps between us, playing peacemaker.

Dido swung her chair at her mother. "Don't interfere. I'm enjoying this. Everything has been plush for Sarah for far too long. But Luke came back and she wanted him again. So"—she laughed in my face—"exit, Niall."

Her excitable triumph was fascinating to watch. Her eyes were like blue stars. I said, "You don't believe a word of that." I crossed to the dressing table. "There's a spade in the lily garden. It has been used. Did you get it and try to move the stone with it? The police will test that and the gun for fingerprints, so you may as well admit it."

Dido was quick in manipulating her chair. She swung toward the dressing table.

I cried, "Oh, no you don't," and dived toward the gun.

Polly got there first. "I'll take that." Her eyes had a hardness I had never seen before; the hand holding the gun was steady. "The police won't find any fingerprints on this." She lifted her linen skirt and wiped the gun carefully. "You see? All gone." She went to her handbag and got out some keys, unlocked the bureau and slid the gun into a compartment. I watched, helpless and fascinated.

The room was very quiet; even Polly's movements had a new control about them—the control of desperation. I looked at Dido and wondered whether the model for Michelangelo's angels resembled her in character, too. *You see,* her look said. *You can do nothing because my mother, my idiotic sentimental mother, is fighting for her darling daughter.*

"And now," Polly said very quietly, "I think you said something about a spade."

I reached the door too late. She was gone,

flying down the hall, shouting to Freda, "For me? Then take a message . . ."

At the same time, I heard the distant roll of thunder. Not even Polly's terror of storms would stop her from getting that spade.

Freda was in the hall, the telephone receiver in her hand, the cord strained as she called Polly back. "It's important. You *must* answer it."

But Polly was out of hearing.

I looked at Freda without really seeing her. I stood with my two hands resting against a tall carved cupboard. My mind was fighting an incredible fact—a knowledge that even Polly accepted, because she knew for certain what I was suspecting and trying to reject. In the quiet of our garden, Dido had tried to kill Niall.

Freda saw me. "That was Francis Lorian on the telephone."

I came slowly toward her, treading cautiously. "Francis . . . Lorian . . . ?" The name scarcely registered.

Freda went to a chair, sat down and ran her fingers along the arms. "He called to say that he has seen Dido's X rays. He said, 'I don't take risks. Tell Mrs. Singleton that I can do nothing that the doctors can't do for Dido. In fact, since I haven't the apparatus, I can't do as much. Tell her I'm sorry.' "

"So his courage failed him."

"I think," Freda said gently, "that, fundamentally, Francis is an honest man. Now I must go and find Polly and tell her."

The thunder came nearer; lightning danced in the distance. I said, "She's in the lily garden."

Behind me Dido's door closed; I heard the key turn in the lock. We had learned once before, when Dido went through a tantrum period and would lock the door on us and sulk, that we must, for her own safety, keep a duplicate key in a cupboard under the stairs. I fetched it, unlocked the door and flung it open.

She turned a blazing face to me. "This is *my* room."

"You were the one who shot Niall that night."

"How silly can you get? How could I?"

"Quite easily. Your father taught you to use a gun in Africa."

"It's so long ago, I've forgotten."

"Oh, no, you haven't. And your mother knows all about it. That's why she wiped the gun and went rushing for the spade."

"I didn't try to kill Niall. Why should I?"

I walked about the room, trying to think. I straightened things, a leather frame with a photograph in it: a child with a jump rope in her hands against a background of mango trees; Dido, years ago; Polly's ruthless, incredible offspring . . . "All right," I said. "Let's put it another way. Why did you take the gun from your mother's bureau?"

"I . . ."

"And don't waste time denying it. Your hysteria when you saw the blood on Niall's arm was terror, wasn't it? You still had the gun hidden in your chair because you hadn't had time to dispose of it. But you found a hiding place in the end, didn't you?" As I spoke, I was thinking with a part of my mind that Polly would have to tell her what Francis had said. There was no miracle for Dido Singleton in Francis' treatment room. For that, I had to try to be gentle.

I pulled Dido's chair near the bed and sat down, reaching for her hand. She dragged it away. "Don't go all sweet and gentle on me. You don't like me, so why pretend?"

"If I didn't like you, I'd probably be calling the police at this moment. As it is, 'like' isn't exactly the word. You're one of us—you're 'family'—and I happen to be rather fond of my people."

"I'm an outsider, here on suffrance because Mother made a mess of her life and can't earn her own living."

"You're hard, aren't you?"

"So would you be if—"

"Why did you shoot at Niall?"

"You're guessing."

"Look," I said, seizing the arms of her chair, imprisoning her, "Niall is missing; the police inquiries will be very searching. I'll have to tell them—"

She knocked my hand away. "You wouldn't—you wouldn't dare. Father would never forgive you."

"Oh, yes, I would—and he would."

I wasn't all that certain about Father but I had to tear the truth out of her somehow. I said, "Tell me why you did it. If you don't, the police will get the truth out of you."

"They aren't interested in the shooting. You and Niall convinced them it was a poacher."

"They're very interested now that Niall is missing."

I had scared her. She said breathlessly, "He

wasn't hurt . . . It was just . . . a graze. That's all . . . I did to him."

"Was it all you *meant* to do?"

Her eyes were defiant. "You can guess that one."

I got up and leaned over her. "Dido—why?"

Sometimes one can't tell just what it is that breaks through a barrier to the truth. Dido leaned her head back against the cushion and closed her eyes. A long sigh escaped her. "He was the man in Africa who left me to die."

I stepped back sharply. She was lying of course. She was just adding lie to lie . . . I watched her open her eyes.

"Do you want to know how I know?"

"I've got to believe you first."

"Oh, it's quite true."

"Then why have you kept it to yourself all these years?"

"I only knew a few days ago."

"All this time later?"

She must have heard the disbelief in my voice, for she said, "I told Mother. She knows it's true. But I've told no one else and I won't admit it if you bring the police here to question me. I won't admit to knowing anything about the gun. I'll say you're jealous of me because Father loves me more than he does you, and so you are trying to make a case against me."

I ignored the childish protest. "So instead of telling us what you had found out and leaving us to deal with Niall, you took the law into your own hands and tried to kill him." And even as I spoke, I thought, *It isn't true—it just can't be.* She was making up some terrible drama. But she held my gaze quietly, without histrionics, and I knew she spoke the truth.

"But I didn't kill him, did I? I'm out of practice with a gun."

"How do you know that Niall caused your accident in Ngorokong? How *can* you know after all this time?"

"You were talking about me at breakfast the other morning when I was on the terrace. Mother asked Niall something about my having treatment from Francis. Mother kept on and on about what happened in Africa, and I could hear that Niall was getting exasperated with her. Then he said that my dog—MacAdam—was with me barking. He wouldn't have known that unless he'd been there, because it was a silly animal and kept going hunting and getting lost and I had only found him that morning after he'd been missing three days. So only the man who hit me knew MacAdam was there."

I said faintly, "And you didn't tell us."

I don't think she heard me. "All these years I've been thinking, 'I'll never know who jumped that wall and left me lying there.' Then suddenly I found him—and I had the power to kill him. It was wonderful."

I looked at her pale, incredibly innocent face, at the mouth with its soft, still-childlike curves.

I said, "But it was an accident. He couldn't have known you were on the other side of the wall."

"Not when he jumped. But I don't know what happened after that. Everything went black for me so I didn't see. But he must have looked back *after* he'd jumped, you do when you think you've hit something."

She was right, of course.

I could see Niall as he must have been—in fear of what he had done . . . in all his neurotic cowardice.

"I hid the gun," she continued. "I had failed that time and I was going to try again. And none of you would ever have guessed that it wasn't Alexandra or someone else who hated him." She wheeled herself to the dressing table and picked up a swansdown puff, flicking it over her face. "I found Theo's spade and when I had dropped the gun onto the ground, I pushed it with the spade under the stone in the place Theo had made for his paints. When I went to get the gun I couldn't reach it, so I had to tip myself up. But I couldn't get back . . ."

"Why did you want to move the gun?"

"The Minerva stone had become uneven and I began to worry that Theo might lift it to fill in the hole and then he'd find what was there. So I found another hiding place for it, a better one—" She smiled at her face in the mirror. "There's nothing you can do about it, you know, Sarah. If you tell the police and they question me, I shall just deny it all. No one can charge me with anything. Mother will see to that. She's quite bright when it comes to defending me." She looked over her shoulder. "So you won't say anything to the police, will you?"

Instead of answering her, I turned and walked out of the room. Downstairs, Freda was picking the dead blooms off the gladioli on the table by the window. Polly was resting both hands on a table, head bent, sobbing.

As I went past her, I paused and kept my voice low. "I know what happened. Dido told me."

Polly turned streaming eyes my way. I said, knowing that, right or wrong, I would never tell, "Don't worry."

Freda heard only my last two words. She scooped up the flabby pink gladioli blooms. "That's what I've told her. Francis has been very honest about it, and now we have to put our faith in the hospital. The doctors have promised that at least Dido won't be tied to that chair all her life."

She didn't know, as Polly did, just what I meant by "don't worry."

19

THE seashore was searched from Launford to the Devon coast. I knew the police came often to the cove below Guinever, but I never looked over the wall. Ironically, after days of gray fretfulness, the sea was quiescent, smooth as stretched blue silk.

Freda and Polly and Father told me what was happening outside my own numb world, and although I had to know, I clung to my conviction that the searching of the coast was so much waste of time. None of us really believed that Niall was dead. So far as Father was concerned, I knew he was thinking with relief, "Whatever has happened, he'll never come back to this house and I'll see that Sarah gets free."

But for me, Niall was still a man I had once loved. And if it had all turned sour during the past few months, nothing could quite erase the earlier memories. He was my husband and he was being hunted. Father could dismiss him with relief. It wasn't like that for me. Whatever he had done, whatever he was, Niall had been part of my life and perhaps you can never quite hate a man who has been your lover.

There were the usual crop of rumors. Niall was seen in London, Belfast, in Paris. He had stepped out of a taxi in Bond Street; he had run down an escalator at Leicester Square and nearly knocked over an old lady with a shopping basket; he had been seen at a racetrack. The public made up their own game of "Find Niall Rhodes," dreaming of their picture in the paper and a press interview. But a week passed and nobody found him.

It is always so easy to tell yourself to be calm. I was so taut that I created the impression of calmness. I hated going into the village; I dreaded the everlasting telephone calls. I lashed out at Father. "Why don't they arrest Alexandra. I believe she knows more than she has admitted. Why don't they take her into custody or whatever they do to suspects?"

Father dropped his drawing pad, rose and reached for me. His big hand patted my shoulder. "This isn't an easy time for you, Sarah, but it's out of your hands now. You must realize that the police are doing their job. They have to abide by certain rules. Holding someone as a suspect for murder without a body is a highly explosive procedure and they don't do it without irrefutable evidence."

I said mulishly, "But they could keep questioning Alexandra."

He hugged me. His coat was rough and smelled of turpentine and paint. I held my cheek against it and felt comforted. I was being unjust. I had no good reason to believe that Alexandra had lied to me, to the police or to Francis.

Father said, "Niall is well out of your life. You know that. If you take him back I wash my hands of you." He held me away from him, glaring into my eyes.

I said, "It's not going to end that way. I don't know what will happen, but there won't be an easy, happy explanation that will put everything right. Life doesn't work out that way."

"You don't use your head with your men, my dear."

"You can't judge me on one mistake."

"There was Luke."

"What's wrong with Luke?"

"Just that he'll never wholly belong to any woman."

"He'll belong to the woman who won't hold him," I said.

Father sat down again, picked up his sketching pad and put a squirl in the righthand corner, darkened a line and then examined it. When he lifted his head to look at me, his hair was as brilliant under the lamplight as the setting sun. "I'm sure Luke does wonderful work, but it's no life for a woman to be married to a man who must always live free."

I didn't answer. It was not arguable. I had long ago lost Luke as a lover who would have married me. Now I possessed him only as a friend. I shut him out of my mind, saying to Father, "The awful thing about Niall is not knowing. He could be out of the country. Or somebody could be hiding him."

The police had found the bullet on the lawn and knew the type of gun from which it had been fired. But the gun itself eluded them.

Rightly or wrongly, it was still a secret among three of us, Polly and Dido and me. I clung to the wild hope that it would never be necessary to tell the truth about it, that the police would solve Niall's disappearance without trying to link it with that other episode.

I had lost my sense of being stalked in daylight and darkness. Wherever Niall was, the plan for his destruction had worked, there seemed to be no more for me to fear from the people who hated him. Yet the tension in the house was so powerful that it was almost tangible. Polly went around doing all the jobs she had always done, but with an air of confusion and terror, watching me, over-anxious to please me, fearful that if she annoyed me I would tell Father the truth about the gun. I gave her no reason to dread this kind of blackmail, but then Polly took to fear like a bird to the air.

I was wrong, I knew, in concealing the truth. But I knew also that it would not in any way help to find Niall; the gun episode was completely divorced from his disappearance. It was so easy to listen to my conscience saying, "You should be honest with the police." But then I would look at Dido at moments when she was absorbed in television or a book and I would wonder how I would feel if I were suddenly brought face to face with the man who had caused me such dreadful physical handicap. How did I know how bitter, how full of revenge I would be? And, equally important, I was certain that she knew no more than any of us about his disappearance.

And so, over the long and awful week I kept silent.

Freda had, as usual, been taking Dido every day for her treatment. It was a long wait for her and I knew it tried her when she had so much to do in the house. Two days a week Dido had to be at Matthews Hospital at half past one for special therapeutic baths.

On the eighth day of Niall's disappearance Freda was in the hall adjusting the collar of her cream coat. I said, on an impulse, "Let me take Dido, today. Please. I want to go into Launford anyway."

Freda was at the door and her expression said quite clearly, "Thank heaven, Sarah's going out and around again." Aloud she said kindly, "Of course, dear, if you would. I've got a lot to do and"—she glanced across the hall—"I rather like to be here to answer *that*."

"That" was the telephone, from which she was still carefully guarding me when Leon or reporters called.

When we were alone together, Dido and I never mentioned the gun but I knew that she resented me even more than she had before, because now she feared me as well.

The road to Launford took us along the rim of the high moors that were an extension of Hardy's Egdon Heath. The trees leaned northeastward, top branches bare, burned by the salt-laden air. The earth was at some parts purple with early-blooming heather, at other places, tawny with bracken. White, balloon-like clouds swooped over the moor. How long, I wondered as I pressed the car to more speed, before houses would stand where the heather blew? How long before apartment blocks and supermarkets would make a graveyard for the golden bracken? I thought, "A man could live in this wild place for days and not be seen." Niall—living rough on Hardy's heath . . . ?"

"You *could* look where you're going." Dido's voice broke the purring stillness.

"I'm on the road and on my right side."

"You nearly ran over a squirrel. It missed the wheel by inches."

"I'm sorry." I had no idea why I was apologizing to her. The squirrel was safe and unhurt except perhaps for a slight quickening of its heart. Dido's reaction interested me. From her voice it was clear that the squirrel's narrow escape had upset her—yet she could take up a gun and aim to kill a man. That she had not was merely because she was not a good shot.

I said, "I was looking ahead of me at the hills. You can just see Corfe—"

"Look at the road," she retorted.

After that we drove in silence. Passing Gordon Terrace, I glanced quickly at Luke's house. There were marigolds in tubs in the small paved garden.

Dido's bitter little laugh reached me from the back of the car. "Oh, yes, he's probably there, Sarah. Enjoying his lunch. Is that where you're going when you dump me?"

"No." I turned in at the hospital gates, determined not to let her mood rattle me.

"It's his fault that Francis won't give me treatment."

"Luke had nothing at all to do with it."

"Do you want me to explain why?"

"I want you to go and have your treatment."

"I'm much too early. But that's nice for you, as well. It means that you'll have longer with Luke. That *is* why you offered to bring me today, isn't it? It'll be his lunchtime."

I did not bother to reply. I got out of the car and came round to open the back.

The porter was busy and I got the ramp and fixed it to the car. Because I was small, it was never easy for me to turn Dido's chair round and get it down the ramp myself, but I managed it this time.

When she was safely out, I pushed the ramp back into the car and shut the door.

"Do you want to go inside by yourself or shall I take you?"

There was no answer. I turned to look toward the hospital building. The glass door was closed; in front of it, geraniums made a semicircle of color. Dido was not there.

I thought irritatedly that, although she was in a bad mood, she could at least have waited until I'd closed the car door or even have said, "I'm going on in." I walked into the building. The porter was helping an old man toward the elevator. I said, "Have you seen Miss Singleton?"

He knew us all so well by now. He shook his head. "She hasn't come this way."

Then where was she? The hospital stood on about half an acre of ground. I looked at the huge clock over the porter's desk. We were early, so she could have gone to look at the flowerbeds, except that Dido wasn't in the least interested in gardens.

I went outside, screwed up my eyes and glanced about me. People sitting on the grass; two children playing round a sundial; a man with his leg in a cast sitting on a bench with his face turned to the sun . . . And then, right at the end of the drive, I saw color. Yellow and blue. The yellow silk shawl that covered Dido's legs, the blue of her dress. She was turning out of the gates, propelling her chair with such speed that when she reached the curb she was forced to pull up with a jerk that sent her chair into a perilous skid. I saw a man reach out and take hold of the bar, saw her look up and say something to him.

I hadn't realized when I drove up and down the hospital drive just how long it was.

As I raced toward Dido, the traffic lights changed to green and the man with her was now wheeling her across the road.

With the malevolence of all traffic signals, the lights changed to red as, panting and gasping, I went out through the gates. I stood on the pavement edge fretting, watching Dido lift her head obviously to thank the man, seeing her start to propel her chair swiftly along Gordon Terrace.

"Oh, no!" I was startled to hear my own voice. Standing helpless and fuming at the curb, I had an awful thought that she was going to Francis. To try to persuade him to treat her? Or to hurl fury at him for refusing?

The lights changed and with my second wind I did a sprinter's dive across the road. Dido had stopped to speak to a postman who was passing. I reached the other side of the road as he opened the gate and pushed Dido's chair up the low step of a house. Luke's house.

I ran toward her. She had propelled her wheelchair onto the path under the window. As I reached the spiked chain fence round Luke's garden, I saw her take something from under her silk shawl on her knees. Before I could get to her, she lifted her arm and flung it with all her force at Luke's window.

As it hurtled through the air, I saw that it was a large book. The pages fluttered; the impact of book and window came with a crash. I heard the splintering of glass, saw the ragged gaping hole. Dido ducked as pieces of glass fell outward onto the brilliant yellow calceolaria growing against the wall.

The gate had swung to, but I hadn't noticed. I plunged at it and almost lost my balance as the wrought iron scrolls resisted me. I fumbled for the latch without taking my eyes off Dido.

Her voice came, clear and carrying in the sudden lull in the traffic.

"That's for—nothing!"

I reached her side. "Are you—mad? Look—"

"I'm looking," she said with pleasure.

As if someone had leaped to the door, it opened. Luke strode out, pushed me aside and seized the chair. Without a word he bundled Dido and her chair ungently up the two steps into the house. The silk shawl had slipped with the force with which she had hurled the book and the end of it caught in one of the wheels.

"My shawl—" she shouted. "You're tearing it."

"Be thankful it's not your neck."

She tugged at the fragile silk and I heard it rip. It came free, suddenly, and jerked her back in her chair so that her arm shot up, the torn silk in her hand like a ragged banner. "Look what you've done."

"No, *you* look—at my window." He

pushed her into the room. I followed without a word. Splinters of glass glittered on the floor, on the smooth lovely polish of a Chippendale table. I saw that the book she had thrown was one I had given her. It was called *Beautiful Women Down the Ages*.

Luke was saying, very quietly, "You spoiled, unscrupulous little delinquent! People—your family, the hospital—do everything they can for you and have you any gratitude? Like hell!"

"I have no one I need be grateful to—and especially not to you. Don't," she cried as he gripped her shoulders. "You're hurting me."

"Good, it's time someone did," he said. "It's damn well time."

"Let her go." I plunged my hands between them, pushing his arms away. "You'll do some real damage."

He turned on me, an angry stranger. "Do you think I don't know how to handle her—physically as well as psychologically? A good shaking won't hurt her." But he drew away and bent to a box on the table, took out a cigarette and lit it. He drew on it deeply.

I said, "I'm sorry about the window. I—"

"It's not for you to apologize. You aren't Dido's keeper. She's old enough to be responsible for herself. And don't, for Lord's sake, offer to clear up the mess."

I hadn't realized that I had automatically gone forward toward the window.

Dido said, "Always doing the right thing, our dear Sarah. Or at least, the *seemingly* right thing. And if you're mad at me because of the cost of the window, don't worry. Father will pay."

" 'Father will pay, Mother will protect me.' For God's sake, grow up. Get yourself something to do, something useful. You've got a good brain if you'll only use it. Oh, but to change the subject," he moved toward her chair again and stood, looking down at her, drawing slowly on his cigarette. "What did you mean, 'That's for nothing,' when you shattered my window?"

Whatever she lacked, Dido had courage. She looked up at him with her angel face and her cold, bitter eyes. "Niall," she said. "That's what I mean. You get the connection, don't you?"

"No, I don't."

My hands were hot and sweaty and I rubbed them down my dress. "About that window—"

"Damn the window," he said quietly, still looking at Dido.

She cried, "For goodness' sake, Sarah, keep quiet. I'm going to enjoy what I have to say to Doctor Luke Ashton. Be quiet." She turned on me as I tried to speak. "This is my party."

"Oh, no it isn't." I grabbed the chair and tried to swing it round.

Luke stopped me. "No, let her get whatever it is out of her system." He walked away and leaned against the mantelpiece. There was a half-drunk cup of coffee on a low table; a newspaper lay where it had been tossed on the floor.

Dido leaned her head back. She said through tight furious lips, "If you had never come back to Launford, Niall would not have disappeared."

I made a movement. Luke signaled again to me to be quiet. He said, "Go . . . on." He was very still, standing in a shadowy patch of the room.

"You don't really need me to tell you. You know it all."

"Go . . . *on*," he said.

"Very well, I will." She took a deep breath. "When you came back to England and met Sarah again, you and she—well—you wanted to get together like in the old days, didn't you? Only Niall was in the way. So, you worked on Sarah to do something about it. And she did."

I said, appalled, "That's . . . vicious." I couldn't think of any other word, nor of anything else to say. I looked quickly at Luke. He was deliberately not glancing my way.

"Wheels within wheels," Dido said, "I've worked it all out—after all, I've plenty of time, haven't I, in this damn chair?"

Luke said calmly, "There's no need for you to have plenty of time on your hands. You could make yourself useful in a number of ways, but we'll skip that one."

"Working out a solution to something that is mystifying even the police isn't a waste of time. And you see, I think I know what happened. I think that Alexandra and Sarah got together—two wives hating the same man—and planned to get rid of him. Alexandra wanted revenge and Sarah"—she gave me a long bitter look—"well, Sarah wanted to be free."

"Whatever your private solution," Luke said, "I fail to see why you broke my window."

"You stopped Father from letting Francis treat me."

"I did?" Luke jerked himself away from the mantelpiece. "You credit me with a very great deal of influence."

I knew that look on Luke's face. It meant, *I will take so much from you and no more.*

I moved between them, saying to Dido, "You've had your say. Now that's enough. No one will believe—"

Again, Luke made a gesture with his hand, silencing me.

Misunderstanding, Dido rushed on. "You used your influence, Luke. I know you did. You probably warned Francis that you'd have the law on him if he dared to touch me."

"How could I stop a man from giving you treatment? Or do I make my own laws? Dear me, so I threaten men, I punish, I manipulate for my own ends. You place me on Olympus, my dear Dido . . . *You stupid, overindulged little brat.*" His voice rose, lashing at her. "Why don't you do something about that imagination of yours? It could be as dangerous as a man-eating tiger—dangerous to you, I mean."

"I'm not easily frightened. I like my imagination to be wild, so there you are!"

The carriage clock on the mantelpiece struck the half-hour.

Luke said, "Where are we?"

I seized the handles of her chair. Someone had to stop them. "You aren't looking at a bunch of murderers, Dido, so don't be so silly."

She tossed her head. "Someone wanted Niall dead. Someone—" and then she stopped. She had turned to me as she spoke and a look in my eyes had silenced her. She had said too much. I knew by her expression that she was remembering the gun under the Minerva stone.

I didn't spare her. I leaned over her. "Yes, somebody did want Niall dead. But that person didn't manage to kill him."

"Don't." It was the first word she could think of to stop me. "Don't. Don't. *Don't*." The word became a scream. She began to beat at me with her hands until I sidestepped and her last thrust thrashed the air.

"Oh, for heaven's sake." Luke lost patience. "Not hysterics! And come to think of it, why? What did Sarah say to upset you?"

"She's just being difficult," I said glibly and began pushing her chair toward the door. "We have to go, Luke. I suppose the strain takes people different ways." Defending her again, as if this sixteen-year-old girl were a child, not knowing what she was saying. I began to see that we must all stop indulging her, Father and Freda and Polly and I.

Luke was saying from behind us, "As I've told you, you'd better get something useful to do—and quickly."

"I'm ill."

"You'll be sick in the mind, too, if you don't use it. They should have left you at Rosehill House and let you have intensified treatment there instead of bringing you home because you had tantrums. They'd have seen that your mind was occupied at Rosehill." He edged me gently aside and wheeled the chair over the step.

Dido said, "Being home and having daily treatment they said, would be psychologically better for me."

" 'They' said nothing of the sort. It was your mother's idea."

"Luke—" I began. "We've spoiled your lunch—"

He turned to me. "And don't say again that you're sorry about all this. Let Dido do her own apologizing."

"But I'm not going to," she said triumphantly.

"Don't be too pleased about it," he said lightly, "because I'm not going to lose any sleep over you. Good-bye, Sarah. Dido . . . brat."

I was halfway down the path when he called me back. I should not have returned at a run, not with Dido watching.

Luke was standing in the hall. "Never let it be said that I don't return other people's books." He handed me *Beautiful Women Down the Ages*.

I took it and said, "About those things Dido said . . ." I was blazing with rage and shame.

"Forget them. She was having a kind of bitter-happy time hating us. I think something must be on her mind that she's trying to exonerate herself for by devising an intrigue between us."

He was nearer the truth than he dreamed.

As I left Luke I knew he would return to his laboratory and forget this scene, which had bored and irritated him. Flames burning under tubes of glass, slides and twisting, multiplying cells under a microscope would absorb him.

Dido was crying when I reached her. As we went down the street to the traffic lights, she said, "Luke won't tell Father, will he?"

"He has every right to."

"But I don't believe he will. Nor will you."

"Don't be too sure." There had to be an end to over-cherishing.

The lights were slow in changing. Dido said very clearly and slowly, *"There is no one . . . I don't . . . hate."*

The terrible little sentence did not shock me. It came from the frustration of leashed vitality, from the overlove of a mother who treated her like a child, from her isolation from the toughness of the world outside Guinever, where she would have to make an effort or sink. But crossing the road with her, I remembered how even at the special school she was sent to when she first came to England she had never made friends. She saw herself even then in the role of someone above ordinariness, a princess. She gave herself airs and expected always to be loved; she threw tantrums if anyone else were praised; she always carried a little mirror in her pocket. I was wrong to blame others for what Dido was. She had a built-in ideal of herself which would have shown itself without physical handicap and parental over-protection.

Just before we entered the hospital I turned her round so that she faced me. "Let's look at you." Her face was paper white, and in wiping away her furious tears, she had smudged her lipstick. Her nose was shiny and she looked like an untidy and not very attractive waif. "Get out your compact and do something to your face," I said. "You can't go in looking like that."

"I'll look exactly as I like."

"Of course. It's your face. But you usually like to appear at your best for the doctors. We all do," I added quickly, afraid of more temper if she thought I were accusing her of special vanity. "Best nightdresses, hair neat, pearls—if we have any." I even managed a laugh, though heaven knew where it came from inside my emotionally exhausted mind. "We take as much trouble with a visit from the doctor as we do with a lover."

"I wouldn't know. I've never had a lover."

"You wait. You will." I opened the door of the station wagon and found my handbag under the seat. "Here, let me give you an *al fresco* beauty treatment." I found some tissues in my bag and folded one. "Hold your face up."

She pushed my hand away. "What are you trying to do? Get round me so that I won't tell?"

"Oh, Lord, not more of it!"

"Yes, more," she hissed at me. "Do you want to know what?"

"Not particularly." I put the tissue back in my bag. "You'll be late for your treatment."

"They can wait for me for once." She gave me a hard stare. "All right. So you could tell the police about my having the gun. But I didn't kill Niall. On the other hand, there's a lot I could tell them about *you*—about your relationship with him. I heard you quarreling. I heard him say, 'You want me dead.' And you didn't answer."

"That's wrong for a start. Niall said, '*Who* wants me dead?' "

"It's my word against yours. And I *know* what I heard."

"You have a gift for eavesdropping and quite a memory for snippets of conversation taken out of their context. Like that time at breakfast when all we were doing was discussing what was best for you."

"But I heard a truth then, didn't I? I discovered who had left me to die—for all he knew—in Africa." She stared up at me. "I write it all down in my diary. You didn't know I kept one, did you? Nobody does. I'm not like my silly mother, locking up something important, like the gun, and putting the key where anyone could find it. No one can find my diary."

"Did you enter in the diary that on the evening of August 17, you shot at Niall?"

She didn't even bother to answer. As I turned from her to call the porter to help me through the doors with her chair, I saw that she had gotten out her compact and was doing swift, covert running repairs to her face.

She saw my glance. "And it's not for your benefit," she said rudely.

"Oh, Dido, what are we going to do with you?"

"Give me legs to walk with."

"You'll walk," I said as the porter came out and took charge of her. "You'll walk, my problem child." But how? Easily, running through the fields? Or with sticks, stiffly like a marionette?

I locked the car door and walked away. The

hospital drive had never looked more gay. An old man was admiring the pink geraniums, the yellow globules of calceolaria. "Doo 'ees 'eart good to see 'em, doan' ut?" His Dorset dialogue was broad and full and fruity.

"They're lovely," I said to the bright weather-beaten face.

I wandered out of the gates and down into the town. A newspaper man had placards propped up outside a supermarket: "POLICE DRAG RIVER."

I bought a paper and stood, jostled by shoppers, reading. The police were searching the River Waveling at Willow Reach. There was a picture of them. The place where the boats worked was exactly where Francis' hired yacht had been moored. I read to the end of the paragraph and still did not know if they were searching for Niall or for the gun. I had no idea whether the gun was considered important. Whenever I had seen the police they had questioned me—and told me nothing.

I tore the paragraph untidily from the page and threw the newspaper in the bin hanging from a lamppost.

I walked aimlessly round the town. The sun beat on the hot pavements, heightening the colors in the shop windows—jewels glittered, oranges and strawberries glowed as if they had been painted, furniture in an antique shop acquired a rich chestnut patina . . . color and richness: summer's impact on Launford. I bought a navy and green scarf I didn't want, two of the thick pens Father liked to use, a tin of Dutch biscuits. I went into a café and had some tea. The parcels on the chair by my side looked gay enough. I could have been just a girl going shopping, and I tried to shut my mind of everything else, to pretend that that was all I was, a nonentity who had never had her name in the newspapers.

The people round me brought me out of my pretense. A man at the next table kept looking at me, covertly, eyes sluing round from a newspaper propped up in front of him. A couple sitting in the corner were very obviously talking about me, heads jerking forward, jerking round, nodding, jabbering . . . I hated them until I realized that someone as notorious as I, whose husband had mysteriously disappeared, would be the focus of my interest, too; if I were one of them seated in a small, not-too-elegant café. A woman passing my table stopped quite still and gave me a long stare. I stared back at her and she walked on, rustling her bill, a silly faded flower from her hat nodding over one ear. I opened my handbag and looked into my compact mirror. I wasn't particularly worth looking at, artistically speaking. Through the last frantic half-hour my hair had become untidy, my skin had a gleamy, glassy look and there was a smudge down the front of my linen dress. But I was Sarah Rhodes and my picture had been in the local newspaper. I was news. Perhaps they were wondering if I had killed my husband in a fit of rage and buried his body. Perhaps they were murmuring among themselves that there were dungeons at Guinever.

I finished my tea in acute discomfort, paid my bill and escaped.

20

I COLLECTED Dido and drove home, glad to be away from the town and among the quiet fields. As we entered the house, Dido said, "About Luke's window—you'll tell . . ."

Polly came running from the kitchen. She wore a huge apron with a bright orange tiger on the front. "Tell what?"

I went toward the stairs, saying to Polly, "I must talk to you."

The wheels of Dido's chair hissed as she followed me to the foot of the staircase. "Where are you going?"

"Up to my room, Polly—*please*—" My voice was sharp, authoritative.

"Mother, don't go with Sarah."

"My darling, what is it? What are you frightened of?" She gave me a quick, questioning look. I grabbed her arm and marched her with me up the stairs.

Dido cried, "Mother, no! Not up there, where I can't go."

Polly tried to drag her arm away from my

hold. "I've got such a lot to do in the kitchen. We could talk there."

"No, we can't."

"Don't go with Sarah. Don't trust her."

"Oh, do be quiet," I shouted back at Dido.

Polly said on a little half-breath, "Sarah, they've told you nothing awful at the hospital, have they?"

"Of course they haven't. Anything the doctors had to say would be said to you."

"Then, what—?"

We reached the room. I shut the door and pushed Polly into the chair by the window. I took the torn-out newspaper paragraph from my bag and showed it to her. I ought to be telling her about the broken window, but that would do later.

She read slowly, nodding her head like a child managing to understand the words and wanting me to know that she did. Then she looked up and sighed. "Oh dear! The inspector called again while you were out with Dido. He's very persistent, but he didn't tell us anything, not even that they were dragging the river."

"The police don't, but they can't stop reporters from seeing what is going on."

Polly gave me a nervous sideways look.

"Freda believes that the police think whoever shot at Niall in the garden tried again and didn't miss the second time."

"Do they?"

"It's just as well, isn't it, that they think like that? It means that we're not suspected—"

"I can't see your argument."

Polly explained in slow, laboured words, "If they're looking for the gun down in the river by that boat, then they must suspect Alexandra. We can leave it like that, can't we? I mean that she tried, and missed, and tried again."

"No, we can't."

She opened her mouth and stared at me in genuine disbelief. "Oh, Sarah, we know that Dido tried to do an awful thing. But it didn't come off. And since I've got the gun, it couldn't have been used to kill Niall, so if they *do* find a gun there, it won't be mine."

"Who says Niall is dead?"

"He . . . he . . . must . . . be. Sometimes I . . . I *know* things . . . it's like having second sight. You know, being the seventh child of the seventh child. It came to me that Niall was . . . was dead."

It was useless to argue with Polly. She

seized on a possibility and made it a certainty, using any means—factual, imaginary or psychic—to prove her point. Polly believed that Niall was dead.

And if they asked me for my opinion, I would say to the police, "I believe my husband is alive. He has chosen to disappear and you won't find him. He is like a star, strong only in ascendancy, when his face value is not shadowed by clouds of doubt. Defeat him and he does not even make a last brave stand. He escapes. He escaped from Alexandra; he has escaped again." This was what I would say. But nobody asked for my opinion. Facts were what the police wanted.

The country was like a photograph taken by an expert—green and russet, crimson and gold, slightly out of focus because of a faint heat mist. It could be entitled "Peace" because that was how it looked from my window, a motionless, exquisite reproof to my inner agitation.

Niall could not be dead. Death was something difficult to understand. My mother had died in a quiet hospital room. I had not been allowed to see her, but there had been no mystery. In fact, when the shock and misery had worn off, my child's eyes had seen it all as a sad and lovely romance. She was the princess who had died from the prick of a rose thorn. If Niall had taken his life, he would have done so here, at Guinever; he would not have gone away to die. Again, violently, came the certainty that he was not self-destructive.

Polly's voice made me start. Staring out at the golden day, my mind had been absorbed. I turned slowly and met her plaintive look.

"I don't know what you're waiting for me to say, Sarah, but I'm not going to talk. I've got a lot to do in the kitchen and I'm going."

I leaped on her before she reached the door and stood with my back to it. "Is the gun still in your bureau?"

She put her hands behind her in an involuntary gesture of evasion and shook her head.

"Polly, where is the gun?"

"It's safe."

"Not if it's in the house, it isn't. The police have stopped believing our story about poachers."

"I'm not going to tell you anything."

"Father won't be so gentle."

"Sarah, you wouldn't! For Dido's sake, oh, no, you wouldn't involve an invalid child."

"Don't strain my sympathy," I said. "It's

high time the invalid child was treated like an adult."

"You're hard."

"On the contrary, we've been hard on Dido treating her as we have. If we'd let her be adult, appreciated the fact that she has a brain instead of encouraging her to atrophy it, if we'd only given her a chance to be useful instead of living this narcissistic life, then none of this would have happened."

Polly's mouth was a tight, straight line. "Nothing alters the fact that Niall ruined her life."

I said gently, "I know. But let's just pass that over for the moment." I leaned toward her trying to emphasize my words. "The police are dragging the river where the yacht was moored. Doesn't that make you see . . . ?"

"See what?"

I checked a flash of furious impatience. "Probably that they suspect Alexandra or Francis of having used the gun and thrown it into the river."

"Well, they won't find it there, so what are you worrying about?"

"I am worrying about the very fact that they *are* suspecting one of them, and my guess is Alexandra."

"Well, you could just let it be, couldn't you?"

The persistent obstinacy of her mouth, the defiance in her pale blue eyes made me angry. "I'm not standing by and seeing someone else falsely accused . . . Polly, are you listening?"

"No."

"Then you'd better, because it concerns you."

"It seems to me that you're more concerned for a stranger than you are for your own family. Or are you now choosing to remember that Dido and I aren't 'family.' "

"Don't be silly."

"Well then, what does it matter to you if they accuse Alexandra?"

"Nothing you say can argue me out of that one. It does matter. I don't care who it is they accuse—my worst enemy if you like—" I could hear my voice rising on a high, wild note. "I won't stand by and see injustice done."

Polly drew herself up and her whole manner changed. With every bone, every nerve, she was firm, quiet, in command of herself. "You can call me wicked if you like. I don't care. But I'm perfectly willing to let someone else take the blame for what Dido did. It's quite unimportant to me who it is. And, after all, Niall was only grazed by the bullet. He wasn't killed."

"No, but the police think they see a connection. The first time, you miss. The second time, you get your target."

"You don't care about getting us into trouble, do you? The truth is that Dido and I are fundamentally strangers . . . *fundamentally,*" she stressed the word, proud that she had found such a long one. "We are of the same blood—just two of us—"

I said furiously, "If, after all Father and Freda have done for you, you're going to talk about 'two against the world,' be careful."

Her face crumpled. "You wouldn't tell, Sarah. You promised."

"It's different now. At first the police seem to work slowly, but they usually get to the truth. And part of the truth will bring them here."

"That doesn't worry me."

I said exasperatedly, "Do you think you can fool them? Sooner or later, if Niall isn't found and they really suspect violence, they'll comb this place from top to bottom, and your room won't be sacrosanct."

She looked at me with awe. "I don't understand you any more, Sarah. Niall was your husband; he's probably dead, yet you are so calm. I'd almost think you callous if I didn't know you. It's as if it's all happening outside your life."

This was no time to tell Polly that she was uncannily right. You can feel so much and then a screen falls between you and emotion and you are an onlooker at your own dilemma. For another thing, I couldn't mourn Niall because I believed that he was alive. I said, "I've warned you, either you give me the gun, or I go to Father."

Quite suddenly her bravado collapsed. She muttered with her head turned away from me, "I hid it in the keep."

"In the room where Father's guns are kept?"

"No, the other one."

"Then we're going there to get it."

"What . . . will you do . . . with it?"

I had no idea, but I didn't tell Polly that. I seized her wrist and held on tightly in case she should try to escape from me. "First," I said, "we'll get the gun. Then we'll discuss the next point."

She came reluctantly, and when we reached the staircase, she hung back. But I clung to her hand and we went down the stairs, Polly pulling back so that she was like a weight I was dragging behind me.

Dido must have heard us coming, for she wheeled herself quickly out of the living room toward me. Her face was very white in the half-light of the hall. "You've been discussing me, haven't you?"

Polly said hastily, "It's all right, darling."

"Nothing's all right while Sarah is around."

I pretended not to hear and went past her and across the living room. I opened the door to the old stone passage, flicked on the light and pushed Polly ahead of me. When we reached the two far doors, I turned the great key of the one that looked out to sea.

Polly drew back, shivering. Behind her I heard Dido shouting at us, but I couldn't hear what she said because I had closed the door to the passage and the handle was too high for her to reach.

Polly cried, "Sarah, I must go back to Dido. You can hear, she's getting hysterical."

"Freda will cope."

"I don't want Freda to cope."

"When Dido realizes we're not listening,

she'll stop." I gave Polly another gentle push and she stumbled into the keep. Immediately she swung round on me, her hands on my shoulders trying to thrust me away. "Let me go. I hate this place."

"You were brave enough to come in here to hide the gun." I locked the door behind me. "Now," I said, "where is it?"

"I'll have terrible nightmares if I stay here." She covered her face with her hands. "I always think that there are walled-up skeletons in those dungeons below us."

"Don't play-act. You weren't squeamish when you hid what I'm tired of asking you for."

I leaned against the cold stone wall. Below us, the sea hissed and sucked at the rocks and the gulls gave banshee wails as they rode on the wind. One wheeled across the window, a shadow between us and the sun. I watched it. Then I was aware of another movement. Polly was sidling slowly toward me, her eyes on my right hand.

"Oh, no." My fingers tightened over the huge antique key. "We're staying here until you give me the gun."

"It's where no one will ever find it."

"Oh, come off it," I said impatiently. "If

you were able to hide it, then it's possible to find it. There are no places you can go to that others can't."

She was nodding her head like a mandarin doll, suddenly childish again. "It won't be found. Ever. *Ever*. So, no one can be accused, can they?"

"Why did you admit that it was here if you didn't intend me to find it?"

She didn't answer me and I guessed that it had been just another of those unthinking statements Polly made in rash moments.

I watched her and saw her eyes slue round towards the nearest window slit and on to the circular wall outside of the keep. It was an involuntary glance, taking up no more time than the flicker of an eyelid. But it was enough.

"I'm not going to play hide-and-seek with you. I'm going to use a little blackmail, instead. If you don't give me that gun, I shall lock you in here and go and fetch Father. There won't be any argument and you won't be able to escape."

She looked at me, her eyes wide and frightened. Then she gave an odd, despairing little cry. "How can you do this to me? How can you . . . ? Oh, Sarah." She stood there, watching for a softening in my expression. Then seeing none, she gave a huge sigh, walked away from me and lifted herself up onto the ledge extending to the window slit.

I watched her crawl half out of the opening.

"Polly, be careful."

I don't think she heard me. I ran to her, creeping near enough to grab her ankles if she threatened to overbalance. "It's . . . here . . ." Her head was far out over the great cliff, her apron twisted over her fat little bottom.

Polly, the timid, the terrified one, was hanging over the cliff with only her sprawled legs and my frantic hands to keep her from falling. I heard her utter small sharp grunts, then, "I've got it . . . ." She wriggled backward, still grunting and panting, until most of her body was safely balanced on the ledge. But her head and shoulders were still hanging over the cliff.

"Here it is, Sarah." She held it up for me to see. Light gleamed on metal; the small, lethal thing was for a moment poised against the sky. "Here it is," she cried again. Her arm lifted. "Here it—*was*." She made an awkward, throwing gesture. I saw the gun, released from her uplifted hand, hurtle through the air. I think I shouted at her or else it was her own wild shout that echoed through me.

She began wriggling backward along the ledge. Inwardly raging, I made way for her. She came, skirt round her knees, fingers clinging to the stones.

"Polly, you fool. Oh, you fool."

She jumped down and stood, disheveled and triumphant. "Now it really *is* safe; it's in the sea."

"The tide is out."

"Oh, I threw it really far . . ."

I said furiously, "You couldn't possibly throw it into the sea from where you were. Don't you know that distances are deceptive from a height like this? It could have seemed that it sailed as far as the water, but it'll fall somewhere on the rocks below, somewhere the police are bound to find it."

"The tide will come in and take it far out to sea long before they start looking."

"It'll be washed up." I made for the door.

She came running after me. "Where are you going?"

"To get it," I said.

"You'll never find it."

All the same, she tried to stop me and for a few moments we wrestled foolishly. Then I broke away from her and ran out of the keep, out of the house and across the lawn.

I didn't stop to think that someone might see me. I tore aside the bushes and climbed the wall at the broken place. But I had to get down to the beach first by way of the ravine and the first cove, then round the rocks to our own stretch of beach. When I was far enough along, I could see, in the first sandy cove, two splashes of bright red and a very fat adult—Lelani and the children. The path was too dangerous for me to watch them. I had to keep my eyes skimmed for the broken places and the fallen rocks that could trip me up. When I reached the ravine, I saw Lelani at the water's edge, watching while Tim kicked at the waves. I looked for Annalise.

She sat cross-legged in the shadow of the cliffs, surrounded by her own and Tim's energetic excavations, the deep sandy trenches and hillocks. She was absorbed in popping the globes of the brown seaweed. Standing over her was Alexandra.

From too great a distance I called. Annalise didn't hear me, but some sort of reverberation must have reached Alexandra, for she turned her head and saw me. Immediately, without a word to the child, she came toward me. I felt a flash of envy that she could walk across the sand as smoothly as an Eastern woman carrying a pitcher of water on her head. I hated walking on soft beaches.

I said, before she could speak, "What do you want with Annalise?"

"Just to talk to her." Alexandra wore russet-colored slacks and a thin white sweater, white gloves and a thick, plain gold bracelet round each wrist.

"Why?"

"Curiosity, perhaps. I wanted to know how they liked their Uncle Niall." Her eyes were screwed up against the sun; the wind blew her hair across her face. She put up a hand and held it back. "And also I wondered if, perhaps unknowingly, they had a clue as to where Niall had gone."

"They haven't. In fact, they've never been very interested in Niall, nor he in them."

She said dryly, "You came along too soon for me to find that out for myself."

"Have the police been to see you again?"

"Oh, yes, they even sent a detective to Poole Harbor to examine the boat. That didn't worry me. There was nothing suspicious for them to find."

I leaned against the rock. "After Niall had

seen you, he didn't take his car—and he hates walking."

"I can't explain that."

"Has it occurred to you that the police follow anything—even the remotest possibility—if they think it could lead to the truth. They might even go to Rome to talk to the woman who saved your life."

Alexandra took her hand away from her hair so that, as she spoke, her face was veiled by strands of soft bronze blown by the wind. "She is dead."

"But you told me—"

"I made inquiries after you came to see me. She died some months ago in Naples."

"There must be others who heard what had happened. People gossip—"

"There can no longer be any direct proof that Niall did this to me." Her hands moved slightly, then were still again.

"Niall doesn't know that the woman is dead?"

"Not unless he has gone to Rome himself to find out."

The police had not found his passport. They had asked me about it and I had told them that I had never seen it. We had not been abroad together.

I watched Lelani, in bare feet, her skirt hitched around her waist, splashing through the water with Tim. Once, she turned her broad dark face, saw me and waved. I waved back. She and Tim were figures in a different world.

There was no reason that I could think of why Niall might have gone to Rome. On the other hand, it was possible that he was out of the country.

Alexandra's face was white and strained in the sharp light. As if she couldn't bear the silence, she cried, "Whatever I did, there's one thing they might accuse me of that I *didn't* do. I didn't try to kill Niall that night in your garden."

"I know."

She turned her head slowly and looked straight into my eyes. "But how can you?"

"I have found out who did."

Her face was radiant with relief. Then a thought struck her and the strain returned. "But you haven't told the police."

I shook my head.

She said hopelessly, "I thought not. Whoever it is, why should you tell them? After the way I involved you, why should you do anything to help me?"

"If Niall doesn't return and it becomes necessary, I shall tell the police. But I still don't believe they were looking for the gun when they dragged the river."

"For . . . Niall?"

"I think it's possible. He was last seen by you and the harbormaster by the riverbank at the end of Willow Lane."

Alexandra said, "You know who shot at Niall, but you don't want to tell. So it must be because it is someone close to you, someone you care for."

It was a statement in the form of a question. I said carefully, "All you have to know is that I won't let you be accused. If it came to that, I would tell."

"But you don't mind that, in the meantime, I am suspected."

"I doubt if you are. You see, before Father and I talked to the police, I went to the Launford Art Gallery. There was a sketch there of the audience at the first night of *The Tempest*. It was the night someone shot at Niall in our garden and you said you were at the theater. But you had no proof. The artist, whoever he is, produced that proof."

"So I'm not suspected of *that?*"

"I told the police about the picture; I said I

recognized the drawing of you—in the audience—your dress, your pendant, your . . . gloves. If they try to work out the possibility that you could have slipped away from the theater, shot Niall and then returned, I shall tell them the truth."

"That someone close to you hated him, too."

"Perhaps. But that shot fired at him in the garden was wild—it grazed his arm, that's all. And it has no connection with his disappearance."

She let a moment of silence go by, then said, "There's nothing more to say, is there?"

I shook my head. We might well meet again, unwillingly, in court. But unless forced to, I felt that we would never see each other again. I said, very quietly, "Good-bye."

She turned away without a word and walked across the sands, slim and long-legged, burnished hair gleaming against the windy sky.

I waved to Lelani and the children and was glad they had become absorbed in a long piece of seaweed. For once, I had no time to give them.

I left my sandals on the beach and padded over the rocks toward the great cliff that guarded Guinever's cove. The rocks were slippery with seaweed, soft and green—we used to call it mermaid's hair. In the pools, starfish rested after the sea's battering, pink and amethyst, lying still in the clear bright shallows.

When I came to the cliff point I saw with dismay that the tide was closer in than I had realized. I stood on the ledge between the two coves, hand stretched to the cliff, steadying myself, debating whether I should make a rush for the cove and search for the gun. But the tide here ran too swiftly and I had no idea just where the gun had fallen. While I searched, I could be surrounded and cut off.

I looked up at the great tower built on the gray rock, saw the window slit from which Polly had hurled the gun. It was no longer my business to find it; it was the affair of the police.

As I watched the waves crash among the rocks, I was certain that the gun had already been sucked down into the dark jade depths and that no one would ever find it.

21

WHEN I returned to Guinever, I heard voices in the living room. I did not want to join them, chiefly because I did not want to face Polly just yet. I knew she would be jumpy with nerves. Had I found the gun? What was I going to do about it? And my father? I could hear her cry, *"Oh God, if Kester finds out, what will happen to Dido and to me?"* But since Polly had not trusted me, I decided that a period of anxiety would do her no harm.

And Dido. I had an uneasy feeling that, given encouragement by the police, she would tell her wild theories to them. I do not believe she either loved or hated any of us, but she needed to make someone a scapegoat for her own bitterness. Caught up in the glare of the limelight, I was the obvious choice, for I was the most vulnerable.

The more I thought about it, the more I realized that I did not dare keep what I knew to myself. I could not tell Father, so I would find Freda and tell her everything, from the morning when Dido overheard our conversation at breakfast and Niall had mentioned the dog barking to the moment when Polly hurled the gun into the sea.

Freda was in the little pantry off the kitchen. The gardening scissors were in her hand and she was humming the dream motif from *Siegfried*. Three luster bowls and the bronze urn from the hall stood ready to be filled with the tall-stemmed delphiniums, the roses and the calceolaria lying in the water-filled sink.

There was a small rush chair by the window. I sat down on it.

Freda said, "I wondered where you were." She looked at me over her shoulder and added quietly, "You've kept things to yourself far too long, Sarah. Are you going to tell me now?"

Penn once said that Freda had a built-in radar system that warned her when someone needed to talk, to ask advice, to give a confidence. I think that she guessed by the way we entered a room, by a look, a hesitancy. Whatever it was, it had always made it easier for us to tell her things when the weight of them became unbearable.

I had no idea how long it took me to tell

Freda about Dido, about the gun, or even whether I was being particularly lucid. But she went on with her job, cutting the stems to required heights, coaxing and bullying the blooms. She did not interrupt me once.

When I had finished, I sat with my hands folded, aware of a huge burden lifted from me onto wiser shoulders. The window was open behind me and drowsy bees hummed among the clusters of campanula.

"Of course, your father will have to be told."

"I promised Polly that I wouldn't tell him."

"But you won't. I will. Polly can't hide her head in the sand any longer." She picked up a yellow rose. "Your father has been saying for a long time that Dido must be sent back to Rosehill or to some place for handicapped adolescents. She will have the same treatment that she gets from Matthews plus occupational therapy. That is what she needs."

"Polly would have to give her consent."

Freda said quietly, "Then she'll have to do just that, won't she? After what has happened, she has no alternative. Six months ago I doubt if Kester would have thought about it, but Dido's character is changing. She needs discipline and that can't be given her by those who have up to now indulged her. She needs fresh, firm influences."

I got up and leaned against the window frame, the sun on my back, the clear tangy air cooling my neck. "Do the police have to be told?"

"Your father will decide that."

"What Dido did has nothing to do with Niall's disappearance. It was his fear of Alexandra and what she was doing to him."

"You must leave it to Kester. All I am certain about is that Dido will be sent away."

"What will happen if, sometime in the future, she finds someone else to hate?"

"Let's not think that way," Freda said. "Let's believe that, in the right hands, she will develop and become adult. At present she is a bitter, indulged child without a sense of responsibility."

I went into the garden and stretched out on the lawn, staring at the periwinkle-blue sky and trying to make my mind a blank. Finding that impossible, I absorbed myself in small things. I began counting the blades of grass under my hand; I searched the distant oak trees for the first sign of autumn. I gave up before I began to count sheep. None of my efforts worked. Niall intruded. So I gave myself up to thinking about him.

People's lives had patterns in kindness and cruelty, good and evil. Niall's pattern of weakness was to run away from trouble. I wondered about his relatives whom I had never been allowed to meet. Perhaps the pattern of escape from censure had developed early in his life and the instances of it had led to the severance of connection between himself and the Rhodes family of Scotland.

But a man could not be two people, each at variance with the other, without breaking. Against the deep-blue sky I saw him as he had stood in front of me, full of fear for his collapsing world.

22

THE gods of television came and went. Autumn blazed over Guinever, the holidays ended and the children went back to school. Niall was already forgotten by those who had put him where he had been—the vast, powerful, fickle public. The programs continued with new men, new voices, new personalities.

For myself, I was empty of the fear that had stalked me for so many weeks. I became more and more certain that Niall would never come back, although I did not share the majority belief that he was dead. I believed that he had escaped to some place where, perhaps under another name, he could make a fresh bid for success in an entirely new field. I doubted if he was still in England. But this did not stop me from hesitating when I turned a lonely corner of the garden or crossed the ravine to Penn's farm. I was always half-waiting for a shadow to cross my path and for Niall's voice to say my name. "Sarah . . ." Sometimes, for a shaken moment, I could almost imagine the grip of his hand pulling me toward him, forcing me with him into exile. But that was just a nightmare I knew to be unreal even as it plagued me. I had plunged into my marriage to Niall as a reckless swimmer plunges wildly through a great wave, knowing a moment's exhilaration before being sucked under.

It was over. I had stepped out of the darkness into—into what? A void, a limbo. One day, I would be judged legally free. Yet, like Alexandra's beautifully gloved hands, I would always carry the scar of that torn year.

For the next few weeks, while the police searched in vain for Niall, I had the merciful release of feverish activity. The lease of the Portland Place apartment had run out. I knew that Niall intended to renew it, but it had never been my real home and I felt nothing for it.

I went to London with the intention of selling the contents of the apartment. But when I walked round it, taking an inventory, Niall's lovely glass, his pictures, his ivories seemed to rebuke me for so easily disposing of them. There was, I felt, some deep betrayal in selling to strangers what someone had once collected and loved—not that Niall had loved anything for itself. His possessions had always been his shop window, and you sold the goods you displayed without a qualm. Yet, as the autumn sunlight glinted on crystal, warmed the ancient yellowed patina of the ivories, burnished the colors of the pictures, I knew I could not sell them. Instead, I had them carefully crated and stored.

For myself, like a bad fortune-teller looking into a clouded crystal ball, I could see no future, make no plans. Emotions were mortal, like the body. I felt as if I were dead inside.

Freda said, "It's reaction, darling. Don't worry. Healthy people are resilient. You'll bounce to the surface again."

On Gordon Terrace, Luke was making plans to let his house. His departure had been delayed for six weeks. During that time he came occasionally to Guinever, but we were never alone and I felt that this was deliberate on his part. I counted the weeks, then the days, then the hours to his departure. At last there was just one bit of one early evening left.

I was thinking about him as I sat in the lily garden with a basket of blackberries I had been picking, resting on the Minerva stone.

The red Graziella lilies and the copper-tinted Sioux glowed on the sunlit pool. I suppose, if one looked at them long enough, one could see in the lovely blooms lying in their nests of leaves a lesson in patience and acceptance. I needed both.

I was so absorbed that I did not hear footsteps along the path outside the hornbeam hedge. A shadow fell across me.

Luke said, "Last time I went away we didn't say goodbye."

An inner trembling seized me as I made a place for him on the soft dry moss near the Minerva stone. "I'm glad you came." My voice was light. By its tone he might have thought that I didn't much care one way or the other. Pride dictated my voice and the way I glanced at him and then looked away.

He sat relaxed, hands clasped round his knees, gazing at the lilies. "I don't know how long I'll be away."

"But you are glad you were chosen."

"I volunteered. It's the kind of life I need—to come and to go."

I said on laughter that I hoped did not sound too hollow, "You slept with a goosefeather under your pillow when you were very young. It's an old wives' saying that if you do that, you become a wanderer."

He nodded. "Will you see me off at London airport?"

I thought with horror, "Oh, no, not that!" A lonely vigil . . . a last hand wave . . . a smile held until there was no one there to see the pain behind it . . . Aloud, I said, "Of course. I'll watch that you don't lose your luggage or drop your passport. I'll be your Girl Friday for an hour." I was talking too rapidly.

Luke stopped me by leaning over and kissing me. "You taste of blackberries."

"Have some." I moved the basket near him. My hand shook.

He noticed and laid his fingers over mine. "Blackberries and the scent of limes, a medieval keep and always the sound of the sea. Guinever, in fact. An important part of me wants to stay."

"But not the essential part. You will always be complete only when you are free."

"I'm not sure that it isn't rather disconcerting to be so well understood."

I said airily, "Oh, I like understanding people. It makes it easier knowing them."

I had been talking from pride, from a masked self that hid desolation.

Luke said, "By accepting what I am, you tie me. Do you understand?"

We looked at each other. The golden leaves made arabesques across his face. I reached out and touched one of the small shadows on his cheek.

He took my hand. "I'm selfish, Sarah. I would even leave the woman I loved for Africa or India or any part of the world where there was a particular opportunity for studying a tropical disease. But I would always come back."

To me . . . to me . . . It was as if I had a torrent inside me. Pride fell like a paper bastion. I cried, "In the old days that would not have been enough. It is different now. I suppose I have grown up."

In one swift movement, Luke held me. "I want to spend my last evening with you. Dinner somewhere, and then . . ."

"To your house."

We broke away, looking at one another gravely.

Luke said, "Why do women like you give to men like me?"

"Why? You tell me."

"I can't. Dear Sarah, God help me, I don't know. All I know is that I want you now, and always."

It would never be easy loving Luke, but I

would rather have it that way than lose him. Later, when I was free for him, people would say, "How hard for Sarah to have a husband who is away for months at a time." They would pity me, but I would laugh inside myself.

Luke drew me to my feet. I was standing on the Minerva stone. It was firm and secure under my weight because it no longer covered a secret-filled hollow.

THE END

This book is published under the
auspices of the
ULVERSCROFT FOUNDATION,
a registered charity, whose primary object is to assist those who experience difficulty in reading print of normal size.

In response to approaches from the medical world, the Foundation is also helping to purchase the latest, most sophisticated medical equipment desperately needed by major eye hospitals for the diagnosis and treatment of eye diseases.

If you would like to know more about the
ULVERSCROFT FOUNDATION,
and how you can help to further its work,
please write for details to:

THE ULVERSCROFT FOUNDATION
The Green, Bradgate Road
Anstey
Leicestershire
England

GUIDE TO THE COLOUR CODING OF ULVERSCROFT BOOKS

Many of our readers have written to us expressing their appreciation for the way in which our colour coding has assisted them in selecting the Ulverscroft books of their choice.

To remind everyone of our colour coding— this is as follows:

BLACK COVERS
Mysteries

★

BLUE COVERS
Romances

★

RED COVERS
Adventure Suspense and General Fiction

★

ORANGE COVERS
Westerns

★

GREEN COVERS
Non-Fiction

ROMANCE TITLES
in the
Ulverscroft Large Print Series

The Smile of the Stranger	*Joan Aiken*
Busman's Holiday	*Lucilla Andrews*
Flowers From the Doctor	*Lucilla Andrews*
Nurse Errant	*Lucilla Andrews*
Silent Song	*Lucilla Andrews*
Merlin's Keep	*Madeleine Brent*
Tregaron's Daughter	*Madeleine Brent*
The Bend in the River	*Iris Bromige*
A Haunted Landscape	*Iris Bromige*
Laurian Vale	*Iris Bromige*
A Magic Place	*Iris Bromige*
The Quiet Hills	*Iris Bromige*
Rosevean	*Iris Bromige*
The Young Romantic	*Iris Bromige*
Lament for a Lost Lover	*Philippa Carr*
The Lion Triumphant	*Philippa Carr*
The Miracle at St. Bruno's	*Philippa Carr*
The Witch From the Sea	*Philippa Carr*
Isle of Pomegranates	*Iris Danbury*
For I Have Lived Today	*Alice Dwyer-Joyce*
The Gingerbread House	*Alice Dwyer-Joyce*
The Strolling Players	*Alice Dwyer-Joyce*
Afternoon for Lizards	*Dorothy Eden*
The Marriage Chest	*Dorothy Eden*

Ulverscroft Large Print Books Ltd.
The Green, Bradgate Road
Anstey
Leicestershire
England